EMP AFTERMATH

Broken World

Chaotic World

Dangerous World

Divided World

This is a work of fiction. Names, characters, places and incidents either are the product of imagination or are used fictitiously. Any resemblance to actual persons, living or dead, events or locales, is entirely coincidental.

RELAY PUBLISHING EDITION, SEPTEMBER 2022

Copyright © 2022 Relay Publishing Ltd.

All rights reserved. Published in the United Kingdom by Relay Publishing. This book or any portion thereof may not be reproduced or used in any manner whatsoever without the express written permission of the publisher except for the use of brief quotations in a book review.

Grace Hamilton is a pen name created by Relay Publishing for co-authored Post-Apocalyptic projects. Relay Publishing works with incredible teams of writers and editors to collaboratively create the very best stories for our readers.

www.relaypub.com

EMP AFTERMATH BOOK THREE

DANGEROUS WORLD

BLURB

You don't survive the apocalypse without making a few enemies…

Laurel has found a safe haven at Lone Oak Hospital. But her loved ones are still back at South Minneha, and her mother desperately needs her. Winter has blanketed the city in impenetrable layers of snow making any chance of returning to her hospital on foot almost impossible. Then disaster strikes Lone Oak Hospital and, in order to survive, Laurel must venture out into the harsh Minnesota winter, and risk everything in a world gone dark and cold.

Meanwhile, Bear has reached South Minneha, only to find Laurel gone. As the temperature plummets, he struggles to keep the other survivors from freezing to death in the brutal cold. And when the blizzard finally lets up, he faces a difficult choice: leave now to search for Laurel, or risk being snowed in until spring.

The Minnesota winters are deadly, but they're not the worst thing out there. Laurel and Bear have made enemies… Savage foes, who hunt them even as they search for each other. And they're slowly closing in.

A new storm is coming. And Bear and Laurel must unite if they are to have any hope of survival.

CONTENTS

1. Laurel	1
2. Bear	11
3. Laurel	21
4. Laurel	28
5. Bear	38
6. Laurel	46
7. Laurel	56
8. Laurel	66
9. Laurel	73
10. Bear	83
11. Britt	92
12. Laurel	97
13. Laurel	107
14. Laurel	116
15. Bear	125
16. Bear	132
17. Bear	140
18. Laurel	151
19. Bear	157
20. Bear	164
21. Britt	172
22. Laurel	178
23. Bear	181
24. Laurel	191
25. Bear	200
26. Laurel	208
27. Bear	216
28. Britt	226
29. Laurel	230
30. Bear	240
31. Laurel	247
32. Bear	257
33. Deb	266
34. Laurel	274

| 35. Bear | 282 |
| 36. Mae | 288 |

End of Dangerous World	299
Thank you	301
About Grace Hamilton	303
Sneak Peek: Divided World	305
Sneak Peek: No Rescue	313
Also By Grace Hamilton	315

1

LAUREL

As Laurel exhaled, her breath formed a cloud in the air. In the dim light of the tunnel, she could see it billowing up toward the ceiling. Walking quickly, she zipped her coat up all the way to her chin and shuddered. It was a big, padded, winter jacket with a furry hood and deep pockets, but it still wasn't enough to keep the cold from seeping into her bones.

It had been snowing, on and off, for three weeks. Thanksgiving had come and gone. It would soon be Christmas. She hadn't seen her mom for… how many weeks was it? She tried to count backward, going through the days and nights in her head. After a while they blurred into one. With no watches, clocks, or phones to keep track of the time, it was easy to forget what month they were in, let alone what day.

The freezing tunnel walls seemed to close in on her as she walked. At the other end — the end she was leaving behind — the door to the outside had been left open. As its muted light drew farther and farther away from her, she shuddered. She'd never been a fan of the dark.

Glancing back at the door, she paused. A few weeks ago, she and an orderly named Marcell had come down here and pushed it open.

Glued up with ice and blocked by a foot of snow, it had taken a considerable amount of effort. They'd forced it back an inch at a time, hooking their gloved fingers through the widening crack to scrape the snow free. Eventually, they'd pushed it open far enough to squeeze through. As they left, a flurry of snow had entered.

After trying, and failing, to make it out of the hospital parking lot to look for supplies, Laurel had suggested they clear the rest of the snow from the door and leave it open. "At least this way, we'll have one accessible exit."

When Marcell had frowned at her, she'd added, "There are solid steel doors at the hospital end. *Locked* steel doors. No one will get through."

Marcell had pressed his lips together, clearly not enthusiastic, despite Laurel's assurances. Since the EMP, the staff at Lone Oak had kept the entrances to the hospital sealed off. Probably a smart move, Laurel had thought; if she'd been a little more discerning when it came to who she'd allowed into South Minneha, she'd be there now. With her mom. But if she wanted to see her mom again soon, she couldn't afford to get totally snowed in.

Reaching the hospital end of the tunnel, Laurel glanced back at the open door. Snow had piled up and tumbled in, making a sludge-slick entrance. In theory, it enabled them to leave if they wanted to, but every time Laurel had tried to brave the elements, she'd been driven back inside by a fresh blizzard or impassable snow. The first couple of times, Arlo had come with her and attempted to help her clear a path through the parking lot, but he soon decided it was better for them to stay put.

Even though she and Arlo had reached something of an understanding over the past weeks, perhaps even a friendship, now that she was stuck in Lone Oak instead of making her way back to *her* hospital, she could feel resentment creeping in. Especially when he tried to convince her it would be better to wait for the weather to turn again.

Now that winter had set in, it was unlikely to break before spring. The cold and the snow were here to stay, which meant Laurel, Arlo and Liam were too.

It was okay for Arlo; Liam was doing well. He was getting the treatment he needed. So he really had no cause to want to leave. But Laurel was desperate to get back to her mother, her friends, and her patients. Especially Peter; he'd be off his chemo meds by now and – although Arlo was happy now that Liam was getting better—Peter's father, Chris, would be climbing the walls waiting for Laurel's return.

Pulling the tunnel door shut behind her, Laurel stamped snow from her boots. This section of the hospital was warmer than the tunnel, but not by much. It was dimly lit — with just a few small windows letting in light — and rarely used.

Laurel leaned back on the door, pulled off her gloves, and puffed a few hot breaths onto her bare hands. Lone Oak's 'Great Migration' had begun a few days ago. Realizing it was impossible to keep everyone warm when they were spread out across different departments, Dr. Hopkins had asked the staff to consolidate their resources.

Having managed a similar operation back at South Minneha, Laurel had helped them plan their maneuvers; the cafeteria had become an eating and living space for the staff and those who were able to get out of bed, while the neighboring ER had been turned into their one and only ward. Trash can fires had been lit around the edges of the rooms, and volunteers put in charge of making sure they didn't go out.

Laurel was heading for the cafeteria, and a mug of hot soup, when Marcell spun around the corner up ahead and almost bowled right into her.

"Dr. Rivera?"

"How many times have I told you to call me Laurel?" She put her hands on her hips and raised her eyebrows at him over the top of her glasses. They weren't her usual prescription. Close, but not quite right. Her old ones had held it together for a good few weeks after the bear attack, but had finally been rendered useless when they fell off her face one day as she bent to lace up her snow boots. Her new ones had been fished out of Lone Oak's collection of spares. They gave her headaches if she wore them too long, were too round for her face, and she didn't like to think about who they'd belonged to before they became hers.

Marcell shook his head but continued speaking. "I was on my way to find you."

"You were?" A familiar knot of worry lodged itself in Laurel's stomach.

"We got Liam's latest tests back. Obviously, they're rudimentary but—"

"But...?" Laurel pushed, her heart pounding.

"He's doing *really* good." Marcell's lips parted into a broad smile that showed off his very white teeth.

Laurel released the breath she'd been holding and put her hand on her chest. "Marcell, you scared me. I thought it was bad news."

"No, no, I just thought you'd want to know." Marcell handed a hand-written chart to Laurel so she could look at it.

"Of course I do, thanks. I guess I'm just used to getting bad news instead of good."

Her eyes scanned the chart. Liam's stats were all up. The meds Dr. Hopkins had put him on were clearly working.

"Any luck out there?" As they started walking, Marcell tipped his head back in the direction of the tunnel.

"It's still too bad to get through without properly clearing it. I'm going to try and put a team together."

Marcell's nose twitched.

"You don't think that's a good idea?"

"It's not that...." He paused, clearly trying to phrase his reservations diplomatically. "It's just that I think most folks are happy to stay put. You know?"

"Don't you think they'll feel differently when the food starts to run out?"

Marcell's brow creased. He tilted his head. "We have plenty of supplies, Laurel. We cataloged them weeks ago. Enough to last a few months at least. We're well stocked. Besides, what's the plan when you're through the snow in the parking lot? You gonna tunnel your way back to South Minneha?"

Laurel sighed. She was glad Lone Oak Hospital had prepared for winter, but frustrated that no one seemed to understand her feelings of urgency. It probably didn't help that she felt like a spare part here; they had few patients and plenty of staff. So, on a daily basis, there was little for Laurel to do except roam the corridors plotting her escape.

She didn't answer Marcell's question. What she was planning to do was find her way to a store where she could scavenge a tent, some proper sleeping bags, shovels, maybe a sled to pull their things — and Liam — if he got too tired to walk.

"It's vegetable," Marcell said as he pushed open the door to the cafeteria.

"Hmm?" Laurel hadn't been listening properly and hadn't noticed that he'd changed the subject.

"The soup. It's vegetable. Sit down. I'll get us some."

Shrugging out of her jacket and taking a seat near one of the fire pits, Laurel rested her elbows on the table in front of her and let her head flop into her hands. Rubbing her temples with her thumbs, she sighed.

When Marcell returned with a mug of soup, she looked up. "And a bread roll!" He presented her with a small freshly-baked piece of bread. Laurel sniffed it. They certainly had been well prepared. Prepared enough to store bread-making supplies.

"I need a tent." Laurel put her mug down and folded her arms in front of her chest. Her wool sweater made the back of her neck itch. "If I'm going to make the journey back to South Minneha, I need a tent, food, equipment…."

Marcell studied her face for a moment. "There are some tools down in the basement," he said, taking a sip from his steaming mug. "I'm sure we could find something to shovel the snow with. I'll help you when I'm not on shift. We'll find the stuff you need."

Laurel closed her eyes and smiled with gratitude. "Thank you."

"No problem." Marcell shrugged and took another large sip of his soup.

But the offer of help hadn't made Laurel feel any better; even if she could source the equipment she needed for the journey, she couldn't leave without Arlo and Liam. Arlo had made it clear to his men that if Laurel returned without him, they were to assume she'd double-crossed him and shoot everyone. They'd never believe her if she told them she'd simply left Arlo behind, and it wasn't like she could get him to record a video message in her defense.

Forcing herself to finish the soup, even though her stomach was woozy with nerves, Laurel headed out of the cafeteria to the ward. Liam was at the far end, boxed in by yellow curtains. The windows and door had been boarded up – partly to keep out people, partly to keep out the cold – and the room was both glum and a little smoky.

"You need to either keep the fires down a little or crack a window," Laurel said — a little more harshly than she'd intended — to one of the volunteers as she headed for Liam's bed. "There isn't enough ventilation in here."

"If we open the windows, won't that defeat the purpose of having the fires?" the teenager replied, folding her arms and biting her lower lip. She had blue-tipped hair, which presumably used to be all-the-way blue, and a silver stud in her nose. "Besides, they're boarded shut."

"Then make sure you keep the ER doors open. We can't let smoke accumulate in here." Laurel pushed her glasses up the bridge of her nose. Her Texan accent had snuck through into her voice and was making her sound more annoyed than she felt. "There are *two* patients in this room on O2 and—"

The girl began to roll her eyes. Now Laurel really *was* mad.

"And," she said sharply, "breathing in smoke isn't good for you either. Coughing, headaches, wheezing… are you asthmatic? Because if you're asthmatic…."

"Okay, okay." The girl raised her palms at Laurel. The gesture reminded her of Mae, and the arguments they'd had when she was a teenager who thought she knew better than everyone –especially her mom.

Turning away, as the girl positioned a chair to prop the doors open, Laurel waved to Liam. He was sitting up eating Jell-O and reading a comic book.

"Well, look at you," Laurel smiled. "You're looking great, Liam."

"I'm feeling good," he said, shoveling in another spoonful of Jell-O. "Doc Hopkins said I'm doing good too."

"I've seen your chart." Laurel smiled. "We're definitely on the right track."

"Does that mean we're leaving soon?" Liam put his Jell-O down on the table next to his bed.

Laurel sat down beside him. "Do you *want* to leave?" She tried to keep her expression blank.

With a shrug, Liam tilted his head. "I mean, it's nice here. But…." He picked at a thread in his blanket. "I'm worried about Peter. We said we'd take some meds back for him and it's been a long time since we left. It's nearly Christmas."

Laurel drummed her fingers on her thigh and smiled. Liam was a good kid. *Such* a good kid. "I think your dad just wants to make sure you're strong enough before we head off. The weather isn't on our side at the moment."

"But we can't wait till *spring*. Peter's meds will run out way before then."

"We won't wait until spring." Laurel nodded resolutely. "I'm working on a plan to get us the equipment we need, so we'll be out of here soon. I promise."

Relaxing a little, Liam rested back on his pillows. "Okay. Cool." He picked up his comic and asked Laurel if she'd ever read it.

"Not that one, no," she said. "But maybe you should bring it with you when we leave so that Peter can read it."

At that, Liam grinned. Lowering his voice, he said, "I might steal a pack of cards, too."

"I'm sure you don't need to steal them," Laurel hissed. "They have at least five hundred packs."

As Liam started to giggle, Laurel noticed movement behind her. She turned to see Arlo striding across the room — chest puffed out, grin on his face. Patting Liam on the shoulder, he chuckled. "My boy," he said. Then he looked at Laurel. "Did you hear the good news? My boy's getting better and it's all thanks to you, Doc."

Laurel stood up, moving away from Liam's bed and warming her hands at a nearby fire pit. "Not all me, Arlo. You got us here." She paused, holding her breath as she readied herself to ask the question that was burning her throat. "Speaking of getting places… I'd really like to try and make it back to South Minneha before Christmas."

Arlo's smile wavered. He swallowed hard and cleared his throat. "That's only a few weeks away, Doc."

"I know." Laurel held his gaze and her nerve. "I'm just worried, Arlo, about Peter. We took half his meds, remember?"

Arlo nodded slowly.

"I'm also worried that if we don't get back soon, your men — the ones you left in charge — will think something bad has happened." She stepped closer. "I don't want my friends or my patients to end up hurt because your guys think something's happened to you."

Scratching his ginger beard, Arlo breathed out heavily. "I understand that," he said, looking over toward Liam. "But Liam barely made it here, Laurel. Do you really think we should risk his health by making him travel forty miles in the snow and ice?"

Laurel chewed the inside of her cheek. No, she didn't. But neither did she want to risk the safety of her friends by staying.

"I'd go alone, but if I turn up without you—" Laurel was interrupted by a banging noise.

Both she and Arlo turned to see where it was coming from. The girl manning the fire looked confused. A nearby nurse stopped what she was doing and looked up.

"What is that?" the nurse asked.

Laurel frowned. "It sounds like it's coming from…."

"Outside," Arlo finished. "It's coming from outside."

Approaching the boarded-up ER doors, Laurel and Arlo pressed their ears to the plywood and listened. The banging was getting louder. They could make out the muffled cries of two, perhaps more, voices.

Laurel stepped back.

Arlo looked at her. "It sounds like someone's asking for help," he said.

Laurel shuddered. "Someone's in trouble. Do we let them in?"

2

BEAR

"We need to light more fires." Bella was smoking a cigarette, one hand slung across her waist. Bear considered telling her that she might be a little warmer if she wore a thick sweater and a scarf instead of her denim jacket and black t-shirt combo, but thought better of it.

"If we do that, we'll need to figure out a way to ventilate the space." Bear looked up at the glass-domed ceiling of the atrium. It was high, which was helping the air to circulate, but if they lit bigger fires, they'd need more than just high ceilings to prevent smoke building up.

Bella was right, though, it was cold in here. And getting colder.

"We can't open the windows in here, they're all electric." Bear leaned back on the reception desk which, over the past few weeks, had become something of an accidental meeting point for him and Bella. Each morning, just before lunch, they'd find themselves here and would discuss whatever it was that Bella needed help with. As if by meeting informally, not actually *requesting* Bear's help, she was still the one in charge.

"Then what do we do?" She put out her cigarette and turned to look at him. Her green eyes narrowed as she waited for an answer.

Bear had been thinking about this for a while. He had an idea for how to build a ventilated fire pit, but he'd need a window. "I might be able to come up with something, but I think we need to move the patients before I do."

"Move them?" Bella looked around the room. In truth, there weren't an awful lot of patients left; even though Bella was now looking after the hospital rather than keeping its inhabitants prisoner, when she opened the doors after getting rid of Murph and his men, many had chosen to leave. Probably they thought it was best to get moving before winter set in.

They'd been right.

"Yes. Move them." Bear gestured to the ceiling. "This space is too big to heat well. When it was autumn and the sun helped to warm it, it made sense. All the glass. It worked great. But it's not autumn anymore. It's winter. The days are getting shorter and darker, and we don't have an endless supply of firewood. We need everyone in a smaller space if we're going to have a hope of keeping them warm."

Bella blinked at him for a moment then nodded. "Okay. Where?"

"Canteen. It's small. There are some windows along the sides that I could use to ventilate the fire pit, and the heat from the stove will add to the warmth."

"Will they all fit?" Bella surveyed the room, then answered her own question. "Not many left now, huh?"

Bear nodded. "If you can start organizing everyone, I'll work on building us a proper heat source."

"Fine." Bella had already turned and was gesturing to one of her guards to follow her toward the canteen. As they headed for the doors,

Bear heard her saying, "We'll create two areas. One for sleeping, one for daytime."

He smiled to himself; she was more capable than she gave herself credit for. And that made him feel better — better about his decision to leave.

"Henry? Can you spare a minute?" Bear waved over to where Henry was playing a card game with Trent and Deb. "Trent, you too."

Deb looked up in mock-annoyance and rolled her eyes at him. "Seriously, Bjorn? Are you in cahoots with these two?"

Bear chuckled and rested his hand on his mother-in-law's shoulder. "Don't know what you mean, Deb."

"I'm *winning*," she hissed, showing him her hand. "Did they ask you to rescue them?"

Bear surveyed Deb's cards and whistled. "I'd get out now, boys, if I were you." He raised his eyebrows at Trent, then at Henry. "She might look like a sweet old lady, but Deb is a card shark. Beat me more times than I can remember."

As Deb protested at his 'old lady' remark, both Trent and Henry promptly put down their cards and stood up.

"What do you need, PB?" Trent hurried to Bear's side the same way Jess used to when she was a puppy. Scanning the room for her, he spotted her with Peter. The boy was sleeping and Jess was curled up next to him, as if she knew he wasn't doing too well and needed some comfort.

Diverting his eyes back to Trent, Bear explained that they were going to build a fire pit and a chimney. While Trent's eyes lit up, Henry's shoulders drooped. When Bear looked at him, he shook his head and rubbed the back of his neck with a look that said, *Another harebrained scheme I've got to get involved with, eh?*

Bear gave him a friendly clap on the back. "Come on. It'll be fun."

Henry didn't look convinced but followed anyway.

In the corridor at the back of the atrium, which led to the ER, Bear paused. Whenever he looked at this place, he still saw bodies. Dropping. Gasping for breath. Being zipped into body bags and dragged outside. When he saw those things, often— mainly at night—they merged with other things. Sights he'd seen in Iraq and tried so many times to forget.

He did his best not to set foot in this corridor. Using the excuse that he liked the fresh air, he'd often walk all the way around the outside of the building to avoid it.

He clenched his jaw and tried not to breathe through his nose; even though the area had long been aired out, he could still smell it. The gas.

His throat started to constrict. He drummed his fingers on his thighs, then raised them to fiddle with his hearing aid. It squealed, but instead of being irritating, the noise helped to snap him out of his thoughts. His breathing began to slow.

"Your battery okay?" Trent asked, frowning.

"Fine. Darn thing's just uncomfortable." They'd located some batteries in the morgue, of all places. Another thing Bear had been trying to forget. It had been Trent's idea.

How about dead people? he'd asked, writing his question in a fresh notebook.

"Dead people?" Bear had almost physically recoiled at the thought.

The morgue. There must be old people there, right? Old people have hearing aids and the metal boxes might have protected the batteries from the EMP? Trent had begun to blush as if it was a silly idea. *Probably a dumb plan.*

"No." Bear had squeezed his arm. "No, kid, not dumb. It's a stroke of genius."

And, just as Trent had predicted, they'd found not one but *four* hearing aids with working batteries. Bear had been using them sparingly — trusting Trent and Jess to keep their ears open at night so he could turn them off — but he figured they'd at least last him until he was able to go out and scavenge for more.

"So, what's the plan?" Henry asked as they neared the ER. For the past few weeks, they'd been using it as an entrance and exit. The doors opened sideways, not outwards, so they could be pulled back even if snow had piled up outside. Now, instead of being Laurel's shiny, impressive emergency room, it was simply a lobby. An almost-empty space filled with nothing but chairs, a few beds, and a line of winter jackets and boots that had been hung up for communal use if people ventured out in the snow.

Trent was heading for the ER, obviously assuming that they were off on a mission outside, but Bear stopped him. "Not that way. This way." He pointed left, down a small corridor that led to South Minneha's small selection of gift stores.

"There's nothing left in the stores, Bear. Anything useful was moved into the atrium weeks ago." Henry stepped in line next to Bear and watched his face.

"What we need isn't in the gift store." Bear put his hands into his jeans pockets. "It's in the garden."

"The garden?"

They'd reached the end of the corridor. Bear pushed the door open to reveal a small square area with a landscaped Japanese garden in its center. The garden was boxed in by floor-to-ceiling glass windows, and four quaint little stores surrounded it: a florist, a bookstore, a store selling gifts and get-well cards, and one selling overpriced and not very practical clothes. It was South Minneha's attempt to make money from the visitors who came from far and wide to be treated at this new, state-of-the-art hospital.

Bear glanced at the florists. A few weeks ago, when he'd still been waiting in excited anticipation for Laurel to return, he'd pictured presenting her with a bunch of dried-up flowers, laughing at how pathetic they looked, making a joke about how he never did manage to pick the right gifts.

"Can I go look in the bookstore?" Trent asked eagerly. It had been picked over since the EMP, but there were still plenty of volumes left to choose from.

"When we're finished." Bear nodded.

"Finished doing *what*?" Trent, for the first time in a while, sounded a little whiny—the way Mae had when she was a teenager and had wanted to talk to her friends on the phone instead of doing chores around the house.

"Collecting rocks." Bear paused for effect, then nodded toward the Japanese garden.

"Rocks?" Henry raised his eyebrows.

"We're going to build a chimney, which means we need rocks. Lucky for us, Robert Sullivan was a big fan of rock gardens." Bear marched over to the double doors and clapped his hands together as he surveyed the snow-covered courtyard. "Perfect," he muttered, then turned to the others. "Right, Trent, go fetch us some jackets. Henry, could you find a couple of wheelchairs or a gurney to transport them with? I'll start gathering."

He began to heave open the doors, letting in a rush of cold air.

Pausing only for a moment, Trent turned and hurried off to the ER to fetch their coats. Henry shook his head and laughed. "You're actually going to build a fireplace?" he asked, looking from Bear to the rocks.

"I'm actually going to build a fireplace."

By sunset, Bella had transferred every single patient to the canteen. They'd positioned hospital curtains down the middle of the room; beds on one side of it, dining tables on the other. She'd then instructed her men to bring in some furniture from the doctors' lounges to make a more comfortable lounge area alongside the dining tables.

Hannah and Bulldog had found a rug in Robert Sullivan's office and had spread it out in front of a large leather couch. Someone else had brought Sullivan's coffee table and a lamp which, although it didn't work, made the place look homelike.

"Tomorrow, I thought maybe I could get everyone involved in painting a mural." Hannah looked at Bear as he parked his wheelchair of stones, and waved her hands at the big empty wall opposite. "One for this end and one for the dorm end."

"Great idea." Bear laughed a little as he pictured Bella's face when Hannah suggested it, but he really did think it was a good idea. If the place looked and felt more like a home, then the people inside it would be more willing to pitch in to keep it clean, safe, and livable.

After all, this was their base for the foreseeable future.

"So, what do we do with them?" Trent was frowning at the big pile of stones Bear had told them to stack up.

"We – *I* — use them to make a cairn. A hollow tunnel to channel the smoke from the fire out of the room." He knelt down, assessing the height of the window and beginning to sort through his stones. Gesturing for Trent to help, he started stacking.

Two hours later, everyone else was finishing supper and Bear was still building. He'd told Trent and Henry to go get their food and had plowed on alone, determined to finish before nightfall so they could have some proper warmth at bedtime.

The past four nights, he'd woken up shivering in the early hours of the morning and he knew others had been doing the same; it wasn't good for anyone, let alone patients like Deb and Peter, to be suffering the cold.

"Bjorn, come and eat your supper." Deb ducked around the curtain that separated the sleeping area from the living area and put her hand on Bear's shoulder. He looked up. Beyond the curtain, he could hear the others talking quietly.

"Almost done," he said, standing up. "I just need to open the window for a moment while I finish the top of the tower."

Deb wrapped her arms around herself. It was already cold in here; if Bear opened the window, it would become practically glacial.

"I know," he said. "I didn't expect Bella to be quite so quick at moving everyone. Still, it has to be done. Keep everyone on that side of the curtains while I finish."

Deb nodded. If she doubted his ability to pull this off, she didn't show it.

With the window open, Bear worked quickly, finishing his chimney, and forming a seal of stones around the opening. Sitting back on his heels, he surveyed his work. He'd created a firepit down below; two large metal trashcans encircled by stones, positioned beneath a chimney that started off wide and got gradually smaller.

In theory, the smoke would be funneled up the chimney and outside, allowing them to light larger fires and keep the whole room warm. If it worked, he could create another on the 'lounge' side of the canteen.

Fetching the fire-lighting equipment, he set about igniting his trash cans. He was mid-way through the process when the curtains behind him rolled back. He turned to find everyone watching him. Everyone.

"Nothing like an audience," he muttered, turning back to the fire.

Eventually, it lit, although it took him longer than normal because his hands were fumbling with both the cold and the pressure of being watched.

Standing back, he held his breath. Trent appeared at his side, craning his neck to peer up the chimney. "I think it's working," he said quietly. Then he stood up and waved his arms. "It's working! PB did it! We have a chimney!"

A slow clap turned into a more raucous one, followed by a few cheers. Mrs. Johnson waddled up to him and took his elbow. "Now, you must eat. I saved you some stew." She dragged him off toward the table.

Suddenly realizing how hungry he was, Bear attacked the stew with gusto. Jess jumped up beside him and rested her chin on the table.

"She's been fed." Trent sat down opposite them and smiled at Jessamine. "She's just trying her luck."

Bear ruffled Jess's ears. "Sounds like her," he laughed, tossing her a crust of bread anyway and smiling as she devoured it.

"You gonna build another one tomorrow?" Trent asked, looking around the lounge for a suitable window.

"Yeah. I will." Bear spooned in another mouthful of stew, then looked down into his bowl. He would build a second fire pit tomorrow. It would be the last thing he did before he left South Minneha.

When he glanced up, a shudder crept down his spine. He hadn't told Trent he was planning to leave. And he hadn't told him that he'd be leaving him behind.

3

LAUREL

"We can't open it." The nurse stepped forward and shook her head. "We agreed. We can't let any more people in. Our supplies won't last."

Laurel clenched her jaw. The staff at Lone Oak had been good to her and Arlo. They'd let Laurel and Arlo inside. They'd helped Liam. But soon after their arrival, there had been a meeting. Patients and staff had been getting worried about the onset of winter, about their resources being ever more thinly spread with each new body they took in off the street. So they'd put it to a vote.

Of course, Laurel and Arlo hadn't been party to this vote; they'd simply heard about it from Liam's nurse, Linda.

"They voted no more strangers," Linda had said solemnly.

"But most of *them* are strangers, aren't they? Patients you found when you went out looking for people to help? People who came and asked for help, like we did?"

Linda had lowered her eyes guiltily; had she voted against helping strangers too?

"It was pretty much unanimous," was all Linda had said in reply.

Turning to the nurse, whose name Laurel didn't know, she put her hands on her hips. "It's below freezing out there. We can't just ignore them. We're a hospital. We all took the Hippocratic oath. We *all* vowed to help people who need us." She looked to Arlo for support. She caught him glancing at Liam.

To Laurel's surprise, without paying the nurse any attention, Arlo turned around and began to tug at the plywood that had been nailed over the door. "Help me," he said, pulling harder.

Laurel bit back a smile.

"No! Stop!" The nurse took a step toward them. As she did, the banging outside stopped and was replaced by an earsplitting scream. Even through the boards and the glass they could hear it — clear as day.

"Help me! My husband is dying!"

At that, the nurse stopped. She lingered in the middle of the room. Her eyes flickered to her wedding ring. Then she ran forward and began to help.

Between the three of them, while the other patients looked on, they freed one of the boards blocking the door. Light streamed in. Snow was pressed up against the door. At least two feet.

A woman in a long red coat and dark brown hat was staring at them with wide eyes. Her nose was red, her cheeks flushed. Laurel noticed a bead of sweat on her brow. Her hands were gloveless. Her fingers must be freezing.

"Please!" she shouted, reaching up to bang her fist on the glass. "Please help me! My husband...." She looked down.

Laurel followed her gaze and gasped. On the ground at the woman's feet, a man was lying in the snow. His pant legs were wet and his sneakers didn't look even a little bit weatherproof. Unlike his wife's, his jacket was thin. Waterproof perhaps, but not padded.

His face was so pale it was almost translucent.

"Get these doors open!" Laurel began to pull on the door. The others did too. She was starting to pant with the effort when she realized one of the other patients had gotten out of bed, an elderly man with frail-looking arms but a determined stare.

A moment later, Liam was up too. Arlo opened his mouth to tell him to go back to bed but stopped when Liam said, "I can help, Dad."

After what felt like forever, finally, the door slid open. When it was wide enough, Laurel waved at Liam and said, "Grab us a wheelchair, Liam. We'll use it to prop the door open."

Wheelchair in place, Laurel scrambled over it. She landed in the snow and instantly shivered. A cold wind whipped across the street. In the distance, she could see the boarded-up old convenience store where Leonora and Frank had given them tea and let them rest. She made a mental note to go and visit them, snow or no snow, as soon as possible.

"I'm Dr. Rivera. What's your name?" Laurel was speaking to the woman but looking at the man.

"I'm Katerina, and this is my husband, Paul. He's sick. Very sick." The woman had an accent. Laurel couldn't place it.

Paul looked sweaty, but he was shivering. Laurel touched the back of her hand to his forehead. He was burning up.

"Let's get him inside." She turned to find Arlo standing behind her. He stooped down and hooked his arms under Paul's shoulders. While

Laurel grabbed Paul's feet, they lifted him awkwardly over the wheelchair. Katerina followed.

"That bed, over there." Laurel pointed to an empty bay in the corner of the room. As the elderly man pulled the wheelchair free from the door, it slid back, sealing them off from the outside. The ER nurse told Katerina to take a seat, but she wouldn't leave her husband's side. Gripping his hand, she whispered to him in a language Laurel didn't understand.

"Can you tell me what happened?" Laurel grabbed a thermometer and tucked it under Paul's arm.

"We were with a group of people, camping out at the train station." Katerina shivered. She was wringing her hands together. Arlo wrapped a blanket around her shoulders. "Many of them got sick. We decided to leave. We'd been traveling for two days. There is a lot of snow. It takes a long time to walk."

Laurel noticed Arlo take a step back when Katerina said that many of their group had been sick. He gestured for Liam to return to his bed.

Discreetly, Laurel pulled the curtain around Paul's bed. "How were they sick? What was wrong?"

"Fevers, headaches, some began to vomit."

Laurel nodded and reached for a pair of gloves. Lifting Paul's shirt, she checked his torso for rashes, then rolled him slightly to look at his back. Relieved to find no signs of anything sinister, she turned back to his wife. "It looks like a nasty bout of flu," she said. "Have you given him anything? Any medication?"

"We had nothing," Katerina replied. "No medicine. His headache is very bad."

"In that case, we'll get you both hydrated and we'll give Paul something for his fever. The headache could be dehydration too." She cleaned Paul's thermometer with a sterile wipe and offered it to Katerina, softening her tone a little. "How about you? How are you?"

"A little headache. That's all." Katerina couldn't take her eyes off her husband. Laurel dipped her head and met her eyes. She smiled and took back the thermometer. "You have a slight fever too, but you're in the best place. You did well to get him here."

Taking in Laurel's words, Katerina visibly relaxed. "Thank you," she said, lowering herself into a chair next to her husband's bed. "Thank you so much."

Laurel stepped around the curtain. She was about to ask the nurse what her name was, so that they could coordinate what to do next, when she realized the nurse was no longer in the room. From beside Liam's bed, Arlo was watching her.

"She's gone to tell someone, hasn't she?" she asked him. "That we let people in?"

"Looks like it." He walked over and folded his arms in front of his chest. Narrowing his eyes, he said, "Listen, Laurel, that woman… she said a bunch of people where she came from were sick? Should we maybe… I don't know. Quarantine them?"

Laurel pressed her lips together. "I don't think it's necessary," she said. "They both have a fever, but it doesn't look like anything more sinister than the flu." She paused and added, "Having said that… Liam's immune system is pretty low right now. It might be worth taking him out of here and setting up in your own room."

"We were supposed to be pooling resources. Sticking to communal areas." Arlo's posture had stiffened. He looked worried, and Laurel knew he had a tendency to become explosive when he was worried.

"If anyone questions it, I'll explain. Go and find somewhere to get Liam settled."

As Arlo gathered up Liam's comics and belongings and took him to find a room of their own, Laurel tried to prise her way into the nearby drugs trolley. Unsuccessful, she stuck her head around the door and looked up and down the corridor. She was about to go and find Linda, to ask for her key, when she spotted a familiar figure in the distance.

Dr. Hopkins strode toward her. As he drew closer, he waved his hands in the air. When he was within shouting distance, he said loudly, "You opened the door? What were you thinking?"

Laurel straightened herself up and pulled the ER doors closed behind her; she didn't want Katerina to hear them arguing.

"Dr. Hopkins, I know you decided not to bring in any new patients, but this couple was desperate. They could have died on your doorstep if we left them out there. They're seriously dehydrated and they're very sick. Flu, it looks like—"

Standing in front of her, older but with broad shoulders and a steely look on his face that made Laurel's stomach clench, Dr. Hopkins folded his arms in front of his chest. "The decision we made wasn't an easy one, but it was for the good of the people we are already looking after and those who might need our help in the future."

Laurel was listening to the doctor speak, but at the same time her own thoughts were whirring. Something had snagged in her mind. The word 'headache'. *Nausea, vomiting, headaches.* Her breath caught in her throat. She'd examined Paul for a rash, but what if... she opened her mouth to speak but Dr. Hopkins raised his palm to stop her.

"Do you think these people are the only ones who'll come to our doors? If we allow everyone who comes knocking into the hospital, we'll have run out of food by the new year. Then what will happen?

What will happen to the people we're already looking after? To the staff?"

"I'm sorry, Sam." For the first time, Laurel used the doctor's first name. For a moment, his eyes softened around the edges. Until she continued speaking. "But there's something you should consider. When I looked at Paul, I assumed flu. He has a fever. No signs of anything else at the moment, but I'm worried—"

"Dr. Rivera, I like you. You're a good doctor. If you were a colleague of mine, I'd be pleased and proud to work with you."

Laurel pushed her glasses up her nose and nodded. "Thank you, but—"

"But this isn't *your* hospital. You don't have privileges here."

At that, Laurel blinked hard. They'd never even talked about whether or not she'd be permitted to treat patients at Lone Oak. She'd assumed that, given the circumstances, it was a case of everyone pitching in; that if she was needed, she'd step up.

"I'm sorry?" She tucked a loose strand of hair behind her ear.

"Those without white coats are civilians, not doctors." Dr Hopkins adjusted the collar of his own white coat.

Laurel self-consciously smoothed her striped, navy-blue sweater over her hips. It wasn't often that she felt as if she'd been taken down a peg or two, but this was one of those moments. Her cheeks flushed. Then she rallied. "I apologize," she said curtly, drawing her shoulders back and raising her chin. "I won't interfere again."

4

LAUREL

As the ER doors closed, Laurel could already hear Dr. Hopkins instructing the nurse who'd accompanied him to go find someone who could put the boards back up over the door.

She set off in the direction Arlo had taken Liam, then stopped, walked back the other way, turned, walked again, turned again. Her heart was racing. For several minutes, she paced up and down the hallway. She felt suddenly claustrophobic, as if there was no air despite the fact that it was freezing and a cold draft was coming from somewhere.

She wanted real air. She wanted to be outside. She wanted to wade through the snow and go back to *her* hospital and *her* people. Her decisions might have got them into a difficult situation at South Minneha, but would she have had it any other way? Would she want to be the kind of person who could so easily weigh up the costs and benefits of saving another human being's life and decide against it?

She stopped and, without thinking, slammed her fist into a nearby wall. It hurt her knuckles much more than it hurt the wall and she recoiled, rubbing her hand. As she closed her eyes and tried to breathe slowly, she heard Bear's voice in her head: "Now, now, Little River. Calm yourself down. It's going to be all right."

That was what he'd called her; his Little River. "A river of passion, emotion, and love," he'd said to her once, cupping her face in his hands, "that's what you are, Laurel."

But that had been before the war and before his injury. Before everything fell apart.

Laurel wiped her eyes with the back of her hand. She was crying. She needed to pull herself together. Up ahead, she spotted Arlo emerging from a side room she thought was once a staff lounge.

"Arlo? How's Liam?"

"He's settled. I stole a bed from an empty ward. I just need to fetch some fire-lighting supplies. Can you watch him for me?"

Laurel nodded. The incident in the ER had put Arlo on edge; the fact he felt he needed someone to 'watch' Liam told her as much.

"I'll find us some supper too," Arlo said, resting a hand lightly on Laurel's shoulder. She smiled at him but he frowned. "You okay, Doc?"

"Got into trouble for opening the doors," she replied, sighing even though she'd tried not to. "Dr. Hopkins reminded me that I don't have a white coat and that in this hospital, I'm no different from any other civilian."

Arlo's expression hardened. A flash of something that might have been indignation crossed his face. "That's ludicrous. You're the best doctor I've ever met. He'd be lucky to—"

"Thank you." Laurel interrupted by moving a little closer to Liam's door; if Arlo was too nice to her, she'd start crying again. "But he's probably right. This isn't my hospital. I should have respected their rules."

"Well," Arlo said, smiling, "that's where you and I are alike, Dr. Rivera."

"Alike?" She put her hand on the door handle.

"Neither of us like playing by the rules. I knew that about you as soon as I met you." He winked at her and the way his face creased made Laurel laugh.

"You're probably right about that, Arlo," she said. "But I'm not sure it's a good character trait to have."

As Arlo walked away, chuckling, Laurel pushed the door open to find Liam sitting on a small gray couch, reading his comic book. He looked up when she entered. "Is that man okay?" he asked. "His wife thought he was dying."

Laurel sat on the other end of the couch and tucked her legs up under her. She was wearing a slightly-too-tight pair of jeans that she'd found in the communal clothes pile. They dug into her hips, so she changed position and leaned forward onto her knees instead.

"It looks like he's got a nasty bout of flu, that's all. Dr. Hopkins and the others will fix him up."

"Just the flu?" Liam asked, relief washing over his face.

"Well, the flu can be nasty," Laurel replied, trying to ignore the niggle in her belly that didn't seem to be going away. "If he hadn't gotten here, he might have ended up very, very sick. But he's here now. I'm sure by morning, he'll be doing much better."

Liam nodded, sitting back on the couch and stifling a yawn that made Laurel yawn too.

"I was thinking," he said tentatively, "that I might talk to my dad about leaving here."

Laurel tried to keep her expression neutral as she replied, "You were?"

"I want to get back for Peter," Liam said, repeating his earlier plea. "And I think I'm strong enough now, I really do." He paused and looked down at his fingers, picking at some loose skin around his thumb. "Would I be able to take my meds with me? Carry on my treatment back at South Minneha?"

Laurel had given this a lot of thought but paused before answering, long enough for Liam to think she was considering the question. "That should be possible."

"And come back in the spring to get me checked over? When it's easier to travel? We could bring Peter then too, if he needed it."

"We could, yes." Laurel had been through the exact same scenario in her head. Back when she'd first been planning to leave with Arlo and Liam, before the snow had started and taking Liam on the journey had felt too dangerous, Dr. Hopkins had told her that if she returned with her mother, he'd do his best to help her. She'd intended to bring her mom, Peter, and Liam back here in the spring. Only now it seemed as if she'd never get the chance to leave, let alone come back.

"Then I'll talk to Dad."

"Liam…." Laurel rubbed her temples then sat up straight. "Are you sure? Are you sure that's what *you* want? Because the journey here was tough on you. The journey back will be harder. Even if we catch a break in the weather and the snow holds off for a few days, it'll be hard going."

"I want to do it," Liam said, barely stopping to think about his answer. "If I stay here and get better, and Peter gets worse, I'll hate myself."

Laurel inhaled slowly. "Don't say that, Liam." She put her hand on his and squeezed his fingers.

"I would, though. He's my friend. I took half his meds. I need to get back to him." Liam's voice had gone up in both pitch and volume. Laurel dipped her head to meet his eyes and nodded at him.

"It's okay," she said. "It's okay. We'll find a way."

"You promise?"

"I promise."

That night, after supper, Laurel fell asleep on Liam's couch. He was in his bed. Arlo was in a chair. By the time she woke, dim, gray light at the corners of the shuttered window told her it was the early hours of the morning.

Despite his determination, Liam hadn't asked Arlo about leaving Lone Oak. While they ate dinner and, afterwards, when they played cards, Laurel had waited and waited for him to bring it up. But he hadn't. So she hadn't either; there was no way she was going to push Liam to go. It had to be his decision.

Swinging her legs around, she pulled on the sneakers she'd been given when she arrived and quietly headed for the door. Sometime in the middle of the night, she'd decided that what she needed to do was test the waters; she'd been assuming that it would be nearly impossible to travel through the snow, but what if it wasn't as bad as she thought? The hospital parking lot was snow-jammed, but out in the streets people could have been working to clear them. She'd have asked Katerina about it if she'd had time. If she hadn't been thrown out of the ER.

Letting the door close gently behind her, Laurel paused and looked up and down the corridor. Back at South Minneha, there had rarely been a quiet moment. Even the early hours had been full of movement, nurses and doctors shuttling from room to room to check on their remaining patients. Here, right now, the silence pressing down on her was deafening and—for perhaps the first time—she realized just how lonely Bear must have felt after his injury.

Laurel moved to the window and looked down at the parking lot. She wrapped her arms around her waist and hugged herself a little. She was still wearing her coat; she'd slept in it and could see it becoming an almost permanent fixture in the coming months. It was a man's coat, khaki green, padded, with a fake-fur hood. It reminded her of one Bear used to wear hunting. She'd worn it once or twice, after he left. For the longest time, it had still smelled of him.

Thankfully, the coat she was wearing now didn't smell like anything except the hospital itself. She didn't like thinking about who used to own the things she was wearing.

Straightening up, she turned instinctively toward the ER. She wondered whether Dr. Hopkins had stayed there overnight to ensure she didn't return, or whether he'd retreated to his office and left someone else in charge. She suspected the latter.

Shoving her hands into her pockets, she sighed. She liked Sam. He was a decent man. He'd helped her without question, and he had done a good job of keeping his hospital safe. But she really was worried about the headaches Katerina had mentioned. And she was worried that he'd dismiss them — just as she had done at first—without looking more closely.

"You've got worst-case-scenario-itis," Laurel muttered to herself. "Headaches, nausea, body aches, and a fever are symptoms of the flu. Just like you thought." As she stopped speaking, her inside voice added, *But they can also be symptoms of something else, can't they?*

Something much more serious. Are you sure you shouldn't investigate?

Just beyond the parking lot, the sun was starting to come up. Laurel focused on the brightening sky and tried to calm her thoughts. Dr. Hopkins was right. This wasn't her hospital. She'd always been a control freak, but at some point, she'd have to trust that other people could do their jobs as well as her. They'd fixed Liam, hadn't they? So what in the world made her think they wouldn't do a full work-up on Paul and Katerina? Rule out everything?

"You look lost...." Linda's voice jogged her out of her head.

Laurel smiled and pushed her glasses up onto the top of her head. With Linda standing next to her, she didn't need them. She sighed a little and shook her head. "Not lost, just ruminating."

"Sounds dangerous." Linda leaned against the window ledge and sipped at a thermos of coffee. She offered it to Laurel but Laurel declined.

After a pause, she said, "You heard what happened?"

"In the ER?" She nodded. "I did."

Laurel didn't ask whether Linda thought she'd done the right thing or not. "Do you know how they are? The couple?"

"I'm on my way now to take over from Jen."

"Oh." Laurel deliberately met Linda's eyes but didn't speak. She wasn't going to ask her friend to bend the rules for her, but if she kept quiet long enough....

Linda rolled her eyes and made a tsking noise. "All right," she said. "Fine. If you come with me and wait outside, I'll give you an update. I know being out of the loop must be killing you."

Laurel breathed for what felt like the first time in too many seconds. "Thank you." As they began to walk, she added, "There's one more thing."

"Of course there is," Linda laughed.

"Do you remember I told you about Leonora and Frank? The elderly couple who helped us before we arrived."

"I remember."

"I need to take them the meds I promised them. I know I can't bring them here. I get that. And they wouldn't want to come anyway. But it's been weeks, and—"

"Just tell me what you need." Linda's voice was calm, resigned, as if she knew Laurel would find a way in the end so she might as well quicken the process.

Laurel reached for her friend's hand and squeezed it. "Thank you," she said sincerely.

"You're going to take them the meds on your own? Will you make it?"

"It can't be that bad out there. Katerina and Paul made it across town." Laurel put her hands into her pockets and shrugged her shoulders as she spoke. What she didn't say was that how bad it was out there was exactly what she wanted to find out; if the journey to Leonora and Frank's store went well, she'd venture farther and find the supplies she needed. Leonora might even have some of them; they seemed to have a bit of everything stowed away in that tiny apartment of theirs. And then – once she was stocked up — she'd leave. With or without Arlo and Liam.

At the doors to the ER, Linda stopped and put her hands on her hips. "Wait here," she said. "I'll come update you in a minute."

The door was open, as Laurel had requested, to help ventilate the fire. Laurel resisted the urge to step around Linda and peer into it.

As Linda moved inside, Laurel almost reached out to catch her arm. She almost asked her to recheck Paul's torso for a rash. To make certain that the symptoms Laurel had diagnosed as flu weren't something far worse. But she didn't. She'd play by the rules. She'd wait for her update.

Not for the first time in the past few weeks, Laurel wished she was wearing shoes with heels; impatiently tapping her sneakers on the floor just didn't have the same impact. Pacing up and down the corridor, she began to wish she'd accepted Linda's offer of coffee.

If Linda was swapping places with Jen, shouldn't Jen have left the room by now? She could hear voices, but they were muffled, purposefully low. Laurel stopped, folded her arms and unfolded them. She inched closer to the door. Someone had closed it. She gritted her teeth.

She was about to push it back open, partly for ventilation, partly to see if she could spot Linda, when the door burst violently open, almost smacking her on the forehead. Jumping back, Laurel was met by a panicked-looking Linda. Behind her, in the ER, someone began to wail.

"What's happening?" Laurel pushed into the room without even waiting for Linda to reply. Shrugging out of her coat and throwing it onto a nearby chair, she passed the blue-haired teenager from yesterday. The girl was staring wide-eyed at the bed in the corner.

"He's seizing." Linda had rushed to Laurel's elbow.

Beside her husband, Katerina had stopped crying and was now silently sobbing, her hands trembling in her lap. But when Laurel looked at Paul, he wasn't seizing. He was still. Jen looked up and me Laurel's eyes. "He's..." she whispered.

Laurel instinctively looked at the clock. *Time of death...* but the clock wasn't working. Moving forward, she spoke gently to Katerina. "Katerina, I'm sorry, but I need to examine Paul."

She could feel Jen frowning at her, Linda watching her, the other patients in the room unable to look away.

"Examine him? He is...." She sucked in a huge gulp of air. Then her shoulders started to tremble. "He's dead," she whispered.

"I know. I'm sorry." Gesturing for Jen to move to one side, Laurel put her glasses back on and lifted Paul's shirt. Without access to proper tests, there wasn't much she could do to confirm what she suspected. But if she found a rash....

Slowly, she checked Paul's abdomen, his back, his arms, his legs. She was about to stop when she glanced at his feet. "Oh no."

"What is it?" Linda had stepped forward.

Laurel moved to block Paul's body from Katerina's line of sight and pointed to the soles of his feet. "Petechial rash. High fever. Excruciating headache. Seizure."

"You think it's...." Linda took a step back.

Laurel nodded. How could she not have spotted it sooner? There had been an outbreak among locals when she was stationed in Iraq. It had spread like wildfire. *How* did she not see it?

Linda's face drained of its color. "Meningitis?"

5

BEAR

As the newly devised South Minneha dormitories shuffled to life, things felt different. Already having started work on the second fireplace, Bear glanced up and watched as hospital curtains were pushed aside and the room transformed into a breakfast area and lounge. Most of the patients here were well enough to get out of bed during the day. But a couple weren't. Glancing around, Bear considered that those patients probably needed their own space, a room where they could have the peace and quiet they needed without the daily hustle and bustle of the main living quarters.

He knew there was a staff room nearby. Before he left, he'd construct a fireplace there too. Then if anyone did need privacy, they'd at least have somewhere warm to go without risk of smoke inhalation.

"You sure made a lot of people happy yesterday," Bella said, uncharacteristically jovial, as she walked over to him and put her hands on her hips. "I feel like I'm at summer camp."

Bear laughed and looked around the room; she wasn't wrong. The atmosphere today was different. It was as if moving into a smaller space had somehow created a community spirit that hadn't been there before. "Well, that's all on you," he said, nodding at her. "It was your idea to make it homey."

As Bella's cheeks flushed, she cleared her throat; clearly, she wasn't used to compliments.

"Listen...." Bear took the opportunity to change the subject. "I haven't told anyone this but—"

Bella crouched down next to him, leaning on her thighs and lacing her fingers together. "You're leaving?" She arched her eyebrow at him.

"How did you...?"

She shrugged. "You were up at dawn knocking stones together. Kinda feels like you're in a rush to get things done."

Bear stopped what he was doing and pulled Jessamine onto his lap. She'd be just as heartbroken as Trent when she found out he wasn't going to take her with him. "I've got to find my wife," he said. "She should have been back by now."

"Your *ex*-wife?" Bella asked.

Ignoring her instead of pointing out what he wanted to—that they were *separated*, not divorced—Bear added, "Not just for me. The hospital needs her, and Peter Jenkins needs more chemo meds."

At that, surprisingly, Bella softened a little. "He's running low?"

"Ran out three days ago," Bear replied tightly. He restrained himself from adding, *From what I hear, your boss Arlo took half of his supply when he left.*

"I see." Bella picked up a stone and weighed it up and down in her hand.

"I'll leave while everyone is asleep. I don't want a big scene."

Bella nodded. "You, ah, want me to give anyone a message?"

Bear blinked at her, surprised by the offer. "Tell them I'll be back and that I'll bring Laurel with me," he said firmly.

"Aye, aye, Captain." Bella offered a half-salute and stood up. "This goes without saying, but take what you need," she said, meeting his eyes for half a second before she turned and walked away.

Watching her head over to the kitchen and ask Mrs. Johnson whether there was anything she could do to help, Bear nodded to himself. Bella was a safe pair of hands. She'd take care of everyone.

As he turned back to the fireplace and continued stacking stone upon stone, he bit his lower lip. Bella's offer to take what he needed was generous, far more generous than he'd expected, and made him feel a little guilty; he never had told the others at the hospital about his truck. The one he and Trent had left in the parking lot when they arrived. The one stocked full of supplies.

As if by some unspoken agreement, neither he nor Trent had mentioned it for weeks. He'd told himself it was because the snow made it pointless to try and get out there and retrieve anything, but deep down, he knew the real reason; those supplies were his escape plan. His 'go save Laurel' contingency. He needed them and, selfish or not, guilt or no guilt, he wasn't going to share them.

He was mentally cataloging what he was going to take from the truck and what he'd leave behind when Trent appeared at his elbow. As Bear turned to him, he grinned. His hands were in his pockets and he was scraping the ground with his foot.

"Why do you look so sheepish?" Bear asked, nodding at Bella as she quietly left the two of them alone.

"Not sheepish," Trent answered. "Hopeful."

"Okay, then why do you look hopeful?" Bear folded his arms in front of him and turned to examine Trent's face. He was going to ask for something; this was his asking-for-something face.

"I was just thinking," he said, in a tone that reminded Bear of the way Mae used to ask to be allowed to attend parties when she was growing up — parties he and Laurel hated her going to.

"You were thinking...." Bear raised an eyebrow.

"That maybe today we could finally have that shooting lesson you've been promising me."

"I've promised you no such thing," Bear replied gruffly. In fact, Trent had been pestering him for weeks and he'd refused every time. Not because the kid was too young to handle a gun — he taught Mae to shoot when she was Trent's age — but because if Trent ended up having to use it for more than shooting rabbits or deer... well, that wasn't something Bear wanted to even think about. No kid Trent's age should know what it was like to fire a gun at another human, but in the new world they were living in, it wasn't an unlikely scenario.

"Oh, come on, Bear. Everyone else is taking turns catching rabbits and squirrels for supper. All I've caught is some mushrooms from the woods that turned out to be poisonous."

"Then maybe we should have a lesson on mushrooms instead." Bear tilted his head, but as Trent rolled his eyes and sighed, resigned to looking perpetually uncool among his newfound hospital friends, Bear's gut twitched uncomfortably. As much as he didn't want to give Trent the power to hurt another person, he also didn't want to be responsible for the kid being unable to defend himself. If Bear was gone, and the hospital came under attack again, he'd want Trent to be protected.

Trent's shoulders had drooped, and he was about to trudge off back toward Peter when Bear said, "All right."

Trent stopped and turned around slowly, as if he might have misheard. "All right?"

Bear nodded. "Get your stuff. Meet me at the back entrance in ten minutes. And be prepared to *pay attention*." He tugged his ear, indicating that Trent had better listen carefully to instructions or they'd have problems.

Trent offered him a stiff salute and stood up straight. "Yes, sir." Then he rubbed his hands together and grinned. "This is going to be awesome."

"Wait!" Bear lurched forward.

Trent lowered the gun, his eyes wide. They'd been practicing for nearly an hour, and the kid was losing his concentration.

"Deb?" Fury bubbled in Bear's gut. "What the heck are you doing out here? First of all, you're gonna freeze to death. Second of all, you're sick. You should be in bed. Third of all, you almost got shot!"

He glared at his mother-in-law who had stopped in front of the bushes, the exact spot Bear and Trent had been aiming for a moment ago. At first, she'd looked panicked, eyes wide, as if she was being held hostage at gunpoint. Now, she put her hands on her hips. She was wearing a padded red coat and a fake-fur hat. He had no idea where she'd found it, but wearing it, she looked more like an extra from an old Hollywood movie than a hospital patient.

"Bjorn Peterson, watch your tone."

As Deb spoke, Trent sniggered a little. Bear nudged him with his elbow and hissed, "You weren't looking, were you? You could have killed her."

Trent pressed his lips together guiltily and said nothing.

Walking forward through the snow, slowly but sternly, Deb fixed her eyes on Bear. When she reached him, she wobbled a little and he reached out to steady her. She tsked. "First of all, I needed some air. Fresh air never killed anyone. Second of all, I might be sick but I'm not dead yet. And third of all, what on earth are you doing out here with a gun in the first place?!"

"She's got you there," Trent muttered.

Bear cleared his throat. "I'm sorry," he said, guiding Deb toward a nearby log because although she said she was fine, she looked a little unsteady on her feet. "I was teaching the kid to shoot. How did you get down there? Couldn't you have walked up near the hospital?"

Deb surveyed the empty beer cans they'd stacked up on the tree stump opposite, not far from where she'd appeared. Ignoring his question, she turned to Trent. "Well, go on then," she said. "Show me…."

With a grin, Trent once more took up his position. He shot once, twice, three times, but missed each one. "I think I got that last one!" he said, turning to Bear for confirmation.

"I don't think so, kid."

"I clipped it. I know I did." Trent ran off to check, even though it was obvious from the fact that the can was still upright that he'd missed it.

As he bounded through the snow, Jess ran after him and Bear caught himself wiping his eyes with the heels of his hands. Clearing his throat again, he glanced at Deb.

"Does he know?" She moved her feet gently up and down in the snow to keep warm.

Bear tilted his head.

"That you're leaving him behind?"

He opened his mouth to speak but Deb waved a hand at him.

"How do I know? Because I know you, Bjorn. I know you can't leave my daughter out there all alone. And I know you love that boy too much to put him at risk by taking him with you."

Bear moved over and sat down next to Deb. "I can't tell him. He won't understand."

Deb reached out a gloved hand to squeeze his. "I'll explain it to him." She paused and let out a small sigh.

Over by the tree stump, Trent gave an exaggerated 'I give up' shrug of the shoulders, but then rallied and picked up a stick for Jess.

"Her too?" Deb asked.

Bear looked down at his knees. "Her too. He needs her."

"*You* need her." Deb nudged Bear's side. "Bjorn. You need her. What if your hearing aids break? Run out of batteries again? You'll need her to be your ears. You shouldn't go alone."

"I can't take her away from the boy."

Deb moved her lips from side to side. "That boy," she said, "is stronger than you think. He lost his parents just a few months ago. His world got turned upside down and look at him — still smiling."

Bear looked over to where Trent was now full-on wrestling Jess in the snow.

"Plus, he loves you. He'd want you to take her."

Smiling a little, Bear nodded. He looked at Deb and shook his head. "You always did know the right thing to say and the right time to say it."

"One of my many talents," Deb replied, tugging on the collar of her coat while she smiled at him.

Bear stood up, chuckling a little. He offered Deb his hand, but as she started to rise from her seat she wobbled and sat back down — hard. She let out a small, "Oh," and put her hand to her head.

Instantly, Bear crouched in front of her. "Deb? What is it?"

For a moment, she didn't look up. She was breathing heavily. But then she raised her eyes. Her face was paler, her eyes wide, but she smiled at him. "I'm fine," she said quietly. Then a little more loudly, "I'm fine. I just got up too quickly."

Bear offered her his arm and helped her up. "You know," he said gently as they waited for Trent to jog back to them, "I know things about you too, Mrs. Rivera." He wrapped his arm around her, so she knew that what he was about to say came from a place of deep love and affection. "I know you ran out of your meds."

There was a pause in which Deb didn't even seem to be breathing. Then she released a slow, quiet breath, raised her hand and placed it on top of his. "Yes," she said. "I did. So, now it's only a matter of time before—"

"Don't say that—"

"It's true, Bjorn." Deb looked up at him. "So, I need you to promise me something."

"Anything." Bear's voice came out hoarse and quiet.

"Promise me that if Laurel doesn't make it back here before I go, you'll tell her how much I love her. You'll tell her she was my sun. Every day. And that I will always be so, so proud of her."

Bear held Deb's gaze for a moment. His mother-in-law's eyes were moist with tears. His were too. Then he shook his head. "You'll tell her yourself. Because I *will* get her back to you. I promise you that, Deb."

6
LAUREL

"This is ridiculous." Laurel spread her arms and looked up at the ceiling. She was in what used to be one of Lone Oak's X-Ray suites. Now it was useless, dark, and freezing cold. Linda grimaced guiltily at her as she handed her a candle. Outside, a janitor Laurel didn't recognize was keeping guard.

"Sorry, Laurel."

"He's keeping me prisoner because I tried to save someone's life?"

Linda narrowed her eyes a little and sighed. "Laurel, this isn't South Minneha. Sam isn't keeping you *prisoner*. He just wants you out of the way so he can do his job without being second-guessed."

Laurel's jaw twitched. Sam was overreacting. Refusing to even talk to her because his nose had been put out of joint.

She let out a throaty growl and spun around to show Linda her back. She wasn't in the mood to be told to 'calm down' or 'let it go'.

"I'll come check on you in a while. Sam will probably come talk to you when he's finished with Katerina."

Laurel didn't reply, didn't even shrug her shoulders to indicate she'd heard what Linda said. She just pressed her lips together and watched the wax pooling around the candle's wick. When the door closed, she finally released her breath and allowed her shoulders to drop. She was so tense that they were almost up under her ears.

For a moment, she lingered in the middle of the room. Then she slumped into a nearby chair and set the candle down on the table in front of her. Leaning back, she closed her eyes and tried to remember Iraq. Was the outbreak she'd encountered there really similar to what was happening here? Or was she connecting dots that weren't there?

She drummed her fingers on her thighs. She was cold. She'd left her coat in the ER and there was no heat in here except for the candle. Somehow, remembering the heat of the Middle East made her feel colder.

She cast her mind back to the medical tent that had served as her field hospital. She made herself remember the first patient, and the second, all the way to the last. Then she shuddered, not with cold but with the lead-heavy knowledge that she was right; Paul died of meningitis. If the group they came from was sick, it was likely Katerina had contracted it too. Which meant that everyone in the ER and — by extension — the hospital was now at risk. Whether it was bacterial or viral, in these circumstances, was pretty irrelevant. Lone Oak wouldn't have enough antibiotics or antimicrobials to treat every one of the hospital's residents if they became ill. And if the staff became too sick to work, that would be a whole different level of difficulty to deal with.

She was about to stand up and march over to the door when it began to open. Linda stepped inside as if she was expecting to be told off by an angry teacher. She glanced over her shoulder. "Dr. Hopkins doesn't know I'm here."

"What's going on out there?" Laurel asked, marching forward to accept the coat Linda was holding out to her. She shrugged her arms into the padded khaki green jacket that she'd become oddly attached to in the past few weeks. Perhaps because it reminded her of one Bear had owned. Perhaps just because its warmth was comforting.

"Dr. Hopkins doesn't agree with your diagnosis." Linda was being characteristically diplomatic, but it didn't do anything to soothe the anger rolling around in Laurel's gut.

When Hopkins had arrived in the ER, he hadn't even listened to Laurel's protestations. He'd just had her tossed out. Literally. The janitor who was now guarding her had frog-marched her down the hall. She'd thought about kicking him in the groin and running back, but had decided against it. For now.

"Did you explain about the rash?" Laurel had implored Linda, as she was dragged away, to make Hopkins examine Katerina.

Linda shook her head. "He asked her if she had a rash. She said no and she said her headache was easing."

"Her husband had just died. How on earth was she even able to answer his questions?" Laurel was almost speaking to herself, twisting the bottom of her sweater between her hands.

"You really think it's meningitis?"

Laurel studied Linda's face, then gestured for the pair of them to sit down. "I don't know why I didn't spot it before. There was a severe outbreak when I was in Iraq. The reason it started was because another doctor dismissed the symptoms as flu. The rash was hiding on the patient's feet. As soon as they saw it, they did tests to confirm."

"But we can't do those."

"No. We can't." Laurel took off her glasses and pinched the bridge of her nose. When she looked up, she met Linda's eyes. Something about the nurse's expression made Laurel tilt her head to the side. "What is it? Is there something you're not telling me?"

Linda scratched at a loose thread in her pants. She was wearing several layers of thermals plus scrubs and a knit cap. "After Dr. Hopkins asked her about the rash and the headache, she started hyperventilating. I took her to the tunnel for some fresh air. We walked all the way to the end, but when we got there—"

Laurel leaned forward onto her knees. "What happened when you got there?"

"She could barely look at the light coming in from outside. She said it was too bright. So I brought her back."

"Damn." Laurel didn't curse often, but in this moment it was the only thing she could think of that conveyed how worried she was. "Did you tell Hopkins?"

Linda shook her head. "I left Katerina back in the ER and came straight here to see you. I thought if I went with you to talk to Dr. Hopkins—"

Laurel shook her head. "Linda, *you* need to talk to Hopkins. He won't listen to me. He sees me as a busybody, someone who's trying to create drama where there is none. It's better if it comes from you... ask him to properly examine Katerina. He's a good man. He doesn't want the people in this hospital to suffer."

"You're sure?" Linda was studying Laurel's face.

"Tell him to start her on intravenous antibiotics, corticosteroids, and an antimicrobial. Maximum dose for all three. Quarantine everyone in the ER and keep a close eye on those who had prolonged exposure to them. Find out which staff are vaccinated. Those who are should be the ones working in the quarantine area."

Linda was blinking fast. She wrapped her arms around herself. "I... I'm not."

Laurel bit her lower lip. Pushing aside her feelings about whether or not doctors and nurses had a moral obligation to vaccinate themselves, she said, "Don't worry, I'm sure you'll be fine. You weren't with them very long. But until you know you're clear, you should probably wear a surgical mask."

"What about you?" Linda cleared her throat and sat up a little straighter.

"I wasn't around them long and I was vaccinated when I joined the military." Laurel stood up and started to move toward the door.

Following her, Linda touched Laurel's elbow. "If this is meningitis and if it's spreading, you should go. Take your friend and his boy and go back to South Minneha."

Laurel stopped and squeezed Linda's hand. She smiled, even though her gut had turned to stone because Liam was too young to have had his vaccine. "Let's take it one step at a time, okay?"

Laurel held her smile until the door closed, but the second she let it drop, the door swung open again. "You can go..." Linda spoke in a hushed whisper. "I persuaded Frank to take a comfort break. Go warn Arlo and Liam to stay away from the ER."

Almost running out of the room, Laurel nodded, "Thank you."

When she reached Liam's room, Laurel stopped and braced herself before opening the door. The sense of panic vibrating in her stomach was not something she was used to feeling; she was used to being in control. See a problem, fix a problem. But she couldn't do that now. She wasn't *allowed* to help fix this problem.

Trying to focus on what she could control — warning Liam and Arlo to stay away from the ER — she pushed open the door and stepped inside. The room was darker than the corridor. It took her eyes a moment to adjust.

Liam's bed was empty. So was the chair beside it. His comic was on his pillow. She turned around slowly, as if Liam and Arlo might be hiding and waiting to jump out at her. When she didn't find them lurking in the corner of the room, her stomach lurched up into her throat. What if they'd gone to the ER?

She was jogging back the way she'd come when a voice from behind made her stop and spin around.

"Marcell?" She smoothed her hands over her hair and tried to catch her breath as she waited for him to catch up with her.

"What's the hurry?" he asked jovially; clearly, he had no idea what was going on.

"I'm looking for Liam. It's urgent."

"He's in the canteen with his dad," Marcell said brightly, jerking his thumb in the direction of the food hall.

Laurel felt herself breathe a little more deeply. "The canteen?" She rubbed the back of her neck. "Okay. That's good."

"What's going on?" Marcell's usual smile had dropped and he was frowning at her.

"You heard about the couple I let in last night?"

"Are you kidding? Everyone heard about that."

"The husband died this morning."

"Of flu?" Marcell shook his head as if it was terrible but understandable news.

Laurel pressed her lips together. She didn't want her friend to expose himself to infection, but at the same time, she didn't want to start an outright panic in the hospital.

"Not the flu?" Marcell folded his arms in front of his chest. "Laurel... you better tell me—"

"I believe it was meningitis that killed him, and I think his wife has it too."

"Oh no," Marcell muttered.

"The only problem is that Dr. Hopkins doesn't believe me. Linda's talking to him now to try and convince him to examine the wife properly, but I think I was a little heavy-handed. Got his back up."

"I'll see if I can help." Marcell put a firm hand on Laurel's shoulder.

"Thank you."

As he began to walk away, Marcell raised his eyebrows at her. "Careful who you talk to about this. Panic spreads like wildfire."

In the canteen, Liam was tucking into a large bowl of oatmeal while Arlo drank from a mug of what Laurel presumed was his usual, strong black coffee. Liam was chattering and had an excited, animated look on his face. Arlo was smiling.

Laurel stopped for a moment and watched them, then took a deep breath and walked over. Sliding into the chair beside Arlo, she pushed her glasses up onto the top of her head. Liam paused mid-flow to grin at her.

"Morning, Dr. Rivera." He narrowed his eyes a little. "You look tired. Are you okay?"

"Since when did you become so perceptive?" Laurel smiled at him but angled herself away slightly so she was facing Arlo and added, "I just need to have a word with your dad, okay, buddy?"

Liam looked from Laurel to his father and nodded. "Sure."

"Arlo? Can we…?" Laurel stood up and gestured for Arlo to follow her.

Still holding his coffee cup, Arlo shrugged and said, "What's going on, Doc? Liam's right. You look like you've got the weight of the world on your shoulders. You still having a beef with Hopkins?"

"Kind of, yes." Laurel lowered her voice as she began to explain. When she got to the part about suspecting Paul had died of meningitis, Arlo's face visibly paled. "Liam hasn't been in contact, I just wanted you to know so you can keep him out of the ER."

Laurel looked at Arlo's hands. They were wrapped around his mug. Were they trembling?

"A kid on my street died of that. I was six. He was ten, maybe eleven. It's bad, right? If you catch it?" Arlo looked toward Liam, who had finished his oatmeal and was now eating some canned peaches. "With Liam's immune system—"

"That's exactly why I wanted you to know." Laurel put her hand on Arlo's forearm and ducked to meet his eyes. "Don't panic. Liam's okay."

"But if it spreads? I mean, is it likely to spread?"

Laurel bit the inside of her cheek. She wanted to say 'no'. But now that she'd remembered Iraq it was hard to forget again. "It could, yes. Especially if it's not controlled quickly enough."

"And right now Hopkins thinks you're wrong?"

Laurel nodded.

"But you think you're right?"

"I'm afraid so."

"Well, I don't think I've known you to be wrong yet," Arlo said gruffly. After what Dr. Hopkins had done for Liam, Arlo trusted him. But it seemed he trusted Laurel more. Steering his gaze back to Liam, as he stared as his son, Arlo said, "We should go."

"Go?" Laurel felt as if she must have misheard him, but as Arlo snapped his eyes back to hers she knew she hadn't.

"We should get out of here. Back to South Minneha. Liam's doing good. He's strong. He told me this morning he thinks we should leave soon because he's worried about Peter." Arlo sucked in a deep breath. "So, yeah, we should go. Now. Before anything bad happens."

Laurel opened her mouth and closed it again. She'd spent the last few weeks desperate to leave Lone Oak and now — in a heartbeat —Arlo was suddenly on board. She should feel elated, but she didn't. How could she leave the doctors who'd helped her if they were about to face a crisis? If the meningitis spread, if it got really bad, they'd need her.

"Let's wait twenty-four hours," Laurel said slowly, attempting to buy herself some time to think. "If we're leaving, we need to get prepped first. Figure out what we'll need to get us back to South Minneha. If the situation in the ER hasn't improved — or it's gotten worse — by this time tomorrow, then we'll go. I promise."

Arlo began to nod. "Twenty-four hours?"

"Twenty-four hours."

"Liam will be okay? If I keep him away from the ER?"

"Keep him in his room. If *you* leave it, wear a surgical mask. I'll find you one."

"And you?"

"I'll do the same. Wear a mask. Steer clear of everyone as much as possible."

"All right then." Arlo turned away from her and waved at Liam. "Time to get going, son. Bring your food with you." Then to Laurel he said, "Looks like we've got some planning to do, Doc."

7

LAUREL

Arlo was pacing up and down Liam's room. On his bed, Liam was watching his father. It was early, the sun only just rising, but they'd been talking almost all night.

Having come up with a list of things they'd need for their journey, including—if possible—a fold-out tent, sleeping bags, and more thermals, they were trying to decide who would venture out to fetch them.

"It's decided then. I'll go."

"And leave Liam?"

"You might be needed here," Arlo said defiantly, crossing his arms in front of his chest.

"We could all go." Laurel sat forward and rested her elbows on her knees. For some reason, she felt decidedly uneasy at the idea of the three of them being separated now that they were united in their plan to leave.

"We don't even know if it's going to be possible to get through the snow once we're past the hospital grounds. Makes sense for me to go alone. Get what we need. Suss out the situation."

Laurel tucked her hair behind her ear and reached for her glasses. They were on the coffee table in the middle of the room next to a map of Lone Oak. She put them on and sat back in her chair, crossing one leg over the other and bouncing her foot up and down. "All right," she sighed. "Marcell said there's an outdoor store…." she leaned forward again and tapped the map, "here. If it hasn't been looted already, you should find what we need."

Arlo nodded and stood up as if he was ready to leave right this second.

"First, you'll need food in your belly and better boots." Laurel glanced at his feet; the ones he was wearing wouldn't get him far. They'd be soaked within minutes of getting outside.

"What's wrong with my boots? They were top dollar. I paid three hundred bucks for these boots." Arlo looked grumpily at his feet.

Liam giggled.

"There's nothing wrong with them, Arlo, but this isn't a fashion parade. It's more important you don't get frostbite." Laurel laughed at him too, noticing him play up his disappointment for Liam's benefit, and picked up her empty coffee cup. "I'll go see if I can find you some in the stores. What size are you?"

"The biggest." Arlo's reply was quick and surprising, and made Laurel snort.

"Of course you are. But if they don't have 'the biggest'?"

"Eleven."

"Great. And I'll bring breakfast. You two stay here."

From Liam's room, Laurel headed straight for the spare clothes store that had been set up in an old on-call room. After a few minutes of rifling through piles, she retrieved what she thought was a suitable pair of boots. She also found some for Liam, a couple of backpacks, scarves, hats, gloves, and some fleeces for each of them.

"Might as well do this while I'm here," she muttered to herself, stuffing the clothes into the bags and lifting both to her shoulders.

When she reached the canteen, however, she instantly regretted not taking the backpacks to Liam and Arlo before going to get breakfast.

Instantly, eyes were on her. "You off somewhere, Doc?" the woman serving up oatmeal asked her.

"Just collecting some clothes for Liam and Arlo. Their winter stuff wasn't really doing the trick."

"Really?" The woman folded her arms in front of her chest, slopping oatmeal into a bowl.

"Could I also take two more protein bars? Liam's eating in his room today, so Arlo and I are staying with him. And two coffees?"

The woman put down her big spoon and narrowed her eyes. "This ain't one of your fancy coffee bars."

Laurel adjusted one of the bags on her shoulder. She wished she'd tied her hair back up; it had gotten caught beneath one of the straps and was tugging uncomfortably. "I'm aware of that," she said politely.

Fishing out two protein bars and gesturing for her fellow volunteer to deal with the coffee, the woman breathed in deeply through her nostrils. It made them flare out to the sides. An awkward silence followed as Laurel tucked the protein bars into her pockets and tried to juggle the bowl of oatmeal with the coffees.

She was about to walk away when the woman said, "We all know what you're planning."

Laurel turned back around. "I'm sorry?"

"Just don't expect to take any of *our* supplies with you when you go. You're a guest here. You want to leave, you'll have to fend for yourself."

Biting back her desire to snappily respond, Laurel simply turned around and stalked back out of the canteen.

When she returned to Arlo, instantly he could tell she was rattled. "What's happened? Is it worse? Did the wife…?" He trailed off.

Laurel shook her head. "No. It's not that. People have gotten wind that we're thinking of leaving. They're not happy about us taking hospital supplies." She dumped the backpacks on the floor and pulled out the clothes until she reached Arlo's new boots.

Pulling them on, he gave a sharp ironic laugh. "Who cares what they think?" He looked at his feet and sighed. "These have seen better days. Was this all they had?"

"I got Liam some too." Laurel handed Liam his pile of goodies. "Plus warmer clothes for all of us and…" She pulled the protein bars from her pocket and handed one to Liam. "Breakfast, as promised."

For a few minutes, they ate in silence, refueling after a restless and talkative night. Then Arlo stood up. "If I'm going, I better go now." He started rifling through his new items of clothing, selected a hat, scarf and gloves, then put them on along with his jacket.

"Be careful, Dad." Liam was sitting on the edge of his bed, still eating his oatmeal. He put it down and stood up to give his father a hug.

"Liam, I'll walk your father to the tunnel and then go get an update from the ER. Stay here, okay?"

"Do as Doctor Rivera says while I'm gone." Arlo added sternly.

Liam nodded at them both.

"Okay, then. Let's go."

As they walked toward the tunnel, and the ER, Arlo glanced at Laurel. "There's only one thing missing, you know."

She looked at him, waiting for him to continue.

"Weapons. They took ours when we arrived. Any idea how we're going to get them back?"

"Actually...." Laurel reached into the back of her jeans. "I already got one of them."

As Arlo raised his eyebrows at her, Laurel handed him the gun she'd been keeping in her pants for the past week.

"How did you…?"

"Saw an opportunity and took it. Linda was flirting with the guy who guards the guns. He'd left his key on the desk. I could only get this one without someone noticing, but—"

"Better than nothing." Arlo checked it over, then put it into his belt.

"Good luck out there," Laurel said as they reached the tunnel. "If you find supplies but can't carry them on your own, try to hide them somehow and I'll go back with you later."

"I'll carry them," Arlo replied defiantly, in a tone that made Laurel almost expect him to flex his muscles.

"Of course you will." She laughed at him and turned around. When she looked back, he'd entered the tunnel and closed the door behind him.

Outside the ER, Laurel paused. The doors were closed. Reaching into her pocket, she found the blue surgical mask she'd been carrying and slipped it over her face, then pushed the door open.

She knew she'd get in trouble, but at this point she was past caring; she needed to know what was going on and had resolved that if Hopkins hadn't properly examined Katerina then she'd just do it herself; they'd have to shoot her to stop her.

But the second she stepped inside, she knew something had changed. The room was eerily quiet. Dimly lit. No fire. And the beds were empty. She whirled around, looking for the patients who had been here yesterday.

"They moved them." A voice in the darkness made her jump. It was the blue-haired girl.

"Where to?" Laurel asked. The girl was sitting down, head in her hands. She glanced up at Laurel.

"A ward upstairs. Said they needed to keep them away from everyone else."

A shiver ran down Laurel's spine.

"Something about an infection. A really contagious one."

Laurel stepped forward. "What are you doing down here? Shouldn't you be with them?"

"Came to find my necklace," the girl said, her voice suddenly less brazen. "My mom gave it to me. I lost it. Figured it must be here."

When she looked up, she was squinting.

"Have you got a headache?" Laurel asked tentatively.

"Worst I've had in my life. Had to sit down." The girl moved her hands to her head and closed her eyes.

"Look." Laurel bent down, spotting a small silver pendant under the chair where the girl had been sitting near the fire. "Is this your necklace?"

A smile broke across the girl's face. "Yeah," she said, grinning. "That's it."

"Then put it on and let me take you back to the ward." Laurel grabbed a wheelchair from the corner of the room and motioned for the girl to sit in it. For a moment, she looked like she was going to object, but then she gave up and sat down heavily in the seat.

"Where is this ward?" Laurel asked as they exited the ER.

"Upstairs. Level three. You won't get the chair up there."

"Then I'll help you walk the stairs," Laurel replied, adding, "By the way, what's your name?"

"Cristobel," the girl said quietly. "But my friends call me Chrissy." She was squinting again. She raised her hand to her eyes. "Dang it, it's bright out here."

Laurel swallowed hard. This wasn't good. It wasn't good at all.

Upstairs, on the third floor, she found the ward that Dr. Hopkins had converted into a quarantine bay.

The patients from the ER were lined up in beds, Katerina at the far end. Jen and Marcell were beside her.

"Dr. Rivera?" From the corner of the room, Dr. Hopkins spotted her and marched over.

"Chrissy was down in the ER. She has a headache and she's sensitive to the light." Laurel passed Chrissy over to Jen, who'd appeared from nearby, and put her hands on her hips as she waited for Dr. Hopkins to respond.

Scanning her face, at first he looked confused. His eyes narrowed. He pursed his lips as if he was considering whether to yell or not. Then, instead of demanding to know who let Laurel out of her guarded room, he scraped his fingers through his hair and shook his head. "Laurel, you were right. I'm sorry. I should have seen it sooner."

Laurel inhaled a deep breath. *Thank God.* "Don't apologize. What matters is what's happening now. Do you need my help?"

Dr. Hopkins shook his head. "Honestly? I don't know what you can do. We're treating them, but it's already spreading."

"The cold doesn't help," Laurel muttered. "It spreads far more easily in the cold." After a pause, she added, "Katerina? How is she?"

"Deteriorating, I'm afraid. Quite rapidly. After her husband died, I'm afraid she lost the will to fight. She seems to be…."

"Giving in to it?" Laurel pinched the bridge of her nose. She wanted to remove her mask but knew she shouldn't. Dr. Hopkins was wearing a mask, gloves, and scrubs. The other staff in the room were too.

"There's really nothing you can do here, Laurel. I'm not saying that because I don't want your help—I admit I should have accepted it earlier—but we need to limit exposure as much as possible."

Nodding, Laurel began to back out of the room.

"I'll let you know if we need you."

At the back of the ward, Katerina had started seizing. Marcell and Linda called for Dr. Hopkins. He ran to them. Laurel watched as the doors swung closed.

For several minutes, she paced up and down the hall outside, unable to leave but unable to do anything to help.

Finally, the doors opened, and Linda stepped out.

"Laurel... you should go."

"I just wanted to see how Katerina is—"

"No, I mean, you should *go*." Linda met Laurel's eyes. "Go now. Get back to your people."

Laurel blinked hard. "She's dead, isn't she?"

Slowly, Linda nodded. "Yes. She is."

"I can't leave. If this gets worse—"

"If it gets worse, there will be nothing you can do." Linda moved to put her hand on Laurel's arm, then stopped herself.

"I—"

"I'll prepare Liam's meds and give you a fresh supply of chemo meds too. For his friend. Peter?"

"Yes, Peter," Laurel said quietly.

"What else do you need?"

Laurel's mind was racing. Despite having spent all night planning what they'd need with Arlo, she was suddenly too stunned to speak.

"Food?"

She cleared her throat. "Food, a first-aid kit, Arlo's out looking for sleeping bags and tents. We have clothes."

"Okay. Food. A first-aid kit. And a gun? Do you need a gun?"

Guilt tugged at Laurel's stomach. "Yes," she said, barely hesitating. "A gun. Thank you, Linda." She shook her head. "Other people aren't going to be happy if you help us."

"Since when have I cared what other people think?" Linda smiled. "I'll bring the stuff to you tonight. You can leave first thing tomorrow."

"All right. Thank you."

First thing tomorrow. Laurel braced her hands on her lower back. She just prayed Arlo had found what they needed.

8
LAUREL

"Ready?" Arlo was standing by the door of Liam's room, suited and booted for the snow, backpack and pop-up tent strapped to his back. Gun at his side.

When he returned yesterday, laden with supplies, they'd spent the rest of the evening going over their route back to South Minneha and waiting for Linda to bring the items she'd promised. True to her word, when it was late and pitch dark outside, she'd knocked and left a bag containing a gun and Peter's meds. Exactly what Laurel had asked for. But there were also some meds she hadn't asked for; antibiotics, steroids, the arthritis medication for Leonora and Frank, and some labeled "for your mom, until you can get her back here."

Closing her eyes, Laurel had held the note to her chest and felt her heart beating faster than normal. Would it be safe? Bringing her mom back here? What if it wasn't?

Quickly, she'd stopped that train of thought; she couldn't go there. Not now.

Arlo, for his part, had managed to secure them a tent, some thermal sleeping bags, and some large packs. But no food.

"I'm really not sure about asking Leonora and Frank for food," Laurel said, shoving her hands into her pockets.

"We're taking them the meds they need. I'm sure they won't mind."

"I know, but...." Laurel was thinking that she didn't want to risk exposing them, even though she was pretty sure the three of them were okay. But she didn't say it. She didn't want Arlo to freak out and change his mind about leaving; odds were they were okay and better off on the road than staying here.

"I don't think we'll need to." Liam's voice surprised her. He'd been quiet all morning.

"Liam?" Arlo tilted his head at his son.

Setting down his pack, Liam opened it up. Laurel and Arlo peered in.

"Where did you get this?" Laurel dipped her hand in and picked up a protein bar.

Guiltily, Liam scraped his shoe on the floor. "From the canteen. I was careful. Everyone was asleep."

While Arlo clapped Liam on the back and said, "Well done, son. Good work," Laurel scraped her fingers through her hair.

This didn't feel good; stealing from the people who'd helped them didn't feel good.

"They have plenty left. Heaps." Liam looked at her reassuringly. "I wouldn't have taken them otherwise."

"See? He wouldn't have taken them otherwise." Arlo nodded once again. "These should keep us going for a while. Now, come on. Before we change our minds."

Biting back the desire to pull the food out of Liam's bag and demand he leave it behind, Laurel closed her eyes and nodded. "Okay. Let's go."

All the way to the tunnel, she expected someone to stop them. Dr. Hopkins. Jen. The angry cook from the canteen. But no one did.

The steel door closed heavily behind them and Laurel focused on the dim light at the other end. It was colder in the tunnel. It would be colder outside.

"It was really okay, yesterday?" Laurel asked, looking at Arlo.

"Not easy, but I made it there and back, didn't I?" he answered, shrugging.

Laurel took a deep breath and nodded. Snow was an anomaly to her. Growing up in Texas and spending a huge portion of her adult life in the Middle East, she was used to being hot, not cold. And she'd yet to live through a winter in Minnesota.

At the end of the tunnel, breathing in the fresh, crisp air from outside, she turned her face toward the brightening sky. *It's going to be okay. Soon, you'll be back home.*

As the thought crossed her mind, it occurred to her that she now thought of South Minneha as her home. Before all this happened, it had been somewhere she tolerated because her mother needed to be there, but now it was the only place she could think of to be.

Perhaps because Bear and Mae were both so far away. Perhaps because she knew she had no way of finding or reaching them, and it hurt her heart too much to even contemplate it. Perhaps because her mother was there.

Whatever the reason, leaving Lone Oak, a weight lifted from her shoulders.

She was keeping her promise. Soon, she'd be back where she belonged. Peter would have the meds he needed. And everything would be okay.

An hour later, Laurel's initial optimism was starting to waver, as was Arlo's. From the hospital, they had made it across the road to drop off Leonora and Frank's medication. Leonora had answered, although Laurel had called for her not to open up.

"There's been an outbreak of meningitis at the hospital, Leonora. I've brought your medication, but I'll leave it here on the doorstep. We're not staying. We need to get Liam somewhere safer. But a friend of mine said she'd come and tell you when it's safe again."

"Oh dear, oh dear," Leonora had muttered through the door.

"How's Frank doing?" Laurel had leaned closer while Arlo tapped his foot impatiently, jogging up and down against the cold.

"The remedies you gave us have been helping, but the medication will be a relief." Leonora sounded like she was smiling. "Thank you, dear."

Along with a note reminding them not to visit the hospital any time soon, Laurel had left Frank's meds on the doorstep and the three of them had made good time traveling down the main street.

Here, in the center of town, the snow had been trodden down by people venturing out of their homes. But as they neared the outskirts, and the buildings became fewer, the snow became deeper.

Liam, having shorter legs than both Arlo and Laurel, was struggling. And Laurel was exhausted already, her legs burning with the effort of plowing through the snow.

"Here, I'll carry you." Arlo stooped down and picked up his son.

Laurel almost winced on his behalf; he was already carrying a tent and a backpack, but with Liam's pack as well as her own, she couldn't help.

They managed only a few more minutes before Arlo had to stop and ask Liam to walk again.

As the day passed, and they drew farther away from the center of Lone Oak, this pattern continued. And Arlo became more and more frustrated. The ease with which he'd made it to the outdoor store yesterday had given him a false sense of how quick their journey would be. In reality, it was quite the opposite; slow, painstaking, and frustrating. While the main streets had been used by others who'd made the landscape easier to cross, as they edged toward the outskirts of Lone Oak, the snow became thicker and their speed slowed to a slow trudge.

"My pants are soaked." Arlo looked down at his pant legs, wet from having to forge a path through the snow. He was wearing long ski socks underneath, but it wouldn't be long before his legs were freezing cold.

"Maybe we should try to find something to help us clear the snow as we walk?" Laurel asked, looking around as if she expected to see a shovel handy.

"Like dig a path?" Liam asked, tilting his head.

"That's ridiculous!" As Arlo turned to look at Laurel, his foot crashed through an extra-large snow drift. "We can't go on like this!" he growled. "It'll take us all year to make it back at this rate."

With wide eyes, clearly feeling very guilty at having to be carried, Liam murmured, "Maybe we should go back? If we turn around—"

"We're not going back," Arlo snapped. "We need to get out of this town. Now."

"Maybe we can fashion a sled for Liam? So we can pull him?" Laurel stepped up to Arlo's elbow and met his eyes. Back in the hospital, more often than not, he'd been affable. Friendly. Easy to talk to. But the flash she saw in him now was the old Arlo; the one who scared her.

If there was one thing she'd learned about Arlo Staaf, it was that him feeling helpless or frightened was dangerous for those around him. And right now, he was both. Helpless against the snow and frightened that, at any moment, they'd come across another sick person who might infect his son. He'd even insisted they wear bandanas around their necks to function not just as warmers but as masks if they needed them.

"A sled?" He helped Liam over the same snow drift that he'd fallen into and tilted his head at her.

"If we could find some wood and some rope...."

"So, now you want to take a detour to find woodworking materials?"

Laurel blinked at him then sucked in her cheeks. "It was just a suggestion." She looked up at the sky. "But there's one thing I do think we should do."

"Yeah, what's that?"

"Find somewhere to camp for the night because, clearly, we're all exhausted."

"Speak for yourself. I say we carry on until nightfall. We have the tent. We don't need shelter."

"Maybe not, but do you want to camp out in the open?" Laurel had stopped and put her hands on her hips. In this mood, Arlo was exasperating.

"Dad?" Liam interrupted her. "I'm sorry, but I think Laurel's right. We need to regroup and setting up the tent inside somewhere sheltered —or at least under the trees—will keep us warmer."

Laurel's lips twitched at Liam's maturity. Had he been reading a survival guide?

For a moment, Arlo said nothing. Then he grunted loudly, threw up his arms, and said, "Fine! You two just tell me when you want to stop."

9
LAUREL

THREE DAYS LATER

It was pitch dark outside. They were hiding out in an empty ground-floor apartment. It was strangely modern, full of gadgets that no longer worked and expensive things that no longer had any value.

Arlo liked it. But he was in a bad mood.

While Laurel concentrated on fixing them some supper from the sparse ingredients in the cupboard—rice, beans, and canned corn—so that they could save their protein-bar rations, Liam attempted to cheer up his father.

"It's going to be okay, Dad. It'll get easier."

"Will it?" Arlo had found an old bottle of whiskey and poured himself one. Laurel wasn't sure that was a good idea; Arlo didn't seem like the kind of guy who would do well with drink, and his mood had been darkening for the past three days.

"Sure." Liam looked to Laurel. "Right, Dr. Rivera?"

"Right. And look at it this way. We're safe. We're away from the hospital. We've found somewhere to shelter each night. We're in a better place here than we were at Lone Oak. With Liam's immune system—"

"You don't need to remind me about Liam's immune system!" Arlo banged his fist on the table, then stalked off into the darkness of the hallway.

As his father left, Liam sighed a big, deflated sigh. Laurel left the rice bubbling and sat down opposite him. "Your dad's just worried about you. He gets stressed when he's worried. As a dad, he feels like it's his responsibility to keep you safe."

"Isn't he supposed to keep me happy too?" Liam met her eyes as he spoke, then quickly looked away. "I shouldn't have said that."

"No, it's okay, Liam. I know what you mean. You guys have had a rough time."

"For a while I thought I was getting the old Dad back, but he's gone right back to how he was. Grumpy. Snapping at me."

Laurel took off her glasses and set them down on the table. The conversation reminded her of one she'd had with Mae not long after Bear returned from the Middle East. In fact, it was heartbreakingly similar.

"Your dad will snap out of it. Just let him feel his big feelings and try not to take them personally," she said, reaching out to squeeze his hand. "Now, while I finish up, why don't you take a candle and go see if there's a kids' room in this apartment? Maybe there are some comics you haven't read."

Eagerly, Liam jumped up from the table, grabbed a candle, and scurried out of the room. Laurel released a small sigh, then went to her backpack and took out the map of Lone Oak; there had to be something they could do to make the journey easier.

She was tracing her finger along a river that joined up with the one they'd lost Liam's wheelchair to when the bear attacked, when Liam returned.

"No kids' room, but I found this." He set down a thick hardbound encyclopedia. "Looks kinda cool."

"Ooh, I used to love encyclopedias when I was a kid. I guess you probably get all your facts from Google?" She pushed the map to one side as Liam sat down next to her and opened the book. "Well," she said, "this is like Google, but in book form."

"Really?"

"Really."

"It can tell me anything?"

"Pretty much." Laurel laughed. "Let's test it. What's something you like? Something you're interested in… I know. Comic books." She went to the index, found the page, then opened it. "There you go… *A comic book is a publication that combines pictures and words in sequential form…*"

"Cool." Liam pulled the encyclopedia closer. "I think I'll look up… gorillas."

Laurel laughed. "Okay then, go for it. Find 'G' in the index."

As Liam searched for his gorilla page, Laurel hunted in the cupboard by the stove and found some oregano. No salt. Oregano would have to do; at least the rice would have *some* kind of flavor.

"You know, Liam, the other day, you sounded pretty knowledgeable when you suggested to your dad that we stop and regroup, and then since then, some of your suggestions…."

Liam looked up and shrugged. Then a smile twitched on his lips and he stood up to fetch his backpack. Reaching inside, he pulled out a battered old book and showed it to Laurel.

"*The Boy Scout's Handbook,*" she smiled. "*1911 Edition...* You've been reading this?"

"Found it in the hospital library. It's got some good stuff in it. Even if it is super old." He began to flip through the pages. "There's a whole section on winter survival."

"Ah. I see. And what do the Scouts suggest?"

"Well," Liam bit his lower lip. "Not so much about dealing with snow. But there's some good stuff about tying knots, making fires, things like that."

"You best keep hold of it, then." Laurel handed the book back to him and returned to the rice.

For a while, as Laurel cooked and Liam read out gorilla facts with gusto, she almost forgot where they were and why they were there. She could have been back home with Mae when she was little, doing homework while Laurel cooked dinner. Leaning back on the countertop and turning the heat off the rice so it could fluff up, she looked around the small family kitchen. Photos lined the walls. Mom. Dad. Two kids, both younger than Liam and with gap-toothed smiles. There were pictures of them at the beach, in a canoe on a lake, hiking with backpacks and big grins on their faces.

Where were they now? One photo showed them outside a log cabin, sitting around a barbeque with an elderly couple who looked like the kids' grandparents. Perhaps that was where they'd gone; to be with family.

Looking at Liam, Laurel swallowed hard. Since this whole thing started, since the world turned upside down, she'd been trying not to think about Mae and Bear. Mostly Mae, because at least she knew roughly where Bear was....

"Thinking about your family?" Arlo's voice made her look up. His features had softened a little. Perhaps some alone time had eased him out of his bad mood.

"Actually, yes." Laurel turned back to the rice, then set about opening the beans and the corn. With her back to Arlo and Liam, she said, "Bear, my husband. He lives off-grid in Canada. He moved there a couple of years back. But my daughter Mae... I don't know where she is." She turned back around, holding the can opener. "She's in the Army. I don't know where she's stationed."

"Wasn't she allowed to tell you?" Liam asked. "Is she doing something super-secret?"

Laurel shook her head and smiled a little. "No, honey, it's not like that. We just haven't spoken for a while, that's all."

"Oh." Liam looked at his dad. "I can't imagine not speaking to you."

Sighing, perhaps at himself for having been in such a foul mood, Arlo sat down beside Liam and put an arm around his son's shoulders. "Me either, buddy."

After a pause, Liam pulled away and looked up at Arlo. "You know, you don't need to worry about me anymore, Dad. I'm doing better."

Arlo was nodding. His eyes looked moist. He wiped them with the back of his hand.

Interrupting, Laurel put her hands on her hips and tipped her head in Liam's direction. "*And,*" she said, "he's been reading up on being a Boy Scout. So we're in good hands."

"Oh really?" Arlo raised his eyebrows at Liam and, as Liam starting rattling off the camping tips he'd learned, Laurel turned back to the rice. Lifting the lid and stirring it a little, she sighed. She liked this version of Arlo, but the last couple of days had showed her that the old Arlo was still in there, lingering just below the surface. And that scared her.

After dinner, they were forced to leave the dishes in the sink. This bothered Laurel, but they had no choice; the water from the tap was thick and brown, and they couldn't afford to waste their drinking water cleaning dishes they wouldn't use again.

"What if the people who live here come back?" Liam asked, looking around as though they might appear at any moment.

"I doubt they will, Liam." Arlo nodded toward the hallway. "I checked out the bedrooms. Their clothes are gone and the kids' toys too."

"They should have taken this stuff." Laurel gestured to the canned goods she'd emptied onto the counter, and to the bag of rice — still half full — and the unopened packet of shortbread cookies that looked mouthwateringly tempting.

"Not everyone can think clearly in a crisis. Probably grabbed what they thought was important—laptops, phones, wallets—for when the power came back."

Laurel shook her head. Laptops, phones, and wallets meant nothing now. Overnight, they had gone from a world in which money meant everything to one in which it was utterly useless.

"It doesn't feel right to sleep in their beds," Liam said, as if he already knew his dad was going to suggest he hunker down in one of the kids' rooms and get a good night's rest.

"We can set up camp in the living room." Laurel moved toward the door. "It'll be easier to keep us warm if we're all together." Looking over her shoulder at Arlo, she asked, "Is there a fireplace?"

He nodded.

"Good. Let's get settled, then. Best make the most of recouping our energy while we can."

In the living room, after lighting the fire, Arlo offered Liam and Laurel a couch each and he took the recliner near the window. For a while, they lay in silence. Laurel looked over at Arlo. His eyes were closed, but he clearly wasn't sleeping. Then she looked at Liam. He wasn't on his couch. She sat up and looked around the room. Instead of trying to sleep, he was at the back of the room, holding a candle while he searched the bookcases that lined the rear wall.

"Find anything good?" Laurel stood up, slipped out of her sleeping bag and walked over to join him. In his chair, Arlo stirred and cleared his throat as he looked up at them.

"They have loads of business magazines, Dad." Liam gestured for his father to join them, but Arlo simply shrugged his shoulders up toward his ears and scratched his beard.

"Not much use now, are they, son?"

Ignoring his father, Liam turned to Laurel. "Dad was in one of these once, weren't you, Dad?"

Again, Arlo grunted.

"Which edition was it? Maybe it's here." Liam's eyes had lit up. Laurel watched him as he sifted through the shelf of *Minnesota Business Monthly* magazines, one by one, desperately trying to find the one with his father's name on the front.

While Liam searched, Laurel scanned the shelves in front of her. Crime novels, some big hardback ones that looked a little too 'literary' for Laurel's tastes, a heap of non-fiction biographies. Then her eyes landed on an atlas. She paused. Her fingers stroked its thick spine. Breathing in slowly, she pulled it free from the shelf and went to sit on the floor in front of the fire.

She was about to open it when Liam shouted, "Here! I found it!"

Rushing over, he shoved a magazine into his father's lap, then quickly took it back and waved it at Laurel. "My mom's in it too." He rushed over and plopped it down on top of Laurel's atlas, flipping it open to the center spread. "There she is."

Laurel adjusted her glasses. There were three photographs on the page. In each one, Arlo was wearing a dark blue suit, a crisp white shirt, and a neatly trimmed beard. His hair was short. His eyes sparkled. Next to him, his wife was wearing an emerald-green dress. Her hands were resting on her stomach.

"She was pregnant in these?" Laurel looked up at Arlo but he was hunched down in his sleeping bag, staring at the dark beyond the window.

"Yeah," Liam answered on his dad's behalf. "It's all about how Dad was this big business man starting a family." He smiled as he tapped the image of his mother's belly. "That's me in there."

"'*Entrepreneur Arlo Staaf on readjusting his priorities as a father-to-be.*'" Laurel read the headline. "Looks like a great article."

Finally, Arlo looked around. "Load of tripe. Allison hated it. 'Why are they interviewing you? I'm the one who'll be giving birth.' That's what she said." Arlo almost smiled, but then pushed his fingers through his hair and shook his head. "They must have been short on stories that month."

"I think it's good," Liam said quietly. "Can I keep it?"

Frowning, as if he couldn't figure out why in the world Liam would want to do that, Arlo nodded. "I suppose so. If it'll fit in your pack." Clearly trying to change the subject, as Liam rolled up the magazine and slotted it into his backpack, Arlo pointed at Laurel's atlas. "You planning a trip?"

Laurel tilted her head to the side. "I was just… wondering how long it would take to get from South Minneha to Thunder Bay."

Arlo sat forward, leaning on his thighs. "All this time desperate to get back to your hospital and now you want to take a road trip? What's at Thunder Bay?"

"My husband. Off-grid in Canada, remember?"

"You mean your *ex*-husband?"

Laurel sat up a little straighter and sucked in her cheeks. "No, I don't." Her Texan accent had snuck through into her voice. "We're not divorced. Just separated."

"I see." Arlo sat back again and folded his arms in front of his chest. He pressed his lips together in a way that made Laurel think he was stopping himself from saying something.

"What?" she asked, drumming her fingers on the atlas.

"Nothing." Arlo shrugged. "It's just… don't you think he'd have come looking for you by now if he wanted the two of you to be together?"

Laurel blinked and swallowed hard. Was Arlo being deliberately cruel? She cleared her throat. "Maybe. But maybe he doesn't know what's happened."

As Arlo scoffed, Liam sat back down next to Laurel and said, "How would he not know? Everyone knows."

"Is Thunder Bay protected by some kind of anti-EMP forcefield?" Arlo was being snarky. The images of his wife had upset him. But Laurel wasn't going to let him get away with it.

"No, Arlo. It's not. But Bear lost his hearing when he was serving in the Middle East. He left because he couldn't stand being around people anymore and he *hated* the hearing aid he had to wear. If he's living alone, I doubt he'll even be using it."

As Arlo looked away, a little guiltily, Liam's eyes widened. "So he really could *not* know what happened?"

"If he'd already gathered supplies for the winter and was hunkering down at the cabin, yeah." She stood up, taking the atlas with her despite the fact she hadn't opened it yet. When she reached the couch, she slotted the atlas into her backpack and looked up at Arlo. "Besides, it doesn't matter if he wants me to find him or not. I need him to help me find our daughter."

Arlo's eyes softened a little.

"She could be anywhere in the world right now. But I'm done sticking my head in the sand. I need to find her. I hoped that *you* might understand that." Before Arlo could answer, Laurel climbed into her sleeping bag and turned her back on him. Her chest was tight with tears that wanted to come, but she squashed them down. She stayed like that for a very long time. Then when she was certain Arlo and Liam were asleep, she let herself cry.

10

BEAR

For three days, Bear had put off leaving. Now, it was finally time. He couldn't wait any longer.

"Ta dah!" Trent beamed as he set down a plate full of roasted hare.

"You caught this?" Bella raised an eyebrow at him. Trent nodded proudly.

"Yep. All me. I mean, Bear was with me, but I shot it myself. Right, PB?"

Bear blinked, distracted, but then nodded. "Right. All you, kid." He looked around the table. "Even skinned it himself."

As the others nodded approvingly, and Trent took on the role of dishing out the meat, Bear took a large swig of water. His stomach was churning with nervous energy. Usually, he'd have said no to food. But with Trent watching him expectantly, he forced down some meat and smiled approvingly.

After supper, and a longer-than-he'd-hoped game of cards with Trent, Deb, Henry and Bulldog, Bear went through his usual nighttime routine. A splash of water to the face. A visit to the hospital's new sawdust toilet block. A treat for Jess.

As Trent settled down for the night, Bear sat on the edge of his own bed. Jess was on Trent's feet, but she was staring at Bear as if she knew something was going on that he wasn't telling her about.

"Night, kid." Bear reached over and patted Trent's shoulder. Trent yawned a huge growl of a yawn and smiled.

"Night, PB. Thanks for today. I can't believe I actually caught something. It was awesome."

"You're welcome, kid." Bear gave the boy's shoulder a squeeze.

As Trent turned away and snuggled down under his blanket, Bear did the same. Luckily, these days, they all slept in several layers of clothing, including coats and hats. But he'd taken his boots off and positioned them at the foot of the bed. Just behind them, tucked underneath the bed, was his backpack. He knew the truck held most of the supplies he needed—he'd been out there to check on it a few days ago—so he'd simply packed a few bottles of water, some medical supplies, the waterproof pants he wore when he went out hunting to protect his own pants from the snow, and the spare batteries for his hearing aid. Just one set; he'd soon need to source more.

Nearby, in the women's section of the canteen, he pictured Deb closing her eyes and drifting off to sleep, safe in the knowledge that he would soon be bringing her daughter back to her. At least, he hoped that was what she was doing. He'd seen the pain in her eyes that afternoon and he hated to think that it was only the beginning for her of a very tough road ahead.

As Trent's breathing became predictably deep and regulated—a small almost-snore coming from his nose on each in-breath—Bear rolled onto his back and crossed his hands behind his head so that his elbows were sticking out to the sides. The fireplace nearby was crackling nicely. He'd done a good job. He'd given the hospital everything he could. Now, he needed to give them Laurel.

"Wake me at midnight," he'd said to Henry, who was on the first fire-shift that night. "I'll take over."

"Sure thing, boss." Henry had picked up his book, seemingly quite happy to sit by the fire and read for a few hours, and offered him a salute.

Bear had wondered in that moment whether Deb had shared Bear's plan with Henry. It wouldn't surprise him, or upset him, if she had; the two of them had grown close. And he wasn't sure he'd have been able to leave Deb behind if he hadn't known she'd have someone to take care of her. Henry was a quiet man, the kind who answered a question when asked but who didn't often offer unsolicited advice. So Bear supposed he'd never be sure one way or the other.

Blinking at the ceiling, Bear breathed out slowly and tried to persuade his body to begin relaxing into sleep. In the military, he'd become adept at catching a few hours' sleep and waking up bang-on when he was supposed to. It was like he had an internal clock he could program. A very useful skill. But tonight, he was petrified it wouldn't work. If he slept in, and Henry—for some reason—didn't wake him either, he'd have to wait another night and he didn't think he could stand that.

So for a few hours he tossed and turned, catching only the briefest slices of sleep until, eventually, he felt Henry's hand on his shoulder. "Bear? Sorry, buddy. Your turn."

Bear sat up quickly and shook his head. "I'm awake," he said. "Thanks, Henry. You go get some sleep."

As Bear stood up, Henry met his eyes. For a moment, Bear thought he was going to say something, but instead he just held out his hand to shake Bear's.

"She told you, huh?" Bear said quietly.

Henry nodded and gripped Bear's hand a little tighter. "She did. And she asked me to give you something." Henry reached into the pocket of his large black coat and handed Bear something pink.

Bear frowned at it. Was it a scarf?

"It's a coat. For the dog." Henry was almost smiling. "She knitted it."

Under other circumstances, Bear would have laughed at that—a great big belly laugh. Instead, he gripped it tightly in his hands and smiled, shaking his head at his mother-in-law's choice of wool color.

"See you soon." Henry patted Bear's arm.

"See you soon." Bear pulled Henry in for a brief hug, slapped his friend's back, then strode over to the fire, sat down, and leaned forward onto his knees. Staring into it, he rubbed his hands together and tried to picture Jess in her new pink coat. It made him smile. When he looked up, Henry was in bed on the other side of the room. Trent was still sound asleep. But Jess was gone.

Bear's heartbeat quickened in his chest. He was about to stand up to look for her when he felt something scrape his leg. He looked down. There she was. Bear scooped her up and put her on his lap. "I know you'll miss the kid," he said, ruffling her ears. "But Deb is right. I need you."

Jessamine sat up and licked Bear's mouth, then his chin, then his nose.

"All right, all right…." He stifled a chuckle. So, she was pleased to be coming with him. At least that was something. "You might not be so enthusiastic when you see your new outfit."

Shoving the dog coat into his pocket for later, Bear settled back into the chair. For the next few hours, he tended to each fire, making sure they stayed lit, and mentally plotted his journey from the hospital to the parking lot.

The snow had stopped a few days ago, and didn't look like it would be starting again too soon, which meant he had a good window of time to make some progress. It would be hard going through the snow, but he'd coped with worse. After all, he'd made it through the Boundary Waters with an infected wolf bite and no winter clothing. Compared to that, it would be a cakewalk.

At least, that was what he was telling himself.

As soon as the sky outside began to brighten, the windows along the top of the room turning from black to gray, Bear stood up and padded quietly to his bed, Jess under his arm. Setting her down and giving her a look he hoped said "wait," he scooped up his boots. Then he slung his bag onto his back, retrieved his rifle, took one last look at the sleeping Trent, grabbed Jess and headed for the door.

As he approached the atrium and the doors leading to the most direct route from the hospital to the parking lot, his thick socks offered little cushion from the freezing floor beneath his feet. Now deserted, the atrium looked sad and empty. A few beds remained—ones they hadn't needed to transport—along with chairs, their old trashcan fires, and some empty drug carts.

Bear weaved through them. He didn't glance behind him; if Jess heard something, he'd see it in her ears.

At the doors, he paused and set her down on the floor. Taking his waterproof pants from his bag, he pulled them on top of the khaki ones he was wearing, then shoved his feet into his thick boots. Jess was waiting patiently. When he took Deb's pink wooly coat from his pocket and tugged it over Jess's head, she looked at him as if he'd lost his mind.

Looking at her, he grinned. "You look great," he whispered. Then he picked up the crowbar they used to pry the doors open and set to work.

After a few seconds of hard pushing, they opened enough for him and Jess to squeeze through. Outside, the snow was deep but there were passable areas where people had walked the past few days—going out for fresh air or to hunt unsuspecting rabbits that might have ventured out of their homes.

Bear headed for one of the trees in the middle of what used to be the manicured lawn out front of the hospital, and scanned the ground. Picking up a branch with lots of small twigs attached to it, that looked almost broom-like, he nodded and retraced his steps.

Then, dragging his branch behind him to cover his footprints, he set off for the parking lot.

As he neared the large concrete structure, however, the snow became deeper and his pace slower. By the time he reached it, the sun was almost up over the horizon. It wouldn't be long before the people inside the hospital woke up.

When Trent noticed he was gone, would he come looking for him? Probably not straight away. He'd assume Bear had taken Jess out to the bathroom or that he was off fixing something or building something. Bear hoped—calculated—that it would be mid-morning at least before the boy realized that he was missing. But he still needed to get away from the hospital grounds as quickly as possible.

Reaching the door to the lower level of the parking lot, Bear stopped. A few weeks back, he'd come out to check the truck was still there. He'd avoiding passing the body bags they had lined up. Bags containing the bodies of men *he'd* killed, Murph, and more. Brought out here because the morgue was too full and there were too many of them. But he knew they were there.

He screwed his eyes shut for a moment, trying to recalibrate. Focus on Laurel. On getting to Laurel.

Feeling himself return to earth, his heartrate slowing, Bear set Jess down on the ground and tucked his branch into the strap of his backpack. Last time he came out here, it had taken him far too many minutes to pry the door open. It had been frozen shut and blocked by more than a foot of snow that he'd had to shovel out of the way by hand.

But today, the snow didn't need clearing.

He crouched down to examine the section of path in front of the door. Someone had swept it.

In his front pocket, he was carrying a bottle of homemade deicer—water with plenty of salt in case he needed it to get the door open. Standing up, he reached for it with one hand while he tried the handle with the other. He'd expected the door to be frozen shut. But it opened with ease.

Quickly, Bear replaced the deicer and, instead, reached for his gun.

He hesitated and glanced behind him. Had it snowed since he'd last been here? Yes. Not much, but it *had* snowed. He hadn't seen any other footprints coming from the direction of the hospital, but a covered walkway led around the side of the parking lot. Someone could have entered that way without leaving a trace….

Giving Jess a signal to stay behind him, he pulled the door back and stepped inside, gun raised, scanning the stairwell. Directly in front of him was the door that led to the lower level. The bodies.

To his left, a staircase wound up to the higher levels of the multi-story parking lot. To his right were an empty vending machine and a ticket machine.

He moved forward. In front of the door to the lower level, he stopped and pressed his good ear up against it. Nothing. He looked at Jess. Her ears weren't twitching. She looked relaxed, if a little ridiculous in her sweater.

At the foot of the stairs, he paused. He had a choice; check every level of the parking lot to see if there was someone here, or head straight for the truck and get the heck out of here.

He rubbed his now-fully-bearded chin—Laurel wouldn't approve, but it was keeping his face warm. If whoever had cleared the entrance and snuck inside was here now, they'd have left wet footprints. There were none, which either meant they'd been here a while or had come and gone.

Either way, it was likely they were looking for shelter or supplies. His truck would provide both. So, skipping all the other levels, Bear headed straight for Level Eight, where he and Trent had abandoned the truck when they'd arrived all those weeks ago expecting to find Laurel.

As he opened the door, he steeled himself for what he might find. Every time he came to check on it, he expected the truck to have been ransacked, the supplies gone. Maybe even the truck itself—although he had no idea how anyone would get it through the snow. Now he'd seen evidence of someone apart from him being here, he braced himself for the discovery that this would finally be the day his fear was realized.

But he was wrong. There she was, just as he'd left her.

As if she knew what they were there for, Jess bounded up to the truck and started sniffing it. Quickly, having already sorted through everything to create a pile of essentials, Bear pulled a second—larger—pack from the passenger seat and began loading it.

Food, mainly protein bars and ration biscuits—the kind astronauts ate in space shuttles; who knew where the owner of the truck had found them—water purification tablets, matches, some empty water bottles, a fold-out cooking pot, two full water bottles, kibble for Jess, ammo, a hunting knife, and a tarp. Then he decanted the contents of his other backpack into this one, attached a sleeping bag to the bottom of it, and slung it onto his shoulders. It was heavy, but he'd carried heavier.

Taking the map from the glove compartment and checking his bearings, he breathed in deeply and nodded. He glanced out at the hospital, shimmering as the sun rose. "I'll be back soon," he said, then jogged back down the stairs and out into the snow.

11
BRITT

Every day since the snow stopped, Britt had traveled across town to sit beside Murph's dead body. The lower level of the parking lot, with its frozen black body bags, had become so familiar it was like home now.

The most she could manage, before the cold started to bite at her nose and fingers, was an hour. She'd been tempted to light a fire, but knew she couldn't risk warming the corpses.

Still, that hour each day was her favorite hour. It was the time she used to plot, and plan, and think of all the ways she'd get revenge on the one who took Murph from her.

Now the hospital was opening up again, people milling in and out to go for walks or to hunt rabbits and squirrels, doors unguarded, she could slip in easily. But how would she find the guy?

Instead, she'd vowed to wait. Wait until the weather turned, then start watching them. She'd figure out who he was, and then she'd figure out how she was going to get him.

Ryan and Bert told her she should stop. Let it go. Focus on finding them somewhere safe, setting up camp, building a new band of brothers and sisters who could help her when the time came to enact her plan.

But she ignored them.

This was her fight. She didn't care whether they joined her for it or not.

She was reaching for the zipper on Murph's body bag, tempted—as she always was—to see him one last time, when she heard something.

Taking hold of her gun, she stood up and hurried to the door. She stood behind it, gun raised, and pressed her ear to it.

Someone was in the stairwell. Someone was *in* the stairwell.

Her heart began to thud. She knew it wasn't either of the guys, because they were too weak to even set foot in the place. What if it was someone from South Minneha? Come to move the bodies again? What if they'd decided it was time to burn them?

She stood back and steeled herself to shoot whoever stepped through that door; no way was she letting them take Murph from her a second time.

But no one came through the door.

She waited.

Still no one came.

Tentatively, she pushed the door open. She could hear footsteps above her, traveling up, pushing another door open. She frowned.

Then she ducked back onto the lower level and sprinted for the opposite end of the parking bays. There, she entered a second stairwell and wound her way quickly up, gently checking each door until, on Level Eight, she saw him—a big blond guy with a big brown beard.

He was on the other side of the parking level, standing next to a big red truck. A dog was at his feet. From the back of the truck, he seemed to be loading items into a backpack.

He fiddled with his ear.

"Well, I'll be damned..." Britt muttered. From the dark of the stairwell, peering through a gap in the door, she knew he couldn't see her. Even the dog hadn't noticed. "It's you, isn't it?"

She squinted. Yes. He was wearing a hearing aid. A big blond guy with a dog and a hearing aid.

Her gut clenched. Her skin started to prickle. It was him. It was *him*!

"Ryan!" Britt was panting with the effort of running through the snow. Ryan and Bert had been waiting for her in the abandoned laundromat near the hospital. The rest of their small gang was still back at the warehouse, but whenever she visited Murph, Ryan and Bert insisted on waiting for her. As if they thought she couldn't be trusted on her own; thought she might do something stupid.

They'd lit a fire and were sitting beside it, smoking and playing cards. Ryan looked up. Bert didn't.

"Britt?" Ryan stood up slowly and put his hands on her upper arms. "What's happened? Are you all right?"

Shrugging away from him, still out of breath, Britt shook her head. "I found him. The one who killed Murph."

"The military guy?" Ryan glanced at Bert, who simply took a long drag on his cigarette.

"Yes. The military guy. He's preparing to leave, so we need to hurry."

"Preparing to leave where?"

"The hospital. I saw him packing a bag."

"Britt, slow down. You saw him packing a bag?" Ryan was looking at her as if she'd lost her mind.

Rolling her eyes, Britt cursed and sucked in a deep breath. Snatching Ryan's cigarette from him, she put it to her own lips and tried to calm down. "I was visiting Murph when I heard someone in the stairwell. He had a truck, hidden on one of the top floors. I watched him. He took a bunch of stuff from the truck and packed a bag. He's going somewhere. And we're going to follow him."

"Follow him?" Bert stood up. "Why?"

At that, the anger and frustration simmering away in Britt's stomach turned into a volcano. "Why?" She lurched forward, grabbing the collar of his jacket, holding the cigarette treacherously close to his sickly gray cheek. "Because he *killed* Murph. And our friends. Or had you forgotten!" She was trembling.

"No, no, of course not. What he did was unforgiveable. Terrible." Bert had begun to stutter. Over the past few weeks, instead of growing angrier like she had, Bert seemed to have just accepted his girlfriend Marianne's death. Britt had told him that after taking down the military guy, they'd go after the woman who killed Marianne, take her out too. But Bert seemed to just want to wallow. Taking action wasn't his style.

Ryan stepped into view and tried to meet Britt's eyes. She was still holding the cigarette and thinking about the sizzling sound it would make when she pressed it to Bert's skin.

"Britt? You want to follow him? Okay. Let's follow him."

She looked at Ryan. He had a kind face. Young, probably her age. Younger than Murph, for sure. If she'd had a brother, he might have looked like Ryan. "Good." She let go of Bert and dropped the cigarette, stubbing it out with her snow-covered boot. "You two go back and fetch the others. I'll follow him. I'll leave a trail for you and we'll meet tonight when he stops."

Clearing his throat, Ryan said, "Let me go with you, Britt. Bert can fetch the others."

Britt tilted her head and studied Ryan's face. He liked her, she knew he did. But Ryan was the opposite of Britt's type, and he clearly had no idea what *true* love was if he thought she would abandon Murph even in death. Still, that didn't stop her from giving him hope in order to get what she wanted.

"No," she said softly, squeezing Ryan's arm and angling him away from Bert. "I need you to go with him. He doesn't trust me like you do. I'm worried he'll tell the others to stay behind, and we've seen what this guy can do. It'll take more than just me and you to take him down. I'm sure of it."

Ryan nodded slowly. Bert was scuffing his shoe on the cold, hard concrete. He was furious with her. But he was also scared of her and didn't want to be alone; she could read him like a book.

"Okay." Ryan pulled his coat closer and picked up his gun from where he'd left it by the fire. Bert did the same.

"Go." Britt checked for her own gun. Patting it made her feel better. Safer. "I'll see you tonight."

12

LAUREL

They left the apartment at dawn. It was tempting to stay, to wait a few more days in the warmth before venturing back out into the cold. But they knew that if the snow started again, their journey would be even more difficult.

"First thing we need to do is find some poles to help us walk with," Liam said as he dragged his small legs through the snow that still covered the sidewalk outside.

"Good idea." Laurel glanced at Arlo. His mood had softened since last night, but only a little. Days in, he was still nervous about the journey, and she could tell he was having second thoughts about whether they made the right decision to leave the hospital.

"I think we should try a different route," he said as he pulled his boot free from a snowdrift.

"A different route?" Laurel glanced at Liam, then back at Arlo. "Why didn't you say something before we left?"

"I was still thinking about it." He scratched his beard with gloved fingers, then gestured to the snow. "Being back out here, I think it's the right decision."

"Think what is the right decision?" Laurel adjusted her glasses on her nose and narrowed her eyes at him.

Pausing, Arlo pulled their map from his pocket. They'd been following the same route back as the one they took to get to Lone Oak, but he pulled his glove off and began to trace a line with his index finger. Laurel tilted her head to look at it. "You want to travel along the side of the river?"

"I know navigating through the trees is more difficult, but if it's more sheltered, it might actually be faster."

Laurel bit her lower lip. Every time she thought about how badly she wanted to get back to South Minneha, her stomach twisted and her heart beat a little louder in her chest. Especially now she knew what she'd do next; find Bear, then find their daughter.

Eventually, she said, "All right. Let's try it. What have we got to lose?"

Nodding at her, Arlo shoved the map back into his pocket, put his glove back on and changed direction. "This way, then."

As Arlo strode out ahead, Laurel kept pace with Liam. This morning, it seemed that he was determined to—quite literally—stand on his own two feet, but she still wanted to keep him close; he had a habit of pretending to be more okay than he really was just to placate his father.

"We could do some foraging down by the river. Could find some useful stuff," he said, looking up at Laurel for approval.

"You've read about foraging in the Boy Scout handbook?" she asked.

Liam moved his head from side to side. "Yeah. A bit."

"I used to do that lots as a kid," Laurel said, smiling slightly as she remembered her father teaching her. "When I moved here from Texas, I thought I might take it up again. I even bought a book about it."

"Shame you didn't have it with you when the lights went out," Liam said, laughing. "'Cos that would have been *real* handy."

"I'm sure I'll remember some of it." Laurel put her hand on his shoulder.

"Cool." Liam smiled back at her, and when Laurel looked up she realized that Arlo had turned and was watching them. He gave her a brief nod, as if to say "thanks for being kind to my kid" then turned and trudged forward.

It took them almost an hour to reach the part of town where the buildings began to thin out. Laurel could see a bridge up ahead. Below it, lined with trees on either side, presumably, was the river.

"This way." Arlo pointed to a copse of trees beside the bridge. "If we head down through the trees, we'll get to the river. Moving along the riverbank should give us the best of both worlds—fewer trees and less snow."

"And the river leads to South Minneha?"

"All the way." Arlo patted his pocket. "You want to check the map?"

"No, no," she replied, following him into the trees, "I trust you."

At that, Arlo smirked a little. "Never thought I'd hear you say that, Doc."

Laurel paused a moment, then laughed. "Never thought I'd say it."

As Arlo had predicted, the ground beneath the canopy of the pine trees was much easier to cross. Although they had to dodge tree roots and keeping their bearings was harder, it was undoubtedly a better choice.

"Wow," Laurel said, exhaling a deep breath, "it's nice not to feel my calves burning."

"Agreed," Arlo replied.

Ahead, now finding it much easier to move, Liam paused every now and then to examine the forest floor.

"Find anything good?" Laurel asked, adjusting her backpack on her shoulders as she stooped to see what he was looking at.

"Nah. Nothing." Liam stood up and sighed. "Thought we might find some berries or some nuts a squirrel had stashed away."

"Well, there are other things we can use." Laurel put her hands on her hips and looked around at the trees.

"Like what?" Liam was watching her.

Laurel pressed her hand to the trunk of the nearest tree. "Bark," she said. "It's nice and dry. Good fire starter." She nodded at Arlo. "We should gather some while we can."

Watching as she stripped some from the trunk, Arlo pressed his lips together. "Do we really want to carry—"

"Dad," Liam interrupted. "When you're out in the wilderness, you have to take what you can when you find it. You have to be prepared."

Laurel smiled approvingly at Liam, then raised her eyebrows at Arlo. "See, your son gets it."

As Arlo rolled his eyes and gathered a token amount of bark, shoving it into his backpack, Liam asked Laurel what else they could take.

"Well, I'm not sure yet," she replied. "Let's see what we find."

For a while, they continued through the trees in the direction of the river. They were heading downhill, which made traveling even easier, and for perhaps the first time in weeks they all seemed to be in brighter spirits. Liam, especially.

"What are these?" He stopped and pointed at something.

Laurel stopped to look while Arlo took the opportunity to stop for a drink of water. "Ah. Dandelions," she said, moving her fingers over the small yellow flowers. "They're struggling. Surprised they haven't been killed off by the weather."

"Oh." Liam folded his arms. "Dandelions are useless."

Looking at him in mock-horror, Laurel shook her head. "Useless? They are *not* useless." Plucking one from the ground, she held it up and brushed its petals with her index finger. "Did you know you can eat every single part of a dandelion? Petals, leaves, stem?"

"Dandelion soup for dinner then," Arlo quipped.

"Really?" Liam was frowning at her as if she was trying to trick him.

"Yes, really. Go on, gather them up." She reached into her backpack and pulled out a small plastic bag. "Put them in here."

"We should be at the river soon," Arlo said, stumbling a little as they navigated a particularly steep drop between the trees.

"Good. I think it's time for a break soon." Laurel and Arlo both turned to help Liam. He was paler than he had been when they left that morning, and his pace was slowing despite the easier terrain.

Laurel even suspected that part of his pausing to forage was to put his father off the scent that he was tiring; here, it would be hard for Arlo to carry Liam and navigate the slope and the tree roots. Even harder than it had been in the snow.

As the trees started to thin and the ground leveled out, Laurel suggested they stop. "Here's a good spot." She gestured to the small clearing they were standing in.

"It's not even mid-morning," Arlo said, folding his arms.

"Yes, but I think we could *all* do with a rest." She met his eyes, hoping he understood what she was trying to say to him; that Liam was the one who needed a break.

"Right." Arlo nodded, glancing from his son back to Laurel. "Right. Okay. Are we cooking up those dandelions?"

"Maybe we'll save those for dinner." Laurel swung her backpack off her shoulders and onto the ground, her back aching with relief. Arlo, who'd been carrying both his pack and Liam's, did the same.

He rubbed his neck, then braced his hands in the small of his back.

Laurel passed out bottles of water and some of the shortbread cookies they'd packed, then sat down on a nearby log. Opposite her, Liam and Arlo sat on the ground with their backs pressed up against a tree.

She watched as Liam closed his eyes and let his head tip back a little. The poor kid was exhausted already and they still had days of traveling to do. Arlo slipped his arm around his son's shoulders and squeezed. The gesture made Laurel smile. Often, these moments she saw between the two of them caught her off guard. They reminded her that, no matter what Arlo had done, he'd done it out of love for his son. Deep, fierce love. And fear that he might lose him.

For a moment, Laurel closed her eyes too. Then she opened them and looked up at the branches above her head. Perhaps, right now, Bear was doing the same thing. Perhaps he'd left his cabin early, gone out to check his traps, taking Jessamine with him of course, then lit a fire and sat outside enjoying the solitude of the woods.

Or perhaps he was still cozy in his cabin. A fire roaring in the grate. A pile of books to read. Food stashed away for the winter. No idea that the world around him had crumbled and changed into something unrecognizable.

Thinking of Bear in his cabin, she realized she had no idea what it was actually like. She knew he was in the Thunder Bay area, but that was it. She'd written to him a few times after he left, care of the local general store, but that was the closest she could get to a fixed location. Her letters had contained mainly perfunctory things like sharing her new job, her mom's trial, how they were doing in South Minneha. He hadn't written back.

Perhaps he wouldn't want her to show up. Perhaps he'd already left.

After experiencing how hard it was to make it the short distance from Lone Oak back to her own town, she was starting to wonder how on earth she'd manage the journey to Thunder Bay. Especially alone, because she couldn't—and wouldn't—ask anyone from the hospital to make the journey with her.

And if that was tough, how would she and Bear even *start* looking for Mae? Her only hope was that Bear might have some idea where she was. Or some contact they could search for who would point them in the right direction.

Lost in her thoughts, Laurel heard Liam and Arlo muttering between themselves. One of them coughed. A bird somewhere sang a slightly melancholy song. She blinked up at the pine branches and frowned. Someone was coughing again.

She looked up, expecting to see Arlo slapping his chest and trying to clear his lingering smoker's cough—she'd noticed it as soon as she'd met him—but it wasn't Arlo coughing; it was Liam.

"You okay, boy?" Arlo slapped Liam's back. It didn't help.

"I'm... fine...." Liam shook his head, wheezing a little between words. He stood up. He looked shaky on his legs but smiled at Laurel. "I'm fine. The cookie just tickled my throat, that's all."

Laurel stood up and walked over, pressing the back of her hand to Liam's forehead. "He doesn't seem to have a fever."

"Doesn't *seem* to have a fever?" Arlo sprang to his feet. Taller than Laurel, when he puffed out his chest and looked at her with that snarl on his lips, it was hard not to feel intimidated by him. "What if he caught it? Before we left?"

"Liam didn't come into contact with anyone—"

"But you did... you could have..." Arlo reached up and pushed his fingers through his hair. "Why didn't I think of this? You could have infected him. Couldn't you?"

Taking a slow, deep breath, Laurel met Arlo's eyes. *He's a parent. I'm a doctor. He's a worried parent. Reassure him.* "Arlo, it's very unlikely that I contracted meningitis from the brief contact I had with the patients. I'm fully vaccinated. It doesn't mean I couldn't catch it, but it's unlikely. Plus, I'm showing no symptoms and, right now, neither is Liam." She put her hand on Arlo's arm, trying to remind him of the times he'd trusted her in the past. She lowered her voice. "It's a cough. Don't scare him."

For a moment, Arlo didn't move, then he nodded. "Fine. But you'll keep an eye on him, right?"

"Right." She nodded.

They waited a little longer before setting off again. With every minute that passed, Laurel felt a wave of relief that Liam hadn't coughed any more. She was pretty certain he didn't have meningitis. Coughing wasn't one of the symptoms she'd expect if he did. But that didn't mean he hadn't caught something else. In Liam's condition, even a bad cold could be dangerous. And, of course, there was the other option; that his cancer hadn't improved as much as they thought it had.

Shoving those thoughts from her mind, because right now the best thing she could do for all of them was get them back to South Minneha as quickly as possible, she led the way toward the river while Arlo stayed a few paces behind to help Liam.

Finally, they were free of the trees and beside the riverbank. Laurel spotted the bridge that they'd crossed and nodded to herself. Arlo was right; walking along the river would be much easier than trudging through the snow. Here, there was barely a smattering of it on the ground.

"It's dried up." Liam was gesturing to her.

"Dried up?"

"The river. It's dried up." Liam pointed down over the bank and she followed his finger.

"Didn't expect that." Arlo said, standing next to Liam and looking down at the sludgy riverbed.

"Maybe we could walk down there?" Liam suggested. "It's sheltered. No wind. Not much snow has settled."

"It's too steep." Arlo pulled Liam back a little, away from the edge of the bank. "We'd never get back up again."

Laurel had moved forward and was peering over the edge. She squinted. Halfway down the bank, she could see what looked like some wheels. "Look." She tugged Arlo's sleeve. "Is that a sports wagon?"

Arlo narrowed his eyes.

"It is." Laurel grabbed his sleeve again. "It's a wagon. That could be *great* for Liam. We used to have one we took to the beach when Mae was little. The wheels go over sand, so they should be able to cope with snow."

"It's too far down, you'll never reach it." Arlo gestured for them to keep walking. "Besides, it's got a Vikings logo on it."

Laurel's eyes widened. "Seriously?" She put her hands on her hips; one of Bear's most appealing character traits was that he was extremely uninterested in football.

Arlo shrugged. "I'm a Packers guy. Now, come on. We'll make good progress on this terrain."

"No, seriously, Arlo." She lowered her voice. "Liam's struggling already. We've got a long journey ahead of us. It's not far down." Laurel looked at her feet. "My boots have good traction. I think I can make it." She was already dropping her backpack from her shoulders onto the ground. "I'll be fine."

She took off her gloves and put them on top of her pack. "Better grip." She wiggled her fingers at Arlo and Liam. Arlo was frowning at her, but Liam looked excited. He really was enjoying all the foraging.

Slowly, Laurel lowered herself to the edge of the riverbank and searched for a good foothold. It was steep, like Arlo had said, but the wagon was only a short way down. Pushing her fingers into the muddy bank, she moved slowly down. Down. Down. Then she reached it.

"Got it!" She pulled it free and waved up at Arlo and Liam.

And at the same moment, her foot slipped.

13

LAUREL

With her limbs tangled beneath her, Laurel fought to catch her breath. She was staring up at a white, full-of-snow sky and every bit of her body was throbbing. She raised a hand to her head. She was bleeding from somewhere near her temple.

"Doc? You okay?" Arlo was shouting to her from the riverbank.

"Think I banged my head on the way down," she called back weakly.

"Is the plant you found good for that?" he replied sarcastically.

"No, Dad. It's dandelion," Liam said defiantly.

Groaning, Laurel sat up onto her knees. The bottom of the riverbed was sludge and slime. She was covered in it. Miraculously, however, her glasses had stayed on her face.

"Can you try to climb back up?" Liam called.

Laurel heaved herself to her feet. Her head was spinning and her fingers were cold. She headed for the bank and tried to find a foothold or something to grab onto.

"There… try there…" From above, Arlo and Liam shouted instructions to her.

She wiped the blood from her face with the back of her hand. "It's no use," she muttered. Then, louder, called, "I can't grab hold!"

"Try harder!" Arlo sounded like he was losing his temper.

"I can't *try harder.* It's useless." Laurel stepped back, out of breath, and leaned forward onto her knees. When she looked up, biting back a pain that she hadn't noticed before in her ankle, she pointed away from the bridge in the direction they were supposed to be moving. "Let's keep moving. I'll see if I can find somewhere less steep."

Arlo was standing with his hands on his hips. She watched him look down where he'd rested his own pack and Liam's at his feet. He picked up Laurel's pack, which was sitting nearby, and held it up for her to see. "I'll have to throw this down to you. I can't carry all three."

Laurel nodded, even though she wasn't sure her aching body could bear to carry it.

Before tossing it down, however, Arlo stopped and called, "Where's your medical kit? I should take it out in case Liam needs it."

Laurel swallowed hard. *In case Liam needs it…* or in case she was unable to get back up and he decided to carry on without her? She pushed her glasses up onto her head and pinched the bridge of her nose. He wouldn't leave her. Would he?

"Laurel? Where is it?" Arlo was moving things around, searching for the medical supplies.

"Front pocket," she shouted. "But leave me some Band-Aids. My head—"

"Got it." Arlo fussed with her pack and she could hear him zip it back up. Moving back to the edge, he called out to her. "Ready?"

"Yeah." And he pushed it over the edge of the bank.

As her pack tumbled down the riverbank, Laurel stood to one side and let it come to rest at her feet. She stooped to pick it up, then winced as she pulled its weight onto her shoulders.

Up above, Arlo and Liam had already begun moving.

She followed them, slowly. Her ankle was throbbing and the feeling of the dried blood on her forehead made her want to stop and scrub it clean.

While Arlo and Liam strode ahead, Laurel struggled to drag her feet through the mud below. Her legs burned with the effort of it. At first she thought the ankle was just jarred, but the pain was worsening so she stopped, waved to the others to wait, and pulled off her boot.

Peeling down her thick sock, she winced. It was swollen, and a deep purple bruise was taking shape.

"You okay, Doc?" Arlo called down to her.

"I need to splint my ankle. I'll be okay. Give me a minute." She pulled her boot back on and looked around for some sticks or twigs she could use. There was nothing sturdy enough.

As if reading her mind, Liam's voice came drifting down. "Laurel? Here…."

She looked up as he threw a short, thick, branch in her direction. She smiled and gave him a thumbs-up. Then she cracked the branch in two and sat back down.

Tugging her pack around in front of her, she pulled out her spare scarf and used it to hold the sticks in place. The splint was uncomfortable and made it hard to get her pants leg back down, but at least it would keep her ankle from giving way and causing another injury.

"Okay," she shouted, heaving herself to her feet. "Let's keep going."

They'd been traveling nearly an hour, and the river had curved around a bend, when Laurel stopped. "This might be a good spot!" she called.

Her heart started to beat faster. She'd lost sight of Liam and Arlo a little way back. From here, she couldn't see them at all. He wouldn't really leave her. Would he?

She was about to shout again when Arlo's flush of red hair appeared. He'd removed his hat and was taking a long drink of water.

"Is Liam okay?" she called.

"He's sitting down. But yeah. He's fine." Arlo shoved his water bottle into his pocket. "You think you can make it up here?"

"Yeah. I don't know. Maybe." Laurel pulled on the straps of her backpack, wriggling her back under its weight. She shouldn't have let Arlo throw it down to her; it was going to be nearly impossible to climb up while carrying it.

Arlo folded his arms. He was becoming impatient.

Pulling her feet out of the mud, Laurel reached out with cold, shaky fingers to get a hold of the riverbank. Even with her gloves on, she was freezing. There was a ledge a little way up that she might be able to reach....

But it was no use. Every time she tried, she lost her footing and ended up back where she started. And every time, the pain in her ankle became worse.

"Sorry, Laurel, but we have to keep going." Arlo looked over his shoulder as Liam coughed. "This was supposed to be quicker. Liam's already been outside too long."

Laurel swallowed hard. Mentally, she was cataloging what she had in her backpack; how long it would last her if she was forced to travel alone until she managed to get out of here.

"Arlo?" Laurel called up.

Arlo folded his arms in front of him. "Yeah?" He looked down at her.

"Don't leave me down here." Her voice wavered as she spoke but she pushed her pride to one side. "Don't leave me. Not after all we've been through."

From where she was standing, she couldn't interpret the look on Arlo's face. Did he nod?

"Keep going," he said, "we'll figure something out."

It wouldn't be long before the sun started to dip in the sky. Laurel was exhausted. For the first time since they left South Minneha all those weeks ago, all she wanted to do was rest. Just stop and rest. But just because Arlo hadn't abandoned her yet, didn't mean he wouldn't.

She hadn't caught sight of either him or Liam for several minutes. "Arlo?" she stopped and looked up. "Arlo? Liam?"

No answer.

"Arlo?!"

Still no answer.

Laurel dropped her backpack from her shoulders. It fell to the muddy ground with a squelch. Leaving it where it was, because no matter what was in it, right now getting out of this river was the most important thing, she flung herself at the bank.

She let out a loud groan as she tried to pull herself up. A jolt of pain shot through her ankle. Her foot slipped but she grabbed hold of a clump of grass and hung on. She expected the grass to give way, pull free from its roots and send her falling backward. But it didn't.

She moved her hand up, searching for another handhold. Her fingers were snaking through the mud when she heard something. Voices. But not just Liam and Arlo.

Holding her breath, Laurel pressed herself against the bank and willed herself to be invisible. If Arlo had left her and someone else stumbled across her, then she was a sitting duck. An easy target.

"Still stuck, Doc?" Arlo's voice made her look up.

She released a fierce sigh. "I thought you'd—"

"Went to get help." Arlo shrugged.

"Help? From where?"

"Well, you wouldn't know from down there, but we're not far from the road now. Just a few trees between us and...." Arlo stopped and shook his head. "Doesn't matter. What matters is, we heard a truck. Took a chance. And found someone with a rope."

"Rope?" Laurel almost felt like crying. "Rope?"

A face Laurel didn't recognize appeared next to Arlo's, thinner than Arlo with a big bristly beard and a bright blue hat. "Ahh, yeah, I see what you mean, buddy. She sure is stuck." The face raised an arm and waved at Laurel. "I'm Jim. Hang tight, ma'am, and I'll be right back."

Laurel closed her eyes and pressed her face against the bank, not caring that her cheek was being covered in mud or that she'd been called *ma'am*, which she usually hated. A few minutes later, something tapped her hand.

The rope.

Up above, Jim yelled at her to grab hold of it. "Arlo and I will pull you up, but you'll have to help."

"My pack." Laurel glanced back, reluctant to clamber back down to get it.

"I have plenty of supplies. Leave it."

Surprised by the stranger's generosity toward someone he didn't even know, Laurel did as she was told; she grabbed hold of the rope and, as Jim and Arlo pulled, she began to climb.

When she reached the top of the bank, Arlo took her arm and heaved her over the side. She lay on her stomach for a moment, breathing deeply.

"Here…" Jim offered her a hand and helped her to her feet.

"Thank you." Laurel looked from him to Arlo. "Thank you so much."

"Your friend was pretty persuasive." Jim nodded at Arlo.

"Persuasive?" she knew what Arlo's version of persuading people usually looked like.

Jim breathed out through pursed lips. "My truck's just about out of gas. Don't think she'll go much farther than a few feet before she gives up. Arlo here said y'all might help me carry my gear. Can't leave it unattended. People are ruthless out here. Take what they want when they want it."

"Carry your gear? Where are you heading?" Laurel was examining Jim's face, trying to get a handle on what kind of guy they were dealing with here, when Liam rushed over and wrapped his arms around her waist.

"I'm glad you're okay," he said. But when he stepped back, he looked at her and frowned. "You hurt your head?"

Laurel nodded. "I'll be fine. Just need to get cleaned up."

"So, Jim, where *are* you headed?" Arlo asked. "You said not far from here…"

Jim put his hands into his pockets and jigged up and down. "Yeah. Just a couple of miles south. A buddy of mine runs one of those survival camps. You know, the kind where they teach you how to survive the apocalypse?"

"Handy," Laurel said, wrapping her arms around her waist as the cold permeated her jacket. With the sun setting, it was getting colder by the minute.

Jim grinned at her, then laughed. "Probably should have attended sooner, but better late than never."

"Well," Arlo cut in. "Like I said. We'll help you get your stuff there, then we'll part ways."

"You're welcome to join me," Jim said as they set off toward his truck. "My buddy will have room."

"Thanks," Arlo replied, glancing at Liam. "But we've got places to be."

For a minute, they walked in silence. Normally, Laurel would have been thinking about what they might be able to borrow or learn from a survivalist camp that would prove useful on the final leg of their journey back to South Minneha. But right now, her brain was too cold and exhausted to think straight.

When they emerged from the trees, Jim gestured to a large truck. "Your boy can sleep in the truck tonight," he said to Arlo. "We'll light a fire, then set off again in the morning. Give…." He turned to Laurel and raised his eyebrows.

"Laurel," she offered, shaking his hand.

"Give *Laurel* a chance to recover from her ordeal."

As Arlo grunted in agreement, Laurel smiled. But something about Jim wasn't sitting right with her; there was something beneath his smile that she didn't trust.

For now, though, while he was offering food and warmth, she decided it was best to keep her thoughts to herself.

14

LAUREL

"Here." Jim handed Laurel a first-aid kit. "For your head."

"Thank you." She dipped to take a look at her head in the truck's side mirror. "I think I need a couple of stitches," she said, wincing as she touched her wound.

Eyes widening a little, Jim put his hands into his pockets and said, "Oh, ah. I don't think I can… maybe your friend?"

Laurel stood up and smiled at him. "It's okay. I'm a doctor. I can handle it."

Relief washed over Jim's face. "Well, that's good. I'm a little queasy with stuff like that."

Interrupting them, Arlo patted Jim on the shoulder and said, "Why don't we leave the doc to sort out her head, and start a fire?" He looked up at the sky. "It'll be getting dark soon."

Jim nodded; they'd agreed to sleep by the truck for the night and head off at first light.

"I'm amazed you even have a working truck," Arlo said as he and Jim started lifting things down from the truck bed to the ground.

"*Had*," Jim laughed. "She's old. But she's been a life saver. Got me across the border from Canada."

At the mention of the Canadian border, Laurel's ears pricked up. She breathed in slowly, hope fizzing in her chest; if Jim had made it here from the border, then surely she could make the reverse journey toward Thunder Bay.

"Shall I hold that?" Liam was standing at Laurel's elbow. He gestured to the first-aid kit. Laurel nodded and handed it to him.

"You doing okay?" he asked as she began to clean her head.

"Shouldn't I be asking you that?" Laurel said, glancing sideways at Liam. He was pale, his skin gray around the edges. She was praying it was just the exertion of the journey that was showing, and not anything more sinister.

"Have you been coughing?" She pulled her glasses down from the top of her head so she could see what she was doing and threaded a needle from Jim's medical kit.

"A little. It's nothing bad."

As she smiled in response, Laurel caught sight of Liam's face in the side mirror. He wasn't telling her the truth. But she wasn't going to press him. Not now.

Finally stitched up, with her ankle still throbbing, Laurel sat down in the driver's seat, letting her legs hang sideways out of the truck, and accepted a bottle of water from Liam.

"You're a bit muddy," he said, pointing to her face and clothes.

"I need a bath, that's for sure." Laurel pulled an 'I wish' face and added, "Ohh, what I'd give for a bath full of bubbles."

Liam giggled, but then his face dropped a little. "Sorry about your pack."

"Oh, don't worry about that. There was nothing important in it." Laurel sighed. Many times, since all this started, she'd wished she had a photograph of Bear and of Mae. She'd wished she'd taken the time to print out those pictures of the spa break she took with her mom last summer. But all she had was memories.

"You look tired." Liam was watching her.

"I'm okay, buddy. Let's go help your dad and Jim." A little shakily, she stood up. Even with the splint, a jolt of pain shot from her ankle up into her shin. "Dang it…" she muttered as she steadied herself on the side of the truck.

"Not broken, is it?" Arlo walked over and looked down at her foot.

"Just a sprain. It'll be fine."

"Here." He reached behind his back and offered her a long, thick branch. "Found this when we were fetching firewood. Thought you could use it."

Laurel tilted her head and examined Arlo's face. "Thanks," she said, taking the branch and leaning on it. "That's better."

Arlo nodded and was about to turn away when Laurel put her hand on his arm. "Arlo? Thank you."

"It's just a stick." He shook his head and looked away.

"Thank you for coming back for me." Laurel dipped her head to meet his eyes. "I mean it. You could have abandoned me back there and you didn't. I'm grateful."

Beneath his beard, Arlo's cheeks began to flush. He cleared his throat, then looked over toward Jim, who'd successfully lit a fire and was rummaging through a box labeled "food." "You hungry?" he asked, changing the subject.

A smile twitched on Laurel's lips. "Sure." She leaned on her stick and followed Arlo. "But I should get out of these clothes first. I'm pretty damp."

Interrupting them, Jim looked up and waved his fingers at her. "I've got some spare clothes in the truck. You could layer up while your jacket dries by the fire."

"Thank you."

"There are some camp chairs in the back too," Jim said to Arlo.

As Laurel sifted through the things in the truck, and pulled out two navy fleeces, Arlo offered Jim a Boy Scout salute and gestured for Liam to come help him. "Chairs coming up," he said.

Ducking behind the vehicle, Laurel peeled off her wet things and put on fresh pants — too big, but warm — a long-sleeved thermal vest, and a pale blue sweater. Then she grabbed the fleeces and put them on too. Hugging herself, she paused and tilted her chin. That smell — it was familiar.

She was pressing her nose to the dark blue fabric when Arlo called, "Doc, grub's up."

Next to the fire, Arlo had set out four chairs and stuck a branch in the ground for Laurel to hang her jacket. She sat down next to Jim and stretched her foot out in front of her.

Arlo started serving up the food Jim had cooked — rice, beans, and canned corn.

"He seems like a good guy." Jim looked up from the fire and tilted his head in Arlo's direction, speaking quietly so only Laurel could hear him. "Good dad."

"Yeah." Laurel wrapped her arms around herself, shivering a little against the cold. "He is."

Once again, she'd been wrong about Arlo. She'd expected him to leave her for dead, but he'd surprised her. Perhaps it was time she started trusting him.

"How are we going to carry all this stuff?" Liam looked like a foreman on a building site, standing with his hands on his hips and staring at the pile of supplies in the back of the truck.

"We'll figure it out in the morning, son." Arlo gestured for Liam to come sit down. Above them, the sky was darkening. Soon it would be pitch black and dotted with stars. "Come sit down. Jim made hot chocolate."

Laurel pulled her coat closer around her neck and adjusted her hat. Even with the fire, it was cold. Very cold. They were sheltered by the trees next to the road. Out of the wind, at least. And the ground here was covered with just a small dusting of snow. But she still found herself longing for the comfort of the empty apartment or their cozy rooms back at Lone Oak.

Shaking her head, she tried not to think about what was happening at Lone Oak.

"Coffee for you, Laurel?" Jim asked, already handing her a steaming mug.

As Laurel wrapped her fingers around it, she felt her muscles begin to relax. She closed her eyes for a moment and breathed in the smell. Despite everything they'd been through, they were okay. And they were nearly back at South Minneha where they belonged.

Perhaps meeting Jim was exactly what they'd needed to help them on the last leg back.

As she sipped her drink, her train of thought was interrupted by Liam saying loudly, "You *stole* it? Who from? Were they bad guys?"

Jim had shifted in his seat and, for the first time, looked a little uncomfortable. When he noticed Laurel watching him, he laughed, but it was a nervous laugh. He patted Liam's shoulder. "Just one guy," he said. "But, yeah. He wasn't a good guy. Offered me a ride when he needed help but I caught him trying to drive off without me. With all *my* stuff too."

Arlo shook his head. Liam was listening intently.

"So," Jim shrugged. "We fought. I won. I took the truck."

Liam breathed out through pursed lips. "Phew," he said. "Well, we're glad you did. Right, Dad?"

"Absolutely." Arlo looked at the large mug of hot chocolate Liam was holding and smiled. "Very glad."

But as Laurel watched Jim, something in her gut shifted. The settled, contented feeling she'd had a moment ago had turned into something else… something that told her maybe Jim wasn't as straight-up as she'd first thought.

She turned her head and, once again, the scent of the fleece she was wearing snagged in her brain.

Bear… the smell reminded her of Bear.

She looked at Jim. He was laughing now, joking with Liam, who was gleefully fishing marshmallows out of his drink. Was it possible? She stood up and walked over to the truck.

"Is it okay if I shift some things to make room for a bed?" she called over her shoulder.

"Sure." Jim nodded at her.

Leaning on the back of the trailer, she reached in and started shifting boxes to one side. She grabbed a sleeping bag and tried to look as if she was preparing to unfurl it. Her heart was hammering in her chest, but she had no idea whether she was being rational or not.

She was sleep-deprived, anxious, and in pain. It was entirely possible she was smelling Bear because her brain still associated him with comfort, warmth, safety.

She was about to stop when she turned around a small cardboard box and saw, etched on the side, the word: KIBBLE. She pulled it closer and ran her thumb over the letters. They were shaky, hastily written. But she could swear she was looking at Bear's handwriting.

"Did the guy you took the truck from have a dog?" Laurel asked casually.

Mid-conversation with Arlo, Jim answered quickly and distractedly. "Ah. No. No dog. Why?"

Laurel closed her eyes and pressed her lips together. Then replied, "I have allergies. Just checking the blankets won't make me sneeze."

Jim looked up at her. From across the campfire, his eyes met hers. His expression was fixed. Unreadable. She smiled at him, but he didn't smile back.

"So, tomorrow we gather up what we can carry and head for your buddy's place?" Arlo asked, rubbing his thighs as he prepared to stand up.

"If you're still up for helping a fella out," Jim smiled.

"I keep my word," Arlo replied.

That was true; he did keep his word. But if Laurel knew Arlo like she thought she did, he'd be interested in seeing this survival camp for himself. Just in case it could prove useful.

"Night, Dad." Liam patted his father's shoulder. It wasn't much past sunset but he looked tired.

"I'll come get you settled in." Arlo stood up and followed Liam to the truck, leaning in and tucking him up in a pile of blankets, then sliding in next to him.

"Nice family." It was the second time Jim had remarked on Arlo and Liam's relationship.

Laurel adjusted her glasses on the bridge of her nose and reached for the pot to pour herself another coffee. "How about you? You have any family?"

Jim's jaw twitched. "I did. Once." He was looking down into his coffee cup. When he raised his eyes, he shrugged. "Now, it's just me." He scraped his fingernail at a muddy stain on the knee of his jeans. "You?"

"I have a daughter." Laurel angled herself so she could see Jim very clearly and added, "And a husband. He lives up in Thunder Bay. Bear. His name's Bear."

Her eyes roved over Jim's face, looking for the smallest hint that Bear's name meant something to him. A flicker of something crossed his features, but it was gone so quickly, perhaps she imagined it.

"You gonna try and find him?" Jim asked, without flinching.

"After I've got Arlo and Liam back to South Minneha, yes." Laurel took another drink from her coffee cup, watching Jim over the top of it.

"Well, if you change your mind, like I said before — my buddy Cal would be glad to have you. A doc would be a big boon for him."

Laurel nodded slowly. She wasn't entirely sure she believed in Cal or this magical survival camp Jim had talked about. In fact, she wasn't sure she believed anything he'd been saying to them.

That night, as she curled onto her side in the back of Jim's truck and tried to get comfortable, ignoring the throbbing in her ankle, she reached under the makeshift pillow she's created and stroked her fingers over the smooth grip of her handgun. She might have left her pack behind in the riverbed, but at least she still had this. And until she'd figured out whether Jim could be trusted, she wasn't letting it out of her sight.

15

BEAR

It was nearing the end of his second day on the road. His legs stung with the effort of moving through the snow. Deeper in places, with a thick crust on top of it, sometimes it held his weight but sometimes he smashed straight through it, his legs sinking deeply and needing to be pulled out. At the end of the first day, he'd sat by his campfire and spent the evening hammering screws into the bottoms of his hiking boots to make DIY cleats. He'd brought the screws with him for this very purpose but had hoped not to have to waste the time doing it.

It was worth it, though, and while still not *easy*, the second day had been easier than the first.

For the most part, Jess was doing okay; she was light enough to trot on the surface of the snow and not break through. And she seemed to be keeping warm in her new pink coat.

Every time Bear got stuck and needed to heave himself out, she stopped and tilted her head at him as if she was surprised that he was holding things up.

"Okay, okay," he'd grumble at her, cursing as he persuaded himself to keep moving.

The first night, they camped in an abandoned gas station not far from the hospital. For the first time in weeks, he'd had to keep his hearing aid turned on and plugged in while he slept. Which was not by any means comfortable.

Now, as the sun dipped in the sky once again, he realized he'd spent the last few minutes humming to himself. In his previous life, back in his cabin in the woods, he'd loved silence. The sound of absolutely nothing but his own thoughts. Now, his own thoughts were the last thing he wanted to be stuck with; all he could think of was the boy. Had Deb told him why Bear left? Made sure he understood? Had she told him it was for his own good? That this wasn't the end of their friendship? Just a hiatus?

Looking down at Jess, Bear rolled his eyes and said, "Okay, okay, so maybe I've discovered I'm not such a huge fan of being alone after all. Maybe Trent got to me. And the rest of them." He sighed and rubbed his gloved hands together.

Wagging her tail at him, Jess lifted a paw and scratched his shin.

"What is it?" Bear frowned at her.

She scratched again and whined this time.

"You want me to carry you?"

Wag. Wag. Wag.

"Seriously?" He'd worried that she wouldn't be able to keep up her sprightly pace, but had hoped she'd manage for a little longer. "Okay. Come on then." Bear crouched down and picked her up. But then he looked at his ski poles. He couldn't use them and carry Jessamine at the same time.

Putting her down again, ignoring the disgruntled look on her face, he unfastened his backpack and took out the smaller pack, which he'd rolled up and put inside in case he found something else he needed to transport. Fixing the big backpack back on his shoulders, he strapped the smaller one to his front, tying it to the larger one, then once again scooped up his dog. Slotting her into it so that her head and paws stuck out the front, he shook his head at himself and scratched his beard. Now he had a dog in a pink coat, *and* he was carrying it like a baby. If Mae or Laurel could see him now, they'd be on the floor laughing.

Jess turned around and licked his face, happy with her new vantage point.

"Just don't blame me if you end up upside down in the snow next time I get stuck," he muttered, ruffling her ears before picking up his poles again.

He was nearing the highway. If he was lucky, when he made it up onto the road, he'd find that the wind had blown it into mounds on either side and that the middle was flatter. Easier to navigate. He stopped and surveyed his surroundings.

There was a copse of trees nearby. Beneath them, there wasn't likely to be as much snow, and he might even be lucky enough to find a rabbit for dinner.

Still carrying Jess, he trudged his way toward the trees. When he reached them, as soon as he was under the branches, walking became easier. Perhaps he should change his plan; travel through the forest instead of out in the open.

The highway would be quicker under normal circumstances, but with this terrain, the trees might be a better option.

Quickly, still wondering what to do, he set Jess down, then began gathering some kindling for a fire. He stooped to pick up a pinecone and was remembering the last time he and Trent had been in the woods, using pine sap to treat their wounds, when he realized Jess's ears had pricked up. She was staring at something.

Bear followed her gaze, reaching for his gun.

Squirrel.

Jess was quivering. Before Bear could tell her not to chase it—so he could shoot it and roast it—she lurched forward. Of course, the squirrel leaped into the nearest tree and disappeared, and Jess was left jumping up and down at the bottom of it.

Telling her to calm down, Bear walked over to where the squirrel had been. Squirrels had awesome memories. Freaky memories. If he was lucky… yep, there it was; a cache of mushrooms and what looked like black walnuts.

Bear wasted no time in raiding it. He sifted through the mushrooms, took the lion's mane for himself and left the fly amanita for the squirrel. He also took most of the walnuts.

Looking up into the tree to where the squirrel was chattering angrily at him, he said, "Sorry, little guy," but shoved a walnut into his mouth anyway and closed his eyes as he chewed.

Watching the squirrel, he looked at his gun. He could shoot it. Right now. Roasted squirrel for dinner. He was still contemplating it when he noticed Jess sniffing at the ground up ahead.

"You found another cache, girl?" He walked over to her and stooped to look at what she'd found.

Not a cache. A print.

Bear tilted his head. As he did, he swallowed hard. A boot print.

He wasn't alone.

His fingers were on his gun. He stood up slowly and peered into the gloom of the thicker trees in front of him. He glanced at Jess, expecting to see her ears pricked. But they weren't. And her tail was wagging.

Before Bear could step forward, Jess ran from her spot and into the undergrowth.

"Jess!" Bear remained stock-still and rolled his eyes at himself. The boot prints must be old. Jess was off chasing a rabbit. Perhaps she'd bring it back for dinner.

He returned to the fire and was setting about lighting it when movement caught his eye. He looked up, expecting to see Jess, then stopped. His breath caught in his throat. He rubbed his eyes.

"Hey, PB." Trent stepped out of the bushes and scraped his boot at the track he'd left. "Tried to cover it but didn't have time."

"Kid? What are you…" Bear trailed off. He was grinning, he knew he was, but he couldn't help it. But the bubble of happiness in his chest was soon replaced with something else. "What were you thinking? You followed me? You've been on your own? For two days? Anything could have happened to you! Are you crazy?"

Watching him, Bear expected Trent to adopt his usual sheepish expression. Instead, he began to grin. "Worried about me, huh?"

"I… that's not the…."

"Admit it. You're pleased to see me." Trent was trying to sound ballsy but something in his voice made Bear's expression soften.

"Ah, for heaven's sake, come here." He held out his arms. Trent lingered a moment, then rushed into them.

"I couldn't let you go alone. You need me." Trent pulled back. He had tears in his eyes. "We're a team, right? I know you were trying to protect me but we're in this together. PB and Trent. Like PB and jelly."

Bear began to laugh. "I need you, do I?"

"Yeah, you do." Trent's voice was surprisingly solemn.

As Bear returned to lighting the fire, Trent sat down and leaned forward onto his elbows. "I'm not the only one following you."

"You're not?" Bear stopped and narrowed his eyes.

"Well, I haven't exactly seen them yet. But I heard them. Before I left the hospital." Trent folded his arms in front of his chest and hugged himself. "I knew you were planning to leave. I saw you go out to the truck that day. So, when I woke up and you were gone, that's where I went. You'd already gone but there was someone else there. I heard her in the stairwell. She was talking to herself. Pacing up and down. Muttering." Trent shrugged at the memory. "She seemed a little...." He tapped the side of his skull with his knuckles. "I heard her say something about Murph, so I followed her. She was camped out at this old laundromat with some others. She told them she'd found the guy who killed Murph... said she was going to follow you."

"And what did these other guys say?"

"They objected at first, then gave in. Seems like she's the one in charge. Her name's Britt. That's what they called her."

"How many of them?"

"Only three, but they said something about 'the others' so I don't know how many now."

Bear scratched his beard with his index finger.

"The way you're moving through the snow, you weren't hard to track."

"Have you seen them?"

"This morning. They weren't far behind me. They stopped but I kept going."

"Did they see you?"

Trent shook his head. "I tried to cover both of our prints but it was too difficult. I thought it would be better to just hurry up and get to you so I could warn you."

"You did the right thing, kid."

Bear pressed his lips together. His mind was moving quickly. Bella had told him about Britt, Murph's sociopath of an ex-girlfriend. If she was after him, she was out for revenge. Which meant he needed to stop her. Once and for all.

"Bear?"

"Mmm?" He was already lost in his thoughts.

"What the heck is Jess wearing?"

16

BEAR

Bear stood just beneath the cover of the trees and peered out. The sun was starting to set. He could see his own track marks in the snow. Trent had entered the trees farther down so, from here, his weren't visible.

"They'll get to your tracks before they get to mine," Bear said quietly.

"Sorry—"

"No. Don't apologize." Bear shook his head. "I'm just thinking out loud... can you show me where you entered the woods?"

Trent nodded.

"We need to cover your tracks and get rid of the fire. Then we'll sit and wait."

"Wait? Shouldn't we leave? Try to outrun them?"

"No. We need to put an end to this." Bear was already dismantling the fire, destroying all evidence they'd been there. Picking a fresh branch with plenty of twigs on the end of it, he told Trent to do the same.

Then—covering their tracks as they went—they headed for the section of trees where Trent had first entered the woods.

"Go clear your tracks," Bear said. "I'll make a hideout here in the bushes. We'll wait here and hope they walk past us."

A smile spread over Trent's lips. "Oh I see, we're turning the tables—the hunted become the hunters."

"Exactly."

Nodding, Trent set about removing his boot prints from the ground.

"Now, create some more, but walk in circles. Confuse them," Bear instructed.

Beneath the trees, there was only a thin layer of snow. Mostly none at all, so by the time they were finished Britt and her gang would be nice and muddled.

While Trent followed Bear's instructions, Bear began putting together a hiding spot. Beneath the boughs of a pine tree, he found some downed spruce branches and used them to create a covered spot. When Trent had finished, Bear beckoned him beneath them, pulled the branches around them, and peeked out from between the needles.

From here, he could see the exact spot where Trent had entered the woods. Hopefully, Britt wouldn't be far behind him.

"It's kinda cold without a fire," Trent said, hugging Jess in his lap.

Reaching for his pack, Bear unfastened the sleeping bag he took from the truck and gave it to Trent. "Get yourself inside there. And keep your hat down over your ears."

"What about you?"

"I'll be okay. I have plenty of layers."

Quietly munching on the ration biscuits Bear had brought with him, the two of them waited. Jess fell asleep. Trent looked like he was drifting off too. It was growing darker outside.

Then, finally, they heard voices.

A man was grumbling, "For Pete's sake, Bert. Did you see any other tracks? Of course he came this way."

"Shhh, both of you," a female—possibly Britt—snapped. "He could be setting up camp for the night. You want to give us away?"

Quiet settled on the group.

Bear and Trent peered through the pine needles. Jess was stock still but Bear put his hand on her collar just in case she decided to make a run for it at the worst possible moment.

"It's working," Trent whispered.

The second of two women in the group, a redhead who had to be Britt, was bending down to look at Trent's fake prints. "They're kinda small," she said, standing up again.

"Guess he wears a small shoe," a tall lanky-looking guy replied.

The redhead rolled her eyes at him and punched his shoulder. "Shut up, Ryan."

"I count six men and two women. Does that seem right?" Bear whispered.

Trent shrugged. "It was just her and those two at the laundromat." He pointed to the one Britt had called Ryan and another who was wearing what looked like a kid's superhero-themed beanie with a pom-pom on the top.

"This way," Britt announced and began to stalk off, following Trent's trail.

"Wait." Pom-pom Hat held up his hand like a school kid at the back of the class. "Britt, what are we actually doing to do when we find the guy?"

Britt whirled around. Her eyes flashed with a look that Bear had seen before; a look Murph had given him.

"Well, Bert, I'll tell you what we're going to do... we're going to kill him, and then we're going to go back to that hospital and kill his little friends, and *then* we're going to go find his lovely doctor wife and kill her too. You remember what she did to Marianne and Rachel, don't you? You remember how she slaughtered them in cold blood?"

Bear swallowed hard and exchanged a glance with Trent. The thought of Britt crossing paths with Laurel made him feel instantly nauseated. But the nausea quickly turned into something else; determination.

As Bert mumbled his reply, Bear muttered to Trent, "We're going to stop this. Tonight."

While Britt and her gang wandered aimlessly around the woods, Bear and Trent remained in their hiding place. After a while, everything went quiet. Then they spotted a very faint glow in the trees up ahead.

"They must have made camp for the night," Bear said.

"What's the plan?" Trent turned to him, waiting for an answer.

"Wait until we're sure they're asleep, then we'll go do some reconnaissance. I want them dealt with. This is a delay we don't need."

Trent offered him a 'yes sir' salute. It made Bear smile. He was in army-mode, but rather than being freaked out, Trent was excited. He reached around to the back of his jeans and, grinning, said, "If we need to defend ourselves, I have this—"

Bear raised an eyebrow. "A gun? Where did you get that?" He tilted his head to check the kid was carrying it with the safety on, but Trent caught him.

"I know how to use it, PB. You taught me."

"Where did you get it?" Bear repeated, folding his arms in front of his chest.

"Bulldog. I told him I was going after you. He said I should be prepared."

Bear bit back a smile. He had to admit, he was more than glad to see the boy's face. More than glad he wasn't doing this alone. And glad the kid had some form of protection. "All right. Well, just remember what I taught you. And let's hope we don't have to use it. Okay?"

As night descended on the woods, Bear slipped a length of rope through Jess's collar. She hadn't been on a leash since she was a pup, but he couldn't risk her stumbling into something she shouldn't. And he couldn't carry her either.

Leaving their packs behind, Bear gestured for Trent to follow him. Thankfully, the moon was bright and illuminated patches of ground where there were gaps in the branches. These were also the parts where snow had fallen, so Bear was conflicted; the snow, still fresh from a flurry the night before, would cushion the sound of their footsteps, but the moonlight would illuminate them for anyone who might be nearby and on the watch.

He decided to stick to the shadows.

"Tread slowly, gently. Don't make a sound. I trust you to be my ears here, Trent. Even with the hearing aid, I can't hear well enough to know if you're being quiet."

"Don't worry. I've got your back."

"And if you hear anything that I miss—"

"I'll give you the signal."

"What signal?" Bear might have chuckled if he wasn't trying to focus on such an important task.

In response, Trent tugged his ear.

"Okay. Let's go."

As they moved away from the safety of their shelter, toward the fire, Bear was hardly breathing. He'd done this kind of stealth observation before. But usually, he had more backup than a kid and a dog.

When they reached the outskirts of the area Britt had claimed as her camp for the night, Bear motioned for Trent to stop and padded forward alone.

From behind a large pine tree, he observed the group. Britt was asleep. Almost all of them were, except for the one she called Ryan, who'd drawn the short straw. No doubt he was supposed to be on guard, but instead, he was poking the fire with a long stick and drawing circles in the earth.

The warmth of the fire was enticing, but Bear did one quick head count—all there, five men, three women—then returned to Trent.

"According to the map, there's a lake nearby. I want to try and find it."

"Now? In the dark?" Trent asked as Bear used a pine branch to sweep away their footsteps.

"If we don't do it now, we'll lose the opportunity."

"What are you thinking?"

As they moved away from the camp, in the direction Bear supposed the lake was, they kept their voices low.

"I'm thinking that Britt could be on thin ice very soon." Bear almost laughed at his own joke.

Trent didn't get it. "Huh?"

"Never mind. Let's just find it."

After a short but slow walk, just as Bear had hoped, they emerged on the shore of a small lake. Its surface glistened in the moonlight. Bear smiled. From his coat pocket, he took out a hand auger that he'd pocketed from the truck. It was long, with a corkscrew end, and he'd wondered whether to bring it. Now, he was glad he had.

"What's that for?" Trent stared at it.

"Wait there with Jess." Bear walked over to the edge of the lake. A few feet away, a tree that had blown down in a storm lay parallel with the shoreline. One of its huge, thick branches stretched out across the water. It had been there a while; the water all around it was frozen. But Bear studied it. He was willing to bet that, although it was frozen, the ice around that branch wasn't as thick as the rest.

Tucking the auger under his arm, he climbed up onto the branch and scooted his way along it on his butt. At the far end, he reached down and, with little effort required, used the end of the auger to pierce the ice. When he removed it, he smiled; the ice was about three inches thick. Perfect.

Before turning around, Bear unfurled his scarf from around his neck and tossed it toward the center—where the ice would be even thinner —then made his return journey.

"We need to lay a trap. Fake some tracks that will lead them here so they think I climbed across the log and walked to the other side of the lake."

"Why would you do that?"

"I'm not going to do it, Trent, I'm—"

"No, I know, but they need to believe you have. So, why would you do it?"

Bear's mouth twitched into a smile. The boy was getting smarter every day. "To double back on myself, to lose them because they can't follow tracks on the ice."

"Right." Trent nodded. "Gotcha."

"So, let's get started...."

Together, they carefully removed all trace of Trent's footprints while leaving Bear's intact. In places where they weren't clear, Bear made sure to make a nice deep impression. Britt clearly wasn't the world's best tracker; he needed to make this easy for her.

Then they returned to the edge of Britt's camp. Again, making tracks that would make it seem as if Bear had come across her and her gang then decided to escape.

By the time they'd finished, they were both exhausted. "Let's get back to the hide. You can sleep. I'll keep watch." Bear put his arm around Trent's shoulders. "I'm glad you're here," he said, surprising himself with his honesty.

"I'm glad too, PB." Trent stifled a yawn. "I'm glad too."

17

BEAR

At sunrise, Bear woke Trent from a deep sleep. He'd spent the night curled up with Jess while Bear kept watch, bobbing from foot to foot, sleeping bag wrapped around him, in an effort to stay warm. Thankfully, there had been no signs of life beyond their hideout. Now, though, they needed to get into position.

"They'll be waking soon. We need to watch them, make sure they follow the trail we left."

Yawning, Trent stretched his arms above his head and shuddered. Without a fire to keep them warm, now that he was out of his sleeping bag, he was feeling the chill. Trent rubbed his eyes. Two days on the road following Bear had taken it out of him. Bear wished he could have offered the kid a good night's rest instead of a hard night on the ground. To himself, he vowed that if his plan worked and they got rid of Britt and her crew, their next stop would be somewhere sheltered. Maybe an abandoned house with a couch for the boy to sleep on.

"Where are we going to hide?"

"Near their camp. Then we'll follow them to the lake."

"What if they don't fall for it?" Trent had started shoving his sleeping bag back into his bag. At the same time, he took a protein bar from his pocket, tore it open with his teeth and devoured it.

"They will." Pulling his own backpack onto his shoulders, and putting the spare one on his front, Bear offered her an apologetic tilt of the head. "Sorry, girl. Just until we're out of the woods." He paused, then chuckled to himself as he slotted her into it. "No pun intended."

"Ready." Trent lifted his pack triumphantly and put his empty food wrapper into his pocket. Then he frowned. "You're wearing her like a baby?"

"You got a better idea?" Bear knew he looked ridiculous, but raised his eyebrows at Trent anyway.

Trent raised his hands. "No, no. You're good. Looks *super* cute. Especially with her new pink coat."

Shaking his head to hide a smile, Bear turned away and grumbled, "Good. This way."

Quietly, as they had the night before, they moved toward Britt's camp. This time, there was more light for them to see by. But there was also more light to expose them. Resisting the urge to hurry, Bear took each step slowly and carefully, glancing to Trent to make sure his footsteps weren't too loud.

Every now and then, Trent nodded at him or gave him a thumbs-up to confirm they were doing okay.

Eventually, he spotted smoke through the trees. Britt had set up camp in a small clearing. Nearby, a large dome-shaped bush caught Bear's attention. He gestured to it. Trent nodded. Together, they inched toward it and ducked beneath the branches. Bear moved the leaves gently aside. Perfect. From here, they could see the whole camp.

Reaching into his pocket, Trent took out a notebook and Bear smiled. Trust the boy to think of that. *Looks like they're still asleep.*

Bear nodded, then made a hand gesture that he hoped implied, *Just wait. They'll wake soon.*

And he was right. Soon enough, someone began to stir. One of the men, sleeping closest to Britt, sat bolt upright and looked around the camp. *Ryan.*

Presumably, one of them should have been keeping watch, because Ryan looked at Britt with slightly worried eyes, then quietly stood up and tiptoed to the outer rim of the small clearing, just a few feet away from Bear and Trent's hiding place.

Brushing down his coat and pulling his hat farther down over his ears, Ryan yawned, then started patting his waistband. Presumably making sure his gun was still there. He was staring absentmindedly at the fire when a look of realization crossed his face; they'd let it dwindle to nothing but smoke. He looked like he was about to start scrambling around to light it again when Britt herself began to stir.

Sitting bolt upright, she shook her arms like a dog shaking off a deep sleep, then leaned forward and rested her elbows on her outstretched legs. "Ryan? What happened to the fire?"

Blinking at her, Ryan—who couldn't have been more than twenty-five years old—opened his mouth to speak, then closed it. When he opened it again, he said, "I was, ah, worried about the smoke."

Britt narrowed her eyes at him, then slowly nodded. "Good thinking." She looked up at the sky. "Now it's light, we don't want him spotting it."

By him, she means me, Bear thought, reaching instinctively for his gun with one hand while he patted Jess's head with the other. He hoped she stayed still—and quiet.

"Spread out the wood." Britt stood up and pointed at the fire.

"Spread it out?" Ryan put his hands into his pockets and licked his lips nervously.

"Yeah. Spread it out. It'll die quicker then. Less smoke."

"Oh, right." Ryan nodded. "Course. Will do."

As Britt took a bottle of water from her pack and sipped from it, she began walking around the clearing, kicking the sleeping bags of her campmates to wake them up. "Anything happen last night?"

Ryan cleared his throat. He was looking at the fire instead of at Britt. "No, no. Nothing to report."

"Did you switch places with Bert?"

Again, Ryan cleared his throat. "No, I, ah, took the whole shift."

"Lazy idiot." Britt gave the sleeping bag nearest to her an extra hard kick. Presumably, this was Bert. "I'll see to it he does tonight's. You look exhausted."

In their hiding spot, Bear shifted from foot to foot. Moving at this pace, he was surprised Britt had ever managed to catch up with him.

"Come on, everybody. Now it's daylight we don't want to waste any time. We know he entered the woods. We saw the tracks. We only lost them because it was dark, so now we need to find them again."

Around her, the six who she'd rudely woken were rubbing their eyes and blinking into the light.

"I said, come on!" She waved her arms and they all started to scramble to their feet.

"Suze, hand out breakfast rations. Ryan and Annie, go look for tracks. Bert…" she paused. Clearly, she and Bert weren't best pals. "Stay put. You're useless."

This was it. Bear exhaled slowly and glanced at Trent. He too was watching, stock still, poised to move when they needed to.

As Ryan and Annie disappeared from the camp, Bear took Trent's notebook and scribbled, *Keep your ears peeled. Don't want to be snuck up on.*

Trent nodded and moved toward the back of their hiding spot while Bear remained focused on Britt.

She was sitting down, eating a handful of nuts and taking slow sips of water, when the trees opposite started to move. Clattering through them, Ryan stopped in front of her, panting, hands on his knees. Beside him, the blonde woman Britt had called Annie was grinning.

"What is it?" Britt stood up quickly.

"We found him, boss." Annie slapped Ryan on the shoulder. "Well, Ryan did."

"You found him?" A smile spread across Britt's face. It sent a chill down Bear's spine. In that moment, he knew that as soon as Britt set eyes on him, she'd kill him. And any guilt he felt about the trap he'd laid disappeared.

"Not *him* exactly, but his tracks. Looks like he stumbled on our camp last night, then legged it toward the lake."

Britt's smile wavered. "And you didn't hear him last night?"

Ryan shook his head. He looked like he was holding his breath.

After a pause, as if she was deciding whether to be mad or not, Britt waved her hand in the air and said, "Doesn't matter. We've got him now." Over her shoulder, she yelled, "Come on, you guys. Let's move." Then she grabbed her backpack and followed Ryan back into the trees.

Bear waited until all eight campers had left the clearing before exiting the hiding spot. When he was certain they were clear, he beckoned for Trent to follow him. Then, moving through the trees and following their own trail, which now mixed with Britt's, they made their way to the lake.

Just before they reached it, Bear stopped and looked down at Jess. Carrying her on his chest like this felt risky. If Britt and the others shot at him, Jess could be hit. So, bending down, he lifted her out of the backpack and tied her leash to a tree that was nicely obscured by undergrowth.

"I'll be back. Stay here and *be quiet*," he said, pressing his forehead to hers.

"Will she be okay?" Trent looked from Jess to Bear as if he was very unsure about this.

"She'll be fine." Bear stood up straight and rubbed the back of his neck. "Safer here than strapped to me if the shooting starts."

"Shooting?" Trent swallowed hard. The kid had shot tin cans and a hare, but never people, and Bear wanted it to stay that way for as long as possible.

"You let me deal with that. Your job is to stay out of sight. Okay? If something happens to me, I'll need you to take care of me. Like you did with the wolf bite. Right?"

"I thought you said my pine sap trick was a dud," Trent smiled.

"It was." Bear squeezed the boy's shoulder. "But I still wouldn't have survived without you."

Then, as quietly as they could, they continued toward the lake.

When they reached it, Britt and the others were standing on the shore arguing.

"Why would he go this way!" Bert yelled, waving his arms. "Isn't it a bit obvious? Leaving a scarf out there so we think he... he..." Bert sucked in a deep breath, trying to swallow down his stutter. "So, we think he w-w-walked out there by moonlight to get to the other side? The *opposite* way he's been heading all this time."

"You seriously think he came out here, laid a fake trail, cleared away the real one, then what? Went back to his bed to have a nice cozy nap? Why would he do that? Why not take us out in our sleep if that was his game?" Ryan was squaring up to Bert while the others stared at them.

Britt was watching them too, biting her lower lip and looking seriously pissed off. As Bear held his breath, she finally yelled, "STOP!"

Bert and Ryan instantly stopped speaking.

Turning to Bert, walking up to him and squaring her shoulders even though he was a good foot taller than her, Britt snarled, "Ryan's right. This guy slaughtered our people. He'd have shot us in our sleep if he found us. He wouldn't have bothered playing silly games."

For a moment, Bear closed his eyes and clenched his jaw. That was really what she thought? She thought he was a cold-blooded killer? No. He'd kill to defend himself. He'd set a trap to give himself time to get away. He wouldn't shoot people in their sleep.

"Plus," Annie had stepped forward and was grinning at Britt as if she was looking for brownie points for agreeing with her, "if he's heading in that direction, it's going to save a lot of time to just go straight across the lake. The trees here aren't too bad, but they're pretty dense on the western side."

"Western side." Bert rolled his eyes. "Like you even know which direction west is—"

Cutting him off, Britt reached for the back of her jeans and took out her gun. With steel in her eyes, she raised it and pressed it to Bert's chest.

"Britt? What the—" Bert's eyes had widened.

Behind him, Annie, Suze, and the others were practically bouncing up and down with enjoyment at what was unfolding in front of them.

"Get rid of him," Annie said, her eyes sparkling.

Looking over Bert's shoulder, Britt smirked. But then she lowered her weapon and took a step back. "I have a better idea." She gestured to the fallen tree. "Bert's going to suss out the ice for us. Make sure it's safe to cross."

Stepping up to Britt's elbow, Ryan, who seemed like he might—deep down—be a good guy who just got mixed up with the totally wrong crowd, said quietly, "Are you sure?"

"Yes." She didn't even hesitate. Looking at Bert, she nodded and waved her arm. "Go ahead, Bert. Lead the way."

For a moment, Bert looked as if he was considering whether to make a run for it. But then he sighed, turned around, and headed for the log.

Bear held his breath. He'd wanted all of them to head out onto the lake, not just one.

With outstretched arms, Bert made his way along the fallen tree branch. Out toward the spot where Bear had tested the thickness of the ice.

"There are no footprints out here. Shouldn't there be footprints on the ice?" he called back.

"Just get on with it!" yelled Annie.

Bert paused. Bear saw his shoulders rise toward his ears as he took a deep breath. Then he crouched down and swung himself onto the ice. As his foot met the frozen surface of the lake, everyone watched with bated breath. Very slowly, he lowered his other leg, then stood up straight. The ice was holding.

Bear gritted his teeth. This could still work. If the ice managed to hold Bert, it wouldn't hold many more of them.

Bert kept going, inching out toward Bear's abandoned scarf. When he reached it, he turned, looking more confident, and swung the scarf around his neck. Taking a bow, he yelled, "Happy?"

Britt wrinkled her nose, then looked at the others and nodded. "Okay, it's safe. Go ahead."

Having, a moment ago, been brimming with excitement, Annie's face dropped a little. "You sure, Britt? I mean…." She lowered her voice. "I thought you were just kidding around with Bert. You really want us to go out there?"

"I want to find this guy. So, yeah. We're going out there." Britt stormed off toward the tree, then stood near the shore and beckoned for the others to go ahead of her.

Annie went first. Then two of the guys with no names. Then Suze. Finally, Ryan hopped up onto the branch and reached for Britt's hand to help her on. A tall guy with a jagged scar on his cheek was last, checking over his shoulder and securing the group at the rear.

Bear looked at Trent and they exchanged a knowing glance. It was going to happen. Any minute now. With all eight of them on the ice, it wouldn't hold.

Tentatively, Annie stepped onto the frozen lake and began to inch her way toward Bert. He was still standing holding the scarf. As Annie got closer to him, he shouted to Britt, "How do we know which way he went?"

"Just go in a straight line. That way. Like Annie said." She flicked a pointed finger in the direction the scarf had been.

Bert opened his mouth to answer her, then closed it again.

Behind Annie, a tall guy with huge feet had paused. "Boss, this don't feel right." He looked up as he spoke.

Annie looked up too.

And then it happened. One second, they were standing there, the next they were gone. The ice opened up with a crack that even Bear could hear and they fell through it. Annie screamed. For a moment, she bobbed up and down, waving her arms and spluttering. Then she disappeared. Next to her, the guy with big feet was gone too. Another was grappling to hold onto the rim of the hole.

"Luke!" Britt lurched forward, but the guy with the scar stopped her.

Dropping to his belly, Bert slid along the ice shouting, "Grab my hand!"

Luke reached for him and Bert began to pull, heaving him out, then plunging his hands into the icy water while he yelled, "Annie! Annie!"

While Luke tried to help him, Bert looked up at Britt and the others. Britt, Ryan, and the guy with the scar were still on the log, but Suze was halfway between the log and the hole in the ice, looking terrified.

"Help me!" Bert was sloshing his arms around in the water, searching for his friends. "Help me find them!"

Bear screwed his eyes shut. He was about to whisper, "Okay, let's go. Quickly," when a familiar sound broke through the trees.

"Jess...." Trent's eyes widened. He was right. It was Jess. She was barking.

"Go get her, make her be quiet!" Bear gave Trent a shove to make him move quickly, but it was too late. As Trent hurtled into the undergrowth to go and find Jess, Britt looked up and started running back along the log. The guy with the scar was in front of her, holding his gun.

"Was Bert right?" Ryan yelled, running after Britt. "Was this all a trick?"

"Just move!" Britt shouted, sprinting across the beach.

Bear waited a beat. He sucked his breath in, counted to five, then muttered, "Only one way out now," and started shooting.

18

LAUREL

"How much farther?" Arlo stopped and dropped the box he'd been carrying to the ground.

Jim had a pack on his shoulders, a popup tent strapped to the top of it, and another bag on his front. He was holding a map, rotating it as if it would help him figure out where they were.

"Can I take a look?" Laurel held out her hand and gestured for him to give it to her. What had started as quickly returning a favor had turned into an overnight hike, and they still didn't seem to be any closer to the camp.

Reluctantly, Jim handed her the map. "It's there." He jabbed his thumb at an open space surrounded by trees.

"Is that a lake?" Laurel asked.

Jim nodded but didn't answer her; he was clearly struggling under the weight of his belongings. Giving in, he dropped the bag on his front to the ground and groaned as he was freed from it. Shrugging out of his backpack too, he stretched his back and groaned again.

Laurel looked up and down the road they were on for any landmarks that might orient them. A sign nearby told her they were on Blue Ridge Road, exit fifty-six. She walked over to an abandoned car and spread the map out on the hood, tracing the road with her index finger.

Beckoning Arlo over, she tapped their location. "We're here."

He nodded.

"The survival camp is here."

"So, how much farther?"

"Not far. We might not make it before sunset, but if we do have to camp overnight, it'll only be an hour or two's walking in the morning."

Arlo sighed through gritted teeth and rubbed his jaw. Behind them, Liam was showing Jim a page in his Boy Scout book. While Laurel remained suspicious and Arlo remained indifferent, Liam seemed to think Jim was hilarious.

"He needs to rest." Arlo smoothed his palm over his face. "Sure wish we'd gotten that wagon out of the ditch."

Laurel grimaced. "Sorry, Arlo."

He shrugged. "Not your fault. You tried." He readjusted the pack he was carrying and looked at the box by his feet, a box Jim had insisted on them bringing. "What's even in here?" he muttered. Looking up at Laurel, he added, "You've got the food and the bedding. Jim's got the ammo, the tent, and whatever else is in that pack on his front. So, what's left?"

Laurel shook her head. She had no idea what could possibly be left to carry and felt horrible that Arlo was having to manage his own pack, Liam's, and Jim's heavy box.

Glancing over her shoulder, remembering the word KIBBLE scrawled on one of the boxes they'd left behind, she paused for a second, then purposefully stumbled sideways, kicked the box, and sent it flying.

"What the...?" Jim looked up as his box toppled sideways and spilled onto the road. As he ran over, Laurel and Arlo peered at the ground.

Laurel looked at Arlo. His face was turning red. Spinning around to face Jim, slowly, with gritted teeth, he said, "Books?"

Jim stopped a few feet away.

"All this time, you've been making me carry *books*?"

Jim's eyes widened. He swallowed hard and raised his hands into the air. "Hey, man, don't overreact."

"Overreact?" Arlo strode forward. He was the same height as Jim but his shoulders were broader and his jaw harder. "My *kid* is struggling to walk. I could have helped him, but instead, I've been carrying your collection of...." He turned, kicked a book, and yelled, "Gone with the frigging Wind!"

Jim began to stutter. "Look. Arlo. You promised you'd help me. I helped your girlfriend over there. In return, you're helping me."

A growl vibrated in Arlo's throat.

Laurel put her hand on his arm. Behind Jim, Liam was watching with wide, worried eyes.

Jim's hand twitched at his waist. He was armed, but so was Arlo.

"Stop." Laurel stepped between the two of them and raised her arms. "The pair of you, stop." She could practically feel Arlo's rage coming off him in waves and she fixed him with a stare she hoped he would interpret as *it's not worth it*.

"Okay, okay." Jim lifted his palms in the air. "Look, we can leave the books. If you want to, we can leave them. If I'd known you were struggling...."

Arlo looked past Jim to Liam, sucked in a deep breath, gave the books another kick, then stalked off to the side of the road to light a cigarette.

"Dad, you said you were quitting." Liam trotted over and put his hand on his dad's arm.

"I am," Arlo replied darkly. "But not today."

As Laurel returned to pick up the map, Jim walked over and stooped to the ground. Nudging the books with his hands, he sighed. Laurel tried to ignore him; she agreed with Arlo that bringing a load of heavy books as an *essential* item was ridiculous. But the look on Jim's face made her pause and crouch down beside him.

"I'm sure there's room for one or two if there's a particular volume you're attached to," she said, eyeing some of the titles.

From among the strewn paperbacks, Jim pulled out what looked like an old hardback. Laurel tilted her head. *Little Women*. Without saying anything, Jim tucked it into the inside of his coat. He didn't look at Laurel as he stood up, and he didn't look back at the books as they started walking again.

A few hours later, having moved quicker now that Arlo was free of his heavy load, they reached an exit that took them away from the highway and down a smaller, tree-lined road. The sun was dipping in the sky.

Laurel stopped and pocketed the map. "I think here's a good place to stop," she said. "We're not far from the camp. If we sleep here tonight, we can set off at sunrise and make it in a few hours."

Arlo, who'd barely spoken since the book incident, grunted and stalked to the side of the road to ditch his things. Liam followed him, flopping down beneath a tree and leaning against its trunk.

Taking a deep breath in, he coughed a little but swallowed it down when Arlo looked at him. "You okay, son?"

Liam nodded. "Fine. Just need some water."

Silently, Jim set about lighting a campfire while Laurel took off her pack and started to sift through their food supplies. "Beans and tuna, beans and rice, or tuna and rice?" she asked, wrinkling her nose.

"Tuna and rice," Arlo and Liam replied in unison.

Laurel turned to Jim. He looked at her and shrugged. "Anything. As long as it's hot."

Taking out the can of tuna, Laurel nodded. "Hot tuna and rice coming up. As soon as the fire's burning."

"I'm on it," Jim replied tightly.

Arlo didn't seem to notice or care that Jim's mood had darkened but – despite her misgivings about him — Laurel was keen to prevent team relations deteriorating any further. At least until they'd kept their promise and could part ways.

Leaving Jim stacking kindling, Laurel walked quietly over to Arlo and Liam. Crouching in front of Arlo, she laced her gloved fingers together and said, "Arlo, you should make up with Jim."

He frowned at her.

Keeping her voice low, Laurel said, "His friend runs a *survival* camp. They might have things we could use, or we might need their help in the future. Best if we try to keep things civil at least."

Arlo narrowed his eyes at her and nodded slowly. "Since when did you become so cynical, Doc?"

"Cynical?"

"I thought you were going to tell me to make friends because it's nice to be friendly, not because we might need to use this guy for something."

"That's not what I said." Laurel pushed her glasses up onto her head, balancing them on her hat.

A smile tickled Arlo's lips. "My bad influence must be rubbing off on you, Doc." He nudged Liam and chuckled. "You reckon, son?"

Liam smiled a little, but it didn't reach his eyes. "I like Jim," he muttered. "No one got mad at me for bringing my book." His Boy Scout manual was sitting in his lap.

"That's because you brought *one* book. One *useful* book. Not a whole library of classics."

"Fire's lit." Jim's voice floated over, interrupting them. He sat back, cross-legged, and pulled off his gloves to warm his hands. When Laurel sat down next to him to start cooking, he simply took his copy of *Little Women* from his pocket and held it in his lap.

19

BEAR

Bear was panting hard. They'd barely stopped moving all day. When he'd opened fire on Britt and her gang, he'd expected them to back up, but they hadn't. They'd come after him, blasting bullets back in his direction even though they couldn't see him through the trees. He'd waited only a few moments before turning and running.

At the tree where he'd tied Jess, he'd found Trent stroking her, whispering and trying to calm her down. "Move!" he'd yelled, bending to untie Jess's leash and shove her back into her pouch.

Behind them, he could hear shouts and gunfire.

"What happened?" Trent's eyes had been wide and frightened.

"No time. Move."

They'd flown back through the woods, back to their hiding spot, grabbed their packs and bolted from the trees.

Outside, they'd barely moved a few feet when it had started to snow again. Trent had suggested going back into the woods, but Bear had shaken his head. "No. The snow will help cover our tracks. We keep going."

Now it was late, the sun was almost setting, and they were both exhausted. The snow hadn't lasted long enough to cover their tracks. It had petered out and left them in the open, glancing desperately over their shoulders to see if they were being followed. Every now and then Trent tapped Bear's arm, pointed to his ear and gave him a look that told him he could still hear Britt behind them.

"How many do you think made it?" Trent asked, struggling to keep up with Bear's pace.

"Two went through the ice. One was trying to help them out. Britt and two other guys were still on the log. One of the others was on the ice but didn't go in. So at least three, maybe five left." Bear grimaced and shook his head. "And at least two of them are the most dangerous. Britt and the guy with the scar on his face looked like they were just waiting for an excuse to shoot." Bear paused and took his water bottle from his pack, took a swig from it, then kept moving. "We need to lose them somehow. It's too open out here."

"Back into the woods?" Trent asked. "It'll be dark soon. We need somewhere to stop and light a fire."

"I don't think we'll be lighting a fire tonight, kid." Bear put his arm around Trent's shoulders. Last night had been hard on them both, sleeping with no fire to keep them warm. He didn't want to do it again, but he would if he had to.

"Woods, then?" Trent gestured toward the woods that ran along the side of the road. Not as dense as the ones near the lake, but enough cover to at least delay their pursuers.

"Okay. Woods."

They'd barely taken a few steps beneath the cover of the trees when Bear's foot caught on something. Unable to steady himself, he fell, twisting himself awkwardly so that he wouldn't land on Jess.

Instead, he landed right on his tailbone and cried out.

"Dude. Did you just fall on your butt?" Trent was trying not to laugh but his eyes were sparkling.

"Yeah." Bear held out his hand so Trent could help him up. "I fell on my butt."

"Poor old Jess. Want me to take a turn carrying her?" Trent was ruffling Jess's ears. She looked distinctly unimpressed and was wriggling to get free.

"Nah. Let her down." Bear unfastened the carrier and dropped her gently to the ground.

"What if she runs off?"

"She won't. Not if we're with her."

Trent nodded. "Okay then. Let's head a little deeper, then set up camp? Find a nice cozy tree to snuggle up with?"

Bear laughed. "Sounds good to me, but we should cover our tracks first."

"Another fake trail? Will they fall for that a second time?"

"Maybe not, but it's worth a shot."

Bear gestured for Trent to follow him and set about walking in circles for a while, looping round, going back on themselves, round and round until he stopped and nodded. "That should do."

Then he headed off in what he hoped was the direction of the road, so that they could camp just inside the trees and be ready to go as soon as the sun came up. This time, as they moved, they used branches to cover their tracks.

They were reaching the edge of the woods, the trees thinning as they neared the road, when Trent grabbed Bear's arm. "Stop." He pointed at Jess. She was scratching at the ground near a bush. She stopped, looked at Bear, then kept scratching. She was trying to crawl beneath it, but there wasn't enough room between its branches for her to squeeze in.

Bear crouched down next to her and lowered himself onto his side to see what she was seeing. It was too dark. All he could see were leaves, branches, and thorns.

Jess let out a small whine.

"There's something in there she wants." Trent sat down on his haunches and peered at the same spot Bear and Jess were looking at. "Stick your hand in there, PB."

Bear frowned up at him. "Stick my hand in? Haven't I taught you anything? It could be a snake."

"They have snakes out here? In winter?"

He furrowed his brow and turned back to the bush. "All right, girl, I'll take a look. But if this turns out to be a gross, slobbery old tennis ball some other canine left behind, we'll be having words."

Jess tilted her head at him and wagged her tail, clearly pleased she was finally being listened to.

Taking a stick, Bear pushed it beneath the bush and started moving it around. It prodded up against something firm. He looked at Trent. "There's something under here."

Trent moved back and pulled a face. "Like what?"

"Dunno. It's not moving." Bear removed the stick, took a deep breath, then went in with his hand. He was wearing gloves, so he figured he at least had one layer of protection.

He also figured that Jess wouldn't be so interested in getting him to tease out a snake or a rat.

Pushing his fingers deeper beneath the bush, Bear held his breath. He moved slowly but he soon found what the stick had found; a large, bulky something.

He prodded it. It didn't move. Taking hold of it, he pulled.

Dragging it free, he sat back and stared at it.

"A rabbit!" Trent grinned and clapped his hands.

"A hare, actually." Bear studied the animal. It was dead, but with the weather so cold it was hard to tell how long it had been dead for.

"Awesome." Trent rubbed his belly.

Scratching his beard, Bear said, "No fire tonight, remember? We have no way of cooking it."

Trent's face fell. "Seriously? PB. Come on… we can't look a gift-hare in the face like that."

Bear's lip curled into a smile, the way it always did when Trent was simply being himself and making lighthearted comments. Looking back at the hare, he rubbed the back of his neck. It looked in good enough condition to eat; no nasty wounds, no blood. In fact, it looked like it had simply dropped dead and lay there waiting for them.

Jess was panting, open-mouthed, looking very pleased with herself.

Bear shrugged off his backpack and opened it up.

"What are you looking for?" Trent asked, peering into the bag.

Bear didn't answer but his fingers soon found what he was searching for; a small tin box. Right now it was full of medical supplies, but those could easily be decanted into one of the pack's inner pockets.

"We'll slice it up. Put what we can in here and pack it with snow." Bear pulled a second bag from the backpack, a plastic one. "Then we'll put the box in here and add more snow. It should stay fresh until tomorrow at least. Give us a chance to get somewhere we can light a fire."

Trent smiled, and his stomach growled loudly at the thought of eating freshly-caught protein.

"Remember how to slice it up?" Bear reached for his boot, took his knife from his sock and handed it to Trent.

Trent nodded. "I think so."

"Better get started then... use that rock over there."

"Right." Trent swallowed hard, then a determined look settled on his face and he nodded again. "Right."

Twenty minutes or so later, Trent's hands were covered in animal blood but he'd done an *okay* job. He'd butchered the hare well enough, and had managed to create a nice pile of thigh and leg meat, sliced into strips, that fitted into the tin box. Leaving room on top of the meat, Bear tossed a few strips to Jess, then stood up and temporarily balanced the lid on the box. "Let's head for the road. We'll camp just inside the tree line. There'll be snow up there we can use to pack this."

Trent nodded, looking down at his bloody hands.

"Best wash those off, kid. Don't want the wolves after us."

Trent had just finished scrubbing and was about to pass the water bottle to Bear when he stopped. He was straining his ears. "Bear, I heard something."

Jess was chewing on a bone she'd pulled free from the pile of discarded hare parts.

"It's just Jess," Bear said.

"No." Trent narrowed his eyes. "It's something else."

Without asking whether it was a good idea, Trent moved forward through the trees. Bear followed him. His heart was beating hard in his chest. He hated having to rely on the kid for things like this, but he was also glad he had him.

"A fire. I see a fire up ahead." Trent pointed and Bear ducked to look in the same direction. He was right. There, through the trees, was the unmistakable glow of a fire. But was it Britt? Or someone else?

Part of him wanted to have one final showdown with Britt, finish her off for good. But a bigger part was tired of fighting. His grip tightened on the tin box. His other hand reached for his gun.

Before he could pull it from his waist, however, he felt movement down around his ankles. He looked down just as a flash of white fur hurtled past him.

"Jessamine," he hissed, lurching forward. "Jess!"

It was too late… Jess had bolted toward the fire.

20

BEAR

"Jess! Jess!" Bear hissed into the dark, praying that the darn dog would turn around and come running back to him.

"What's got into her? She never runs off!" Trent whispered, looking nervously toward the glow in the distance.

"Probably smelled food. Another hare cooking on the fire." Bear scratched his beard and narrowed his eyes at the flicker between the bushes, which was undoubtedly a campfire.

"What do we do?" Trent asked, adjusting his backpack on his shoulder.

Bear sighed. He glanced behind him. Somewhere back there, Britt and her gang were still following them. His fake trail might have put them off the track, but it might not have. If whoever was up ahead was friendly, they could be useful. On the other hand, if they weren't….

"We'll go check it out. Stay quiet and follow me. I don't want to be seen until we're sure who we're dealing with."

Trent nodded and stepped into line behind Bear.

As they started moving through the undergrowth, Bear found himself holding his breath. "Can you hear anything?" he whispered.

"Voices. Quiet ones. Can't make out what they're saying."

"How many?"

"Not sure."

Bear gritted his teeth. Not for the first time, he wished he had full use of his senses.

The glow became brighter as they inched toward it. Every now and then, Bear stopped and hissed, "Jess," under his breath. But she didn't reappear.

Soon, they were close enough that even Bear could hear the voices. He gestured for Trent to stop. "Wait there." He held up his hand to prevent Trent from going any farther, then slipped into the shadow of a large, thick-trunked pine tree.

Here, the smell of pine tickled his nostrils; whoever lit that fire must be burning pinecones.

He rested his hand on the tree trunk, felt the rough bark beneath his fingers, and tried to slow his breathing.

"She's so cute! Look at her little pink coat." A kid's voice, a boy, younger than Trent.

"She must have run away from someone," a man replied.

"It's funny...." A female voice. Bear tilted his head, angling his good ear toward the campfire. That voice. It was familiar. "She looks just like...."

Bear's breath caught in his throat. It couldn't be.

As he told himself to slow down, his feet began to move. Before he could think about what he was doing, he'd stepped out from the shadows.

"What the heck?" A ginger guy with a big beard stepped in front of him. He had a gun. But Bear wasn't looking at it. He was looking past it. "Stop. Stop right there, buddy." The ginger guy raised his gun and squared his shoulders.

Bear hadn't even taken his own weapon from his belt. He moved forward and raised his arm, placing a hand on the barrel of the guy's gun and moving it gently to one side.

Whoever this guy was, he was looking at Bear like he was crazy. "I said stop. Take one more step…"

"Dad, don't!" The boy's voice. Bear glanced at the kid. Jess was sitting in front of him. He had his hand on her back. She was wagging her tail.

"Arlo, don't." The woman. She stood up. She was staring at Bear. Her face was dirty, her hair pulled up into a ponytail but with wisps of it flying free and surrounding her face. "Don't shoot… it's my husband."

Bear's ears were ringing but he knew her voice even without hearing it properly. "Laurel?" He moved closer and reached out to touch her. He stopped with his hands hovering above her forearms. But she didn't stop. She flung her arms around his neck. She was laughing. Or was she crying? He could feel her shaking as she held him tight.

He put his hands on her waist, then folded them around her. "Is it really you?" he whispered.

Laurel was nodding, wiping tears from her eyes, but smiling as she stepped back and took him in. She was exactly the same. Sure, her hair was tangled, she was covered in dirt and bruises, and she looked like she needed sleep and a good meal, but she was the same. Same sparkling smile. Same hypnotic eyes.

Shaking her head, as if she'd realized there were others present, Laurel put her hand on Bear's arm and turned to face the guy with the beard. "Arlo, this is Bear. My husband."

The guy — Arlo — raised his eyebrows. He looked from Laurel to Bear, then slotted his gun back into his belt and held out his hand. "Nice to meet you."

Bear was mid-shake when he realized that this was *Arlo* he was being introduced to. "Arlo Staaf? The guy who kidnapped you?" Bear looked at Laurel. He was taller than Arlo, bigger, and willing to bet he'd be a lot meaner if he had to be. If he had to protect Laurel.

"He did it for me." The boy had stood up. "To get me help. My dad's a good guy really."

"You're Liam?" Bear folded his arms in front of his chest.

The boy nodded.

"I met your pal, Peter. He misses you."

"You met Peter?" Liam grinned.

"You met Peter?" Laurel repeated.

Bear breathed in slowly. He had some explaining to do. But so did Laurel. Was she friends with this guy Staaf now? "I'll explain," he said. "But first, there's someone I want you to meet."

Turning toward the spot where he'd left Trent, Bear put his fingers in his mouth and whistled. "Hey, kid. It's safe."

A moment later, Trent's gangly frame appeared from the shadows. Bear gestured for him to come forward, and put his arm around Trent's shoulders. "Kid," he said, grinning. "You're not going to believe this. But this..." he turned to smile at Laurel, "is Laurel. My wife."

Trent's eyes grew so wide they looked like they might pop right out of his head. "Laurel? You're kidding! *You're* Laurel?" Trent let out a small whoop and smacked his knee in a rather dramatic fashion. "Ma'am, you have no idea what PB's gone through to find you. We came all the way from Thunder Bay. Through the Boundary Waters. He got bitten by a wolf. Fought off some guys who tried to take our truck. Saved the hospital!"

"Trent, maybe slow down. That's a lot of information," Bear muttered gently.

Laurel was watching the pair of them closely. Pushing her glasses up onto the top of her head, she laughed. "Well, it certainly sounds like we have a lot of catching up to do."

As their initial elation at seeing one another began to fade, Laurel stepped to the side and put her hands behind her back. Suddenly, she seemed shy. Was she remembering that it had been two years since they saw one another face-to-face? Was she remembering the reasons why?

"Trent's been my travel companion since I left Thunder Bay." Bear changed the subject and again squeezed Trent's shoulders. "He's saved my life more than once."

"Well, then I'm *very* glad to meet you." Laurel pulled Trent in for a hug. As she released him, Bear noticed Trent's gaze settle on something. He followed it. There was someone else here.

Trent's body had stiffened. He pulled back from Laurel.

From the shadows, a figure Bear recognized lifted his palms. "Hey, buddy."

"Bear… is that…?" Trent grabbed Bear's arm, ducking behind him slightly.

"What are you doing here?" Bear instantly reached for his gun. As he lifted it, Arlo raised his too, but pointed it at Bear.

"Jim." Bear almost spat on the ground. In front of him, Jim smiled a thin smile. Turning to Laurel, only just stopping himself from putting his arm around her and pulling her away from the guy, Bear growled, "This guy *stole* my truck and left us for dead. What is *he* doing here?"

For a moment, their small campsite descended into chaos. Trent starting yelling, trying to tell Laurel and the others what had happened. How Jim had shot him and stolen all their things. Forced them to travel through the Boundary Waters with nothing but the clothes on their backs and one small bag.

In protest, Jim shook his head and muttered a string of, "Let me explain… it wasn't like that… I've changed since then…."

Jess started barking. Arlo told her to shut up. Laurel told Arlo to leave the dog alone.

The only one who was quiet was Liam.

Then something broke through the quiet. Bear only just caught it, but the others froze and the looks on their faces told him he was right.

A gunshot.

Bear looked from Laurel to Arlo. "We've got to go." He'd deal with Jim later.

Softly, not moving, Laurel said, "What's going on, Bear?"

Arlo's jaw twitched. "You being followed?"

"Some crazy chick called Britt," Trent answered for him. "Bear killed her boyfriend Murph and now she's out for revenge."

"Murph?" Arlo's eyes widened. "You killed Murph?"

"It's a long story. We don't have time." Bear waved his arms, gesturing for the others to get going. Why were they all just standing there? "But, yeah. She's been following us from South Minneha. She's out for blood."

"Well, she was after us too a while back." Laurel reached for one of the packs on the ground, wincing as she pulled it onto her shoulders and starting kicking dirt over the fire.

"I thought we put an end to her back at the farmhouse." Arlo grabbed his pack too, then his kid's.

"What about the rest?" Jim was looking forlornly at the other bags on the ground.

"Take what you can, but hurry," Laurel stepped in. "We've got to move. You don't know what this woman's capable of." As she turned, she caught Bear's eyes. "How many are with her?"

"Not sure. I tried to lose them. Got rid of a few but don't know how many are left."

"However many she's got, it's too many." Arlo checked his weapon. "Let's move, everyone."

Scooping Jess into his arms, Bear deposited her into her sling and started jogging. When he realized Laurel wasn't at his side, he looked back. She was limping, leaning on a branch she was using as a walking stick. He slowed, grabbed the pack she'd attached to her front and heaved it onto his own shoulder instead.

She looked at him wide-eyed as if she was about to object.

"Concentrate on moving." He pointed at her ankle. "We need to get out of here."

She nodded. They'd gone just a few paces when she turned and met his eyes. "Bear?"

"Yeah?"

"I never picked you as a dog-wearing type. But it suits you."

21
BRITT

"Britt, up ahead." Ryan grabbed Britt's elbow and hissed at her.

Pulling away from him, she growled. Under the cover of the trees, it was almost pitch dark, impossible to see ahead. But this time, she hadn't relied on sight. As the others had scrabbled around looking for a trail to follow, Britt had stood stock still and just listened.

"Quiet," she'd snapped.

The others had fallen still.

"That way." She'd pointed. "He's heading that way."

Now, as Bert stood shivering behind her, she didn't need to use her ears anymore. Ryan was right; there was light up ahead. Firelight.

"Britt. I don't feel so good—" Bert's teeth chattered as he spoke.

"Maybe you should have thought of that before you plunged into a frozen lake." Britt's stomach twisted with rage. She still couldn't believe they'd fallen right into such an obvious trap. And she couldn't believe Bert was the only one who'd seen it.

"He needs to get warm." Ryan took off his scarf and offered it to Bert.

"Well, I think we've established there's a fire up ahead. Help me take this guy out, you get a seat front and center."

"Britt, I don't think I can…" Bert's words petered out. He slid to the ground, leaning against the nearest trunk. Britt was pretty sure that if it wasn't too dark to tell, his face would look blue.

"Leave him," Karl snapped. As he turned his head, his scar caught a slash of moonlight. Britt would have shuddered if she hadn't been so sure that he was on her side. He and Murph went way back. And Karl was still pissed that he'd missed the opportunity to fight at the hospital because he'd been scouting the area looking for Arlo.

Arlo… Britt's jaw twitched. As soon as they'd taken care of this Army guy, Arlo was next.

"You think he's alone?" Ryan asked.

"Why would he stop and light a fire? He knew we were on his trail." Karl adjusted his gun on his shoulder.

"He's an arrogant jerk." Britt pulled her hat down over her ears. "Thought he'd fooled us twice." She gestured for the others to stay put. "I'll be back. Wait here."

"Britt. You shouldn't go alone." Ryan's whiney voice made Britt's skin twitch. She bit the inside of her cheek, trying to resist the urge to turn around and tell him to shut up.

"Stay. Here." She repeated herself as firmly as she could and stalked into the undergrowth.

Slowly, she inched toward the light. As it flickered, she blinked to push the image of Murph's face from her mind. Now, whenever she saw him, it wasn't the real him. It was the cold, unmoving, wrapped in a black body bag version of him.

She stopped when she heard voices, crouched down, and moved so she could see through the branches up ahead.

There he was. *Him.* Standing there with his arm around some kid.

Britt blinked. He'd moved to one side and in front of him... it couldn't be. It was the woman. The doctor from the farmhouse. The one who'd been with... "Arlo Staaf." Britt's mouth became instantly dry.

At first, a flutter of panic rocked her gut; Arlo and the guy who killed Murph *knew* each other. They'd joined forces. Of course they had. And now she had to take them both out at once.

But as she stayed and watched, and listened, she realized she was wrong; Arlo had never met this guy before. They hadn't joined forces, they'd just been thrown together. And they all looked the worse for wear.

The doctor was limping. Arlo's kid looked like he was about to keel over. And was that a dog in a pink coat? Geez.

Britt smiled to herself as she slipped back into the shadows. While they were busy playing catch-up, this was her chance.

As quietly as she could, in case the dog heard her, she returned to the group. Karl was standing, like a general, in front of the others. Ryan was crouched down in front of Bert. He'd wrapped a blanket around him and taken off his own jacket to put around Bert's shoulders.

"Well?" Karl strode forward.

"It's him, but not just him." Her lips spread into a grin; Karl would like this. "Arlo Staaf is with him. Looks like they just stumbled on one another. And the doctor. The one who killed Marianne and Rachel."

Karl's expression didn't change. "Staaf is here?"

"Just up there."

He nodded slowly, his jaw setting into a determined line.

"They're totally off guard. If we move now, we've got them." Britt turned to the others but before she could rally them, Ryan stood up.

"Britt, seriously, Bert needs help."

"Oh, for heaven's sake, Ryan, you don't see anyone else complaining. Just leave him here." Britt's eyes flashed wider. "Have you forgotten what we're doing out here? What we're trying to do? For Murph?"

"Britt, Murph's dead." Ryan's face paled as he spoke. "I mean, it's just…" he stuttered.

"You want out? Then why don't you stay here with him? Play nursemaid. Leave the fighting to those of us who can handle it." Britt turned and put her hand on Karl's arm. "Let's go."

"No…." The voice came out of nowhere, shaky but loud. Bert was staggering to his feet.

"Shhhh," Britt hissed at him. "What are you doing?"

"No one's—" Bert sucked in a deep breath. "Going anywhere." Then before Britt had time to realize what was happening, Bert lifted his gun and fired into the air. One. Two. Three shots.

"What are you doing?" Britt pointed her gun at him but before Bert could mirror her, another gun shot. Bert clutched his chest and fell to his knees.

Britt turned to look at Karl.

"You shot him!" Ryan looked from Karl to Bert. Bert had slumped over, face first on the frozen forest floor.

"Yeah," Karl replied. "I did. And now we gotta move. 'Cos your friend here just told our other friends that we're following them."

Britt reached up and grabbed a fistful of her own hair. Letting out a loud growl, she spun around and kicked at the ground.

"You shot him." Ryan was still staring at Bert's body. Slowly, he looked up. "You're going to let him get away with that?"

"Do you have a problem with me, kid?" Karl broadened his shoulders. His thick neck twitched.

"Guys. Stop." Suze stepped forward, looking from Ryan to Karl as if she was actually pleased about what was happening.

"Yeah, I have a problem." Ryan reached for his gun. "I have a big problem." He lifted it but before he could fire, Karl did the same.

BANG.

Britt jumped back and slammed her hands over her ears. When she opened her eyes, Ryan was writhing on the ground clutching his leg. "Britt, he shot me." He rolled over, groaning.

Karl didn't move, just watched him with an amused expression on his face.

"Dammit, Karl." Britt rolled her eyes and bent down to look at Ryan. Snapping her head back up to Karl, she said, "Go. Follow them. Lay a trail so I can find you. *Don't* start shooting until I get there."

Karl opened his mouth to speak but Britt didn't give him chance.

"Do it. The rest of you, with Karl." She stood up slowly, still looking at Ryan. "I have business to settle here."

"Britt?" Ryan mumbled, his eyes widening as he looked at her.

Next to Karl, Suze grinned and licked her lower lip. "You gonna shoot him, Britt? Put him out of his misery?"

Britt tilted her head and narrowed her eyes. "Why are you still here?" She looked from Suze to Karl. "Go!"

As the others hurried off into the undergrowth, Britt closed her eyes, breathed a deep breath, then opened up her pack. Dropping it to the ground, she muttered, "Keep still. It's not that bad." She ripped Ryan's pants leg open and examined the wound.

"How'd you know?" Tears were streaming down his face.

"Because I've been shot before and this ain't bad." She pulled the first-aid kit from her bag. "Now, keep still."

For a moment, neither of them spoke. Then Ryan lightly touched her hand. "Britt? Why'd you help me?"

She paused. He was watching her intently, an almost hopeful look on his face. She swallowed down her desire to pull her hand away. "Because we're friends," she said tightly.

"We are?"

Ignoring his question, she lowered her eyes and concentrated on sterilizing Ryan's wound, ready to stitch up the bullet hole. But as she looked at the bloodied mark on his skin, the only thing she could think about was Murph. Getting revenge for Murph.

Which was precisely why she needed Ryan; he was the only one she could trust to do exactly what she told him to when she told him to do it. She was so close to justice, and she was not going to let it out of her grasp. Not this time.

22

LAUREL

As they began to run, Laurel looked sideways at her husband. Her husband who had appeared, like a ghost, from the woods. Who'd come all the way here, with Jessamine and a teenage boy in tow, to find her.

There were so many things she wanted to ask him; how long ago he left Thunder Bay, *why* he'd come looking for her, what had happened at South Minneha, how her mother was, what he'd been planning to do once he found her.

But there was no time. Bear had brought danger right to their doorstep. Britt, who they'd already fought off once, was back. And if she found out that Bear was now traveling with Arlo—well, Laurel didn't want to be around when that happened.

"I'm sorry," Bear panted, as if he could read her mind. "I'm sorry I led her here."

Laurel shook her head at him. "It's not your fault." She smiled a little; caught between being so pleased to see him she wanted to do nothing but stop and look at him, and feeling like she should hold back. "I'm glad you found me."

From up ahead, Arlo spun around and snapped, "Less talking, more moving." Next to him, Liam was struggling to keep up. Arlo looked at his son and then, without warning, stooped and picked him up. Liam tried to object, but Arlo simply shushed him and strode forward.

"Any idea where we're headed?" Bear asked. Laurel could tell he was struggling to slow himself to her pace. She wished she could ditch her stick, but her ankle simply wasn't strong enough yet.

"We were going to a survivalist camp. Jim helped me out of a ditch and in return we agreed to help him get his stuff to his friend's camp."

Bear's jaw twitched but he didn't say anything.

"When I last checked the map, it looked like we weren't far out. A couple of hours." She looked up at the sky. "Obviously, I hoped we'd be making the trip in daylight so I could navigate properly."

Bear stopped and gestured for Laurel to take out the map. She held it into the fading light and indicated the camp and the road they were on. In a low voice, Bear said, "We could leave him. Laurel, he's a thief and a liar. You do *not* have to keep your promise to this guy."

Laurel adjusted her glasses on her nose. "That might be true," she said. "But right now, a survival camp, people with guns… that sounds pretty good to me."

Breathing in heavily, Bear nodded.

"Do we have time for this?" Jim had stopped up ahead and jogged back toward them. He looked at the map, then glanced behind Laurel and Bear.

They couldn't see or hear anyone. The gunshots had stopped. But that didn't mean Britt had disappeared.

"Here." Jim jabbed his index finger at the map. "It's right here. We know where we're going, so if this woman's as crazy as you say she is, let's go."

23

BEAR

"There. There it is." Bear pointed at a tall fence with no sign and barbed wire along the top of it blocking their way in.

Silhouetted against the dark, star-spattered sky, the camp was bigger than Bear had expected.

"How do we get in?" They stopped in front of the entrance. Bear looked at Jim.

Ignoring him, Jim strode forward and banged on the gate. As he did, it opened. He hesitated, looked back at the others, then straightened his shoulders and strode through.

"Cal?" he called.

Bear put his hand on Laurel's elbow and nudged her forward.

"Cal?" Jim called again. "Where are they?" Jim spun around, as if tents and people might spring up from nowhere. But they were met by nothing but a large empty field.

Bear looked back at the gates. No guards. Wide open. The place was abandoned.

"Is this some kind of joke?" Arlo was still holding Liam but was looking around, staring through the moonlit field with a look verging on disgust on his face. "You said it was a *survivalist* camp? There's nothing here!"

Jim opened his mouth to reply but nothing came out.

Moving a little farther into the field, up ahead, Laurel pointed to something. "There's the remains of some tents over there."

Bear followed her gaze. She was right; a collection of abandoned tents lay collapsed on the ground, blending into the dips and humps of the landscape.

"Looks like your buddy moved on to *survive* elsewhere." Arlo lowered Liam to the ground and patted his son's head. Liam leaned into Arlo's side; the kid was exhausted.

"They can't have gone." Jim strode forward, ignoring the tents. "They can't have."

"Maybe they didn't have enough supplies for the winter." Laurel bent down and nudged a piece of tent fabric to look underneath it. "I wouldn't want to try and survive the cold out here."

"But he said…" Jim seemed truly shocked. "He said they were building cabins. Like a commune. He said—"

Putting a firm hand on Jim's shoulder, resisting the urge to squeeze too hard, Bear said gruffly, "Looks like he lied to you. Not great, is it? Being lied to?"

Jim shrugged out of Bear's grip and wrapped his arms around himself. As he strode off through the snow, his orange coat reflected the moonlight.

"He's like a walking flare," Bear muttered, stepping up next to Laurel.

"Maybe he should read Liam's Boy Scout book," she replied, meeting Bear's eyes and smiling.

Heading forward, Bear adjusted Jess's weight on his front. He was tempted to set her down but didn't want to risk her running off again.

"We're not staying here, are we?" Arlo asked, his arm around Liam's shoulders.

Laurel turned to survey the camp. "I don't see that we have much choice. If Britt's behind us—"

Bear nodded. "We should find something to block the gate with. If we can seal it off, we'll be pretty secure in here." But it was dark, and they were surrounded by nothing but open space and abandoned tents. It would take them hours to scour the place in the dark.

"There are some trees over there." Trent pointed to the outskirts of the camp. "Maybe we could find some logs or something."

Bear looked at Laurel. She was biting her lower lip. She looked cold and tired, and he wished he could put his arm around her to warm her up. Snapping out of his thoughts, he shook his head. The thick forest of trees that hugged the outer rim of the camp stood in ominous darkness. It afforded them some protection. But the chances of finding something big enough to block the gate, and being able to drag it back here in time to use it, were slim to nonexistent.

"There. Cal could be in there." Jim was a little way ahead and had turned to call back to the rest of them. In the distance, Bear could make out a cabin. Squinting, he realized it was in front of a lake, positioned on some sort of struts so it was raised from the ground.

It was hugged on one side by limestone bluffs and the lake on the other. The bluffs almost gleamed in the moonlight.

"Maybe everyone's sheltering in the cabin." Jim gestured for them to follow him as he moved quickly forward.

Laurel and Bear exchanged a skeptical look. Leaning toward her, he said, "I'm telling you now, this place has been abandoned. But if we need somewhere to hide for the night, that cabin looks to be as good a place as any."

Laurel was nodding in agreement when Trent came jogging up behind them. "I can hear them," he said, taking hold of Bear's arm and waving toward the gate. "I was looking for something to block it with. I heard them. Behind us. They can't be far."

Bear looked at Laurel to see if she'd heard what Trent was hearing. She was stock still, straining her ears. Then her eyes widened. She waved to Arlo, then pointed back in the direction of the gate.

As Arlo scooped Liam back into his arms, Bear heard what the others were hearing. Shouts and hollers. Threats floating toward them in the darkness.

"Ready or not, here we come... I hope you're ready for us, Rambo."

Bear shuddered. There was no time for the gates. Laurel was right, they'd be better off in the raised cabin or whatever it was. With the lake and the bluffs shielding it, it was the best protection they were going to get.

Jim was already heading for it, so Bear beckoned for the others to follow and moved as quickly as possible through the snow with Trent and Laurel at his sides.

They made it to the steps. Laurel was limping badly. She'd ditched her walking stick but was clearly in pain from pushing herself too hard. Bear wished he could scoop her up and carry her, but she'd probably hit him over the head for trying. Plus, he still had Jessamine strapped to his chest.

"Be careful." Arlo tugged Liam back and looked around at the others. "I'll go first. Someone watch Liam."

Behind him, Jim stuttered, "Ah, guys, don't you think I should go first in case Cal is up there?"

No one answered him.

"I'll help Liam." Trent hurried to Liam's side while Bear gestured for Laurel to go next.

As Arlo started to climb, it became clear that the cabin wasn't what it used to be. The wooden steps that zig-zagged up the side to the sheltered platform above were slippery and Bear didn't trust that they wouldn't give way.

"Test each step before you put your full weight on it," he told the boys. "And make sure you've got a good grip on the step above."

Both boys nodded. Arlo was about ten steps up when a loud crack broke through the strained silence. Bear looked up as a large splinter of wood fell, grazed the side of his face, then plummeted to the ground.

"Step broke!" Arlo yelled. Luckily, his other foot had been on the step above and he was gripping one farther up with his hands. "Others seem okay."

Painfully slowly, they ascended the steps. In her carrier, Bear could feel Jess shaking, and he wasn't sure if it was because of the height or the cold.

"It's okay, girl, nearly there. Nearly there."

"Girl?" Laurel looked back at him.

"Sorry, I was talking to the dog." Bear offered her what he hoped was one of his more charming smiles; not that he'd used a smile like that in a while.

"Of course you were," she chuckled.

When they finally reached the top, Arlo looked back at them. "This place isn't so much a cabin as a glorified treehouse." He tested the platform before climbing onto it then called back, "It's nothing more than a roof and a room, like a fishing hut or something." He disappeared, but as Bear heaved himself up, he saw Arlo inching his way around the outer rim of the platform before ducking beneath the shelter roof.

"I thought you said," muttered Bear as Jim dragged himself and his belongings up the steps, "that this place was some kind of haven? A survival camp? Bad enough there's nothing but a field and some old tents out there, but this..." Bear looked up at the shelter roof and around the empty interior. "Like Arlo said, it's hardly any better than a fishing hut."

Jim stood up and brushed himself down. He looked forlornly at the shelter. "Cal told me it was...."

Bear blinked at him. Just looking at this guy's face made him clench his fists.

"Look." Jim shoved his hands into his pockets and took a step forward, sucking in a deep breath and squaring up to Bear. "Does it matter? I brought us to a shelter, didn't I? It's better than being out there in the open. Besides, *you're* the one who brought that gang here. Not me!"

Bear's muscles were twitching, his jaw tensed, when Laurel nudged his elbow. "He's not wrong, Bear. About being safer here. It's bright tonight and with the open space, the lake, and the bluffs, there's no way Britt will be able to sneak up on us. It's better than being outside or hiding in the woods."

Bear nodded slowly. Arlo was still out of sight inside the shelter. "We should—"

Laurel spoke at the same time. "We should go inside and see what resources we've got. Jim, can you stay out here on lookout?"

Bear tilted his head. Somehow, he'd thought that he was the one in charge, but as always, Laurel was clear-headed in a crisis and ready to whip them all into shape.

Jim bit his lower lip. "You want me to stay out here alone when I'm unarmed?"

"Yes," Laurel said bluntly. "If you see anything, there's plenty of time for us to get out here and rescue you."

Inside, they found Arlo settling Liam into a corner and tucking blankets around his legs. The cabin was small, the rear wall home to some low worktop units and a camp stove.

Laurel walked over to them and opened each cupboard door in turn.

"Anything?" Bear stepped up beside her.

"Some old kerosene lamps. Some cleaning stuff." Laurel reached in and pulled out a plastic bowl. "A wash bowl."

"Real hard-core prepper stuff," Bear laughed dolefully.

"And this." She held up a small black case and tried the lock. It wouldn't open.

Bear took it from her, tried it, then set it down on the worktop.

Without skipping a beat, Laurel clapped her hands together and said, "Right, looks like there's nothing useful here except walls and a roof, so what weapons have we got?"

"Trent and I are armed." Bear gestured to Trent, who showed them his handgun.

"Can you use it?" Laurel asked. "Because if you can't—"

"He can use it," Bear interrupted. "I taught him myself."

"Good. Arlo and I are armed too. We both have full clips."

"Mine's partial," Bear said.

"I have almost a full box," Trent added. Then, glancing at Bear, he said, "Bulldog made sure I was well stocked."

Laurel adjusted her glasses on her nose, then frowned, pulled off her hat, and pushed them on top of her head. Noticing Bear watching her, she said, "Mine broke. These are the wrong prescription. More of a hindrance than a help."

Tugging his ear to draw her attention to his hearing aid, Bear nodded. "Tell me about it."

"You're seriously going to trust this teenage kid with a gun but not me?" Jim had ditched his post and was standing, hands on his hips, looking from Bear to Arlo as if they were the ones in charge and not Laurel.

"What happened to the guns in my truck?" Bear asked. "The ones you stole from me? The ones you used to shoot the boy with?"

At that, Laurel blinked hard. Her mouth opened as if she was going to say something, but then she changed her mind and closed it.

"Long story," Jim grunted.

"Well, we don't have time for stories, so why don't you get back out there and do what we asked you to do?"

"Actually," Laurel stepped between Bear and Jim, "Jim, could you take care of Liam? He needs food, painkillers, and to stay warm." As if she sensed he was going to object, she added, "I don't think we told you this, but Liam is being treated for leukemia. He really does need rest."

Bear noticed Jim's eyes soften, a movement that seemed uncharacteristically genuine.

"I'm okay." Liam clearly wanted to help, like Trent, but even Bear could tell that the boy needed to sit down for a while. "You need him on lookout."

"Trent can be on lookout duty." Laurel nodded at Trent. "He's armed and Jim isn't, and we could use your dad's help seeing what's around here that might be useful."

For a moment, Jim's expression remained fixed, staring at Liam, but then he nodded. "Okay." He smiled and crouched down next to him. "Come on, kid. Let's get you settled."

While Jim unpacked some water and food for Liam, Bear told Trent to keep watch.

"What's taking them so long?" Trent asked, taking up position in the shadow of the bluffs so that he was obscured from view from the ground.

"I don't know. But they'll be here." Bear shivered a little. "We didn't have time to cover our tracks and if they followed us here, it wouldn't take much to figure out where we'd be hiding. Not long now, they'll find us."

Behind him, Laurel and Arlo were examining the small, padlocked case.

Setting it down on the floor, she tilted her head. As she did, the moonlight caught the side of her face. Bear watched her and smiled. He knew this look; this was her "I mean business" look. The one she adopted whenever she was concentrating hard in a crisis.

Reaching back, she pulled a hairpin from the top of her ponytail, straightened it out, and began to wriggle it around in the lock.

"You've turned into a master criminal since we last saw each other?" Bear quipped.

Laurel shrugged. "Saw a video on YouTube once."

Just when he thought she was going to give up... click. The case pinged open. Laurel looked up and grinned, then opened the lid.

"Okay, we've got... an old thermos, some questionable hard candy, a flashlight, which I'm guessing doesn't work anymore and," she gestured to Bear, "a flare gun."

Bear crouched down. Laurel was right. A single-use flare gun.

Now that, he thought, *might come in handy.*

24

LAUREL

"Can we light a fire? The boy's freezing." Jim tapped Laurel's shoulder and she turned to look at him. "It's not like they're not going to know we're here."

"I don't think we can risk it." Laurel glanced at Bear, who shook his head in agreement. "If they didn't, it'd be like putting up a huge flashing sign."

"I'm just worried about him." Jim wrapped his arms around his waist. Up here, despite the roof, it was perishingly cold. An icy wind whipped through the tower, making them all shudder.

"I'm sorry." Laurel looked past Jim to where Liam was sitting looking at his Boy Scout book. It seemed, recently, he'd ditched his comics in favor of more practical reading. "There should be extra clothes in his pack and Arlo's. Wrap him in some more layers and get him into a sleeping bag."

Nodding, Jim turned and headed back to Liam. When he spoke to him, his face was different. Brighter, like he really *enjoyed* being in his presence.

"Didn't care too much about *Trent's* well-being when he shot him and stole my truck," Bear muttered, as if he could read her mind and knew she was having sympathetic thoughts about someone he clearly hated.

Deciding it was best to say nothing, Laurel pressed her lips together, then took her glasses off and put them in her pocket. "Better to be able to see long-distance right now," she said when she caught Bear watching her.

Tilting his head a little, he said, "Well, I'll be your eyes if you'll be my ears."

"Deal." She smiled but then caught herself and stopped; this was no time to be smiling.

Tapping Laurel's elbow to indicate that she should follow him, Bear stalked off toward the outer edge of the platform. Enclosed by a small wooden fence, it must be at least fifty or sixty years old. Watching the way Bear placed his feet, slowly and deliberately, she could tell he felt the same way she did; as if the whole thing might give way at any moment.

"Anything?" Bear spoke to Trent as if he was so much older than his teenage years. As if he was a friend. Laurel wondered if it had always been that way between them, and what they'd gone through together to make them so close.

"Nothing yet. Problem is, if they approach through the trees instead of the gate, we won't see them until they're almost on us." Trent paused, then said, "You think the fence goes round the forest too, or stops at the edge of it?"

Bear shook his head. "No way to know. Might be that the gate's the only way in. But we still have the advantage of height up here. Wherever they come from, we'll see them."

To their left, the sound of feet on wooden boards made both Laurel and Trent turn their heads. Trent nudged Bear; he hadn't heard it.

"Arlo? Everything okay?" Laurel was speaking quietly, even though their voices wouldn't carry on the wind from all the way up here.

"No way they can approach from that direction. They'd have to scale the bluffs, and unless they're superheroes or mountain goats…" Arlo told them.

"Good. At least we only have to keep watch on one spot," Bear replied.

On Bear's chest, Jessamine started to wriggle. Poor girl had clearly had enough of being carried. "You should probably put her down," Laurel said gently. "If Britt starts shooting—"

Bear nodded solemnly. "Just worried the crazy dog will fall off the edge."

"It's enclosed. She'll be fine." Laurel reached over and started to help him undo the straps of Jess's carrier. "Plus, she's smart." As Bear lowered her to the ground, she caught him whispering something in the little dog's ear.

Laurel inhaled slowly, then sighed; Jess had always been Bear's dog. They'd adopted her when he returned from Iraq, to help him get over his injury. Mae had suggested it and Bear had reluctantly gone to the pound just to look, and had come home with the little dog. Laurel had been so desperate to do something to help him, she didn't mind that Jess preferred him and always had.

Jess hadn't been a miracle cure. But she had eased his pain.

"Go sit with Liam, Jess." Laurel pointed toward Liam and Jim. Jess looked up at her.

"She's confused," Bear said, straightening himself up. "She remembers what Jim did. Isn't sure why you're asking her to hang out with him."

"I'm not." Laurel kept her voice steady. "I'm asking her to hang out with Liam. A kid who needs some comfort."

She could tell that Bear's hackles started to rise every time he looked at Jim. But she did not want to start arguing about him. Not now. Whatever he did to Bear and Trent sounded terrible, but people could change with the right impetus. Look at Arlo. A few weeks ago, she'd never have believed that they'd end up as friends. But as much as she'd doubted him when she was stuck in the riverbed, he'd proved that *friends* was exactly what they were now.

"PB. I see something," Trent hissed, ducking down as if he was trying to hide himself from view.

Instantly, Bear was at Trent's side. As Laurel took out her gun, she made a mental note to ask Bear what *PB* meant when all this was over.

"There." Trent pointed toward the trees near the lake's edge. "Three o'clock. You see? It looks like they have something burning. Is that a torch?"

Bear narrowed his eyes. Laurel did the same. Trent was right—there in the tree line, something flickered in the moonlight. The glint of metal. Guns being raised.

"Get ready." Bear looked at each of them in turn. Arlo already had his weapon raised. "But conserve your rounds—"

"We don't have endless ammo," Laurel added, finishing his sentence. "Fire warning shots only unless they approach past that oak." She pointed to a large oak tree, which served as a good marker of how close they could afford for Britt to get.

Laurel was about to suggest they spread out a bit more when Trent said, "There! I see someone!"

A slim shadowy figure had stepped out of the trees and was running full tilt toward them. Trent fired his gun. He didn't hit him, but Laurel wasn't sure he was trying to.

She looked at Bear. He could take this guy out if he wanted to. Why wasn't he?

Bear's jaw twitched.

Arlo fired too. Trent again.

Bear was hoping the guy would turn back. Laurel could see it in his eyes; the desperation *not* to have to shoot him. He was almost at the oak tree when Bear gave in.

Two shots.

The guy fell.

By the time the sun began to rise in the sky, illuminating the horizon in shades of pink and gold, too many bullets had been spent trying to prevent Britt from getting close to the cabin.

"We've kept them at bay but...." Arlo checked his rounds. "I'm nearly out."

"Jim, do you have any spare ammo in those bags?" Laurel pointed to the haul that Jim had managed to carry from the truck.

"I just brought food and water," he said, looking a little embarrassed. "Sorry."

"And books," Arlo muttered. "Books but not bullets. Good thinking."

In the corner of the shelter, Trent and Liam were sleeping while Bear kept watch. There had been no movement from Britt in the past few hours, but now that it was getting light, they probably didn't have long until that changed.

"Maybe we should make a run for it while they're sleeping," Jim suggested.

"We'd be dead before we got to the bottom of the steps," Arlo countered.

"Arlo's right." Laurel took a long swig from her water bottle. "They'll be watching us just the same as we're watching them."

"Then what do we do?" Jim held his hands up. "We can't just sit here. If it becomes a case of waiting us out, they'll win. We'll run out of bullets."

Laurel breathed in slowly and drummed her fingers on her thigh. Jim was right. They had to think of something.

Standing up, Arlo walked quietly toward the back of the shelter. While it had a roof, it also had large open doorframes on each side. He stood beneath the rear frame and looked up at the bluffs behind it.

"What if we climbed onto the bluff? It's close. If we could find a way across, it looks like we could get a foothold and climb up it."

"Arlo, there's no way…." Laurel stepped up beside him and put her hands on her hips. "We'd never make it."

"We'd have to leave our stuff." Arlo looked at their packs lying on the floor. "But if we could get up onto the roof—"

"We'd need a ladder, *something*." Laurel met his eyes and shook her head.

"How else do we get off of here, then?" Arlo's eyes flashed with annoyance. "'Cos Jim's right. We're sitting ducks up here. We never should have—"

"Stop arguing." Trent's voice interrupted them. He yawned and stood up, pushing his hands through his curly black hair. "Arguing *never* helps."

Laurel smiled at him. "Sorry, Trent. Go back to sleep. You didn't get much shut-eye."

"I'm fine." Trent straightened himself up.

Ignoring him, Arlo refused to give up. "I still think that if we could get over there—"

"Arlo." Laurel's jaw twitched. His pig-headedness hadn't softened, that was for sure.

"Fine then. I'll do it myself. If I can get back to South Minneha and get my men, we'll win this thing hands down. We'll outnumber her—"

"Dude… your men are—" Trent widened his eyes as he spoke, then bit his lower lip as if he wished he hadn't said anything.

"What?" Arlo moved toward him. "My men are what?"

Trent sucked in his cheeks. He glanced at Bear, like he was wishing he could rescue him, then said quietly, "Your guys are dead. Most of them, anyway. Murph attacked the hospital. Bear managed to fight back. Killed Murph and a bunch of others, but most of *your* guys?" Trent winced and shook his head. "They're gone, man."

For a moment, Arlo didn't move. He simply stood staring at Trent, unblinking. Then he turned and rammed his fist into the wall behind them. He was breathing heavily, shoulders shaking.

Laurel put her hand on his arm. "Arlo, I'm sorry."

Without speaking, Arlo shrugged her off and stormed outside.

"I shouldn't have told him." Trent looked at Laurel.

"No, honey." Laurel put her hand on his shoulder. "It isn't your fault. He had to know. Besides, we're too far away from the hospital for him to fetch help and bring it back here. It'd take days, and we don't have that kind of time."

Breathing in slowly, watching Arlo grip the edge of the balcony and breathe deeply, Laurel could feel his pain. But she also couldn't help thinking: *Perhaps if you hadn't left them holding my hospital hostage, they'd have kept their lives.*

She was about to go after him when Bear whistled. "Front and center," he called. "Now."

Laurel, Trent, and Arlo rushed forward just as Britt herself came into view. Stepping out into the open, she raised her hands in the air.

"She's not armed," Bear said quietly.

"It's a trick." Arlo lifted his gun.

"Arlo!" Britt's voice penetrated the air and sent a shiver down Laurel's spine. "I'm *so* happy to see you. I was worried you'd miss all the fun. But it seems it's your lucky day."

Laurel swallowed hard. Something flickered in the tree line. Was that a torch? Before she even had chance to realize it was happening, the oak tree went up in flames.

"Go!" Britt yelled.

Moving dangerously close to the flames, Britt's soldiers charged forward. Firing into the flames was pointless. The figures were obscured by smoke. Then one of them emerged.

They were holding something. Bear tried to fire but couldn't get a good angle from where he was standing.

"Bear! He's got a Molotov!" Laurel raced to the corner of the terrace. Arlo tore after her. But they were too late.

The Molotov hit the side of the structure.

25

BEAR

As the Molotov hit the side, Jessamine started barking. Liam had woken up and was sitting, wide-eyed, next to Jim.

Laurel had called for Bear, but Arlo was closer to her. "It hit one of the struts!" she called, looking back at him over her shoulder. "He's retreating."

Bear ran toward Laurel, then swung himself down onto the top of the creaky wooden steps. Hanging on with one arm, he leaned out, aimed, and fired.

The guy who threw the Molotov staggered a few more paces before dropping to the ground. Bear looked away. As he turned his head, he caught the smell of smoke. He'd been praying the structure wouldn't catch fire, but his prayers had gone unanswered.

"It's on fire," Bear shouted to Laurel and Arlo as he heaved himself back up onto the platform. "Water. We need water."

Nodding, Arlo waved at Jim. He was still sitting with Liam, arm around the boy's shoulders, watching them closely. "Bring the water. Quickly."

Jim clambered to his feet, steadying himself by leaning against the wooden walls of the shelter. He hesitated, then when Arlo repeated his request he grabbed hold of the large canister of water that he'd carried all the way from the truck and dragged it over.

Laurel and Arlo were standing directly above the strut that was on fire, watching it over the rim of the balcony. Arlo grabbed the canister. Laurel helped him lift it.

This small display of teamwork made Bear blink. He'd expected Laurel to have nothing but hatred for the man who'd forced her to leave South Minneha, but she seemed to like him. Trust him. Whatever had happened since they left South Minneha all those weeks ago, Arlo Staaf didn't seem like the same person who'd been described to him by those he met at the hospital.

"If we use it all, what'll we drink? What if we're stuck up here for days?" Jim pressed his lips together. He was scared. It was written all over his face.

"Then we'll melt some snow from the roof." Laurel turned her back on Jim. "If we don't put this fire out, the entire structure will go up in flames with us in it."

Bear shoved his gun into his pocket and strode over. "Here," he said, "let me help." While Laurel and Arlo balanced the canister between them, Bear unscrewed the top. When the lid was loose, he stepped back so the two of them could lean forward and pour a steady stream of water down onto the crackling flames.

At first, it sloshed awkwardly, missing the strut entirely. But then they got the angle right and the flames started to die.

"It's out." Laurel finally stepped back and lowered the now almost empty canister to the ground. She rubbed the tops of her arms as if they hurt with the effort of holding it up.

"It's done some damage, though." Arlo motioned for Bear to look, and pointed. As they looked down, assessing how bad the damage really was, Trent called to them from his lookout spot.

"They're coming again," he said. Liam was next to him, pointing in the same direction as Trent. When Arlo saw that his son had left the shelter, he strode over, put his arm around him and beckoned for Jim to take him back inside.

This time, two approached at once, weaving around one another, darting behind trees, making it almost impossible for Bear and the others to take them out. Then one broke free, a thick-necked guy with a scar on his face. He was holding another Molotov. It was burning in his hand. The guy was insane. If the glass bottle cracked while he was holding it….

Bear ran to the spot where Laurel had poured the water. That was what scar-face was heading for. That was what Bear would have done; go after the already-weakened strut and bring the entire thing to the ground.

Arlo was already there, leaning over. Bear joined him, both aiming for the same guy. "Dang it, the tree's in the way," Bear growled.

"I think I can—" Arlo heaved himself up onto the railing of the balcony.

"Careful." Bear grabbed his foot to steady him. Arlo was balanced precariously, holding onto the edge of the roof with one hand and aiming his gun with the other while Bear kept a grip on his leg.

Arlo narrowed his eyes. "Gotcha." He fired. And just as he was about to throw the Molotov, the guy with the scar dropped to the ground.

A grin spread across Arlo's face. Bear held up his hand, gesturing for him to get down. A few feet away, Laurel took aim at the one still running toward them while firing. This time, she almost got him. He turned and ran for the trees.

Arlo was still holding onto the roof with one hand. Then he wavered. His fingers loosened on his gun and it bounced off the railing, falling to the ground. Bear reached for him at the same time Laurel did. They pulled him back onto the platform, but he seemed unable to support his own weight. They lowered him to the ground and Laurel crouched over him.

"Arlo?" She was already undoing his coat. "Were you hit? Arlo?"

Arlo groaned and tried to speak, but no words came out.

Laurel tugged open his coat. A large bloody stain had seeped into his sweater. She lifted it and Bear flinched, turning away.

As Laurel started to whisper to Arlo, "It'll be okay, we'll fix you right up," Bear scraped his fingers through his hair. Inside the cabin, Liam was huddled next to Jim. When he looked up, he caught Bear's eyes and the color drained from his already pale face.

Bear had never been good at lip reading, but he knew what Liam was saying. "Dad… What's happened to my dad?"

"Oh no!" Laurel was gripping the railing The color had drained from her face. On the floor behind her, Arlo lay motionless. She turned to look at Liam, who was being bear-hugged by Jim as he tried to run out onto the platform.

"It's okay, it's okay. It'll be okay." Jim was trying to soothe him, but Liam was sobbing hard. His face turned red, contorted with rage or heartbreak or both.

"Dad!" He dug his nails into Jim's forearms. "Let me go! I want to see my dad!"

Liam hurtled toward them, almost falling over his own feet. When he reached Arlo's body, Laurel stepped in front of him. Bear did too. But he pushed them aside and knelt down next to his father. His hands fluttered out to hover above his dad's now blood-red sweater. Then he bunched his fists and sank back.

"Liam." Laurel crouched down and put her hands on Liam's upper arms. "Liam, you don't want to see your dad like this. Trust me, honey. You don't want to see." She met his eyes. "I did everything I could, but he's gone. It was quick. He wasn't in pain. Liam, I'm so sorry, but he's gone."

For a moment, Liam sat stock still, trembling. Then he dipped his head and began to silently cry.

Bear looked up, searching for Trent. He was watching Liam with an expression that said he knew exactly how the kid was feeling and almost couldn't bear to see it.

Tentatively, Jim walked up to Liam and wrapped a blanket around his shoulders. Helping him to his feet, he said softly, "I'm so sorry, kid. Come on. Come with me." Then with surprising delicacy, he turned Liam slowly back toward the shelter and guided him away from Arlo's body.

As Liam sat down, tucked his knees up under his chin, and cried quietly into his arms, Bear pulled Laurel close and kissed her forehead. He knew he shouldn't have. That wasn't what they did anymore, was it? But he couldn't help it. She was hurting, and he'd never been able to watch her in pain.

"Liam... the poor boy. He lost his mom and now his dad." Laurel pulled away and wrung her hands together. "If I'd had my medical kit...."

Bear stood back and met Laurel's eyes. "Laurel, you and I know that wouldn't have made any difference."

She paused for a moment, then sighed deeply. "I know."

Down on the ground, it seemed that Britt's men were regrouping. The guy Arlo shot must have been important, because when he went down, they retreated into the woods and now all was quiet.

Bear pressed his lips together, then said, "I'm sorry, Laurel, but I can't ask Trent. We need to move the body."

Laurel swallowed hard. "Yes." She nodded, glancing to where Jess and Trent were both helping to comfort Liam. "Round back. We'll cover him with a blanket for now."

"For now." Bear squeezed her arm. "We'll give him a proper burial later."

Having finally given in and lit a fire, because it wasn't as if they were hiding anymore, Jim made them all a cup of coffee. "Two sugars each. No sense rationing it now," he said bitterly.

Beside them, Liam was sleeping. He'd cried so hard that, eventually, sleep was the only logical thing left to do.

"So, what now?" Trent asked, wrapping his hands around his mug. "We've taken out three of her guys, right? She can't have that many left."

"Maybe, but we're not out of the woods yet," Bear said. "We're stuck up here. We're outnumbered. And the strut that was weakened by the Molotov is concerning me. If Britt succeeds next time and takes it out, we'll be in trouble. So we need to think fast."

"I'm not sure—" Laurel squeezed her eyes closed. "I'm not sure I can. I just keep seeing Arlo…."

Bear met her eyes. "Don't go down that road. Not now. I need your brains here, Rivera. What do we do?"

Laurel paused, then opened her mouth to speak. Before she could make a sound, another voice drifted toward them on the wind.

"I'd like to propose a deal!" It was Britt. Bear's jaw twitched. He thrust his coffee into Jim's hand and exited the cabin. Edging closer to the railing, Laurel at his side, he gestured for Trent to stay back.

"I don't negotiate with terrorists," Bear shouted down.

In response, Britt offered him a slow exaggerated clap. She was by the edge of the lake, past the smoldering oak tree. She tugged on the scarf she was wearing, then took off her hat. "I don't want any more of my people to die." She held up her hands. "So, give me Arlo Staaf and the rest of you can leave."

"Arlo?" Laurel muttered.

"She doesn't know he's dead," Bear replied.

"If he loves his kid the way he says he does," Britt yelled, "I'm sure he'll agree it's a fair swap. One life in exchange for… how many of you are there? *Four* others?" She moved sideways as if she might be able to catch a glimpse of Arlo if she looked past Bear and Laurel. "Come on, Arlo! What do you say?"

"We'll think about it," Bear called down. "Come back at midday. You'll have an answer."

Britt looked up at the sky. It was still early. But then she dipped her head and widened her arms. "Midday. Fine. See you then, friends."

"She wants Arlo?" Jim had left Liam with Trent and the three of them were huddled as far away from him as they could get, so he wouldn't overhear what they were saying. "Well, just tell her the truth. We don't have him! If all she wants is Arlo dead, then—"

"That's not all she wants," Bear interrupted him, folding his arms in front of his chest. "It's a ploy. We give her Arlo, she shoots him, then we're a man down and she comes for us anyway."

"Are you sure?" Laurel asked.

"Trust me, she's not going to let me go. Arlo might have feuded with Murph, but I *killed* him."

"Then what do we do?" Jim looked from Laurel to Bear.

"I have no idea," he said. "No idea."

26

LAUREL

Laurel felt as if she was floating out of herself, watching them all from above. Every now and then the image of Arlo's broken body, lying beneath a blanket, flashed in front of her eyes and made her wince. And when she looked at Liam, she felt as if her heart was breaking.

He'd been through so much. He and Arlo had just started to bond again, become what a father and son were meant to be. And now Arlo was gone, just like that. Taken away without Liam having a chance to say goodbye.

She pictured Arlo dancing with Liam and Chris Jenkins' son Peter, back at South Minneha, before they left and made their treacherous journey to Lone Oak. Nausea lurched into her chest and she turned to grip the railing.

Behind her, Liam was awake and crying again. She could hear him.

"Hey." Bear put a firm hand on her shoulder. Even through her coat she could feel the warmth of it. "Don't do this now. We need you."

When she turned her head to look at him, he gestured to Liam. "The kid needs you."

Jim was watching them both. He moved from foot to foot as if he felt awkward, like he was intruding on a private moment he wasn't supposed to be part of.

Laurel breathed in slowly. She looked at the sky, less pink now and more white. Was snow moving in?

"We have a couple of hours to figure out how we're going to play this," Bear said gruffly. "Unless she's the one playing us and she's going to attack us anyway."

Bear stopped and looked at Jim, then past him to Trent and Liam. Trent wiped his cheek with the back of his hand. He was crying. "Jim, swap places with Trent."

When Jim didn't move, Bear gritted his teeth and added, "Trent's folks were killed when the EMP hit. Car went off the road. He watched them drown. He's a good kid, but he's still just a kid. He can't handle his own feelings as well as Liam's."

To Laurel's surprise, Jim didn't react to Bear's disdainful tone or try to suggest that—as Trent had barely fired his gun—*he* should be the one to take control of it. Instead, he simply nodded and said, "I understand."

As Jim walked over to Trent, the platform creaked. It did *not* like movement.

"That's awful," Laurel said, pulling off her hat because the wind had dropped and she suddenly felt warm. "What happened to Trent's parents."

"Found him in town, near Thunder Bay. I had no idea about the EMP until he told me. After that, I kinda got stuck with him." As Bear spoke about Trent, his top lip curled into a smile. Laurel knew that, beneath his beard, his cheek would be dimpled. Seeing him like that soothed her a little. It reminded her of the way he looked at Mae when she was little. Proud. Loving.

Before Laurel could reply, Trent appeared at Bear's side. Jess was with him. Bear scooped her up and ruffled her ears. "You both okay?" he asked, looking from Trent to Jess.

"We're okay." Trent breathed in sharply and looked down at his gun. "I didn't get a good shot. Just hit the ground and that tree over there."

"You did *good*." Bear grasped Trent's shoulder and squeezed. He ducked his head to meet his eyes. "You did good."

Trent smiled weakly.

"While Jim watches Liam, can you be our lookout? Britt said she'd give us until midday to decide whether to give up Arlo—"

"Arlo? But he's—"

"I know. So we've got a couple of hours to figure out what we're going to tell her. While Laurel and I do the thinking, we need to make sure Britt's not pulling the wool over our eyes and sneaking up on us."

"Got you." Trent nodded firmly and when Bear dropped Jess gently to the floor, patted his leg for her to follow him.

Unfortunately, the best lookout point, sheltered from view from the ground, was on the same side of the tower as the stairs and the spot where Arlo was shot. Laurel watched as Trent positioned himself almost parallel with the bloodstain Arlo left behind, then fixed his eyes on the near distance, purposefully avoiding looking at the floor.

"Okay," Bear put his hand on Laurel's arm and guided her away from the railings, being careful to stay out of earshot of Liam and Jim. "Seems to me that our only option is to divide forces."

Laurel blinked at him. "Divide forces? You mean split up?"

Bear nodded. "The way I see it, we can't all stay up here. We're a man down and we can't all leave at the same time. So Jim and I will stay and cause a diversion while you take the boys and run."

"Take the boys and *run*?" Laurel's skin began to prickle. "You want me to take the boys and *run*?"

Not catching the annoyance in her voice, Bear simply nodded and continued. "We don't know how many people Britt has left. The boys are our priority now. Jim and I will distract Britt. Hold her off. You get back to the hospital and bring as many people back here as you can."

Laurel inhaled slowly and folded her arms in front of her chest. She was tapping her foot, but it didn't have the same impact in snow boots as it would have in high heels. "It'll take at least a week to get back to South Minneha from here. Then another to return. And that's *if* the snow holds off." She gestured to the sky, which seemed to be growing more and more ominous by the minute. "You think you can last two weeks with barely any ammo or food?"

Bear's expression didn't waver; he was staring at her with steely eyes that said he'd made his position clear and didn't intend to compromise on it.

"I'm not doing it, Bear. There's got to be a better plan." Laurel's voice began strong and clipped but ended a little shaky as it dawned on her exactly what he was suggesting. "You're doing this because you know bringing people back here is futile, aren't you?"

A moment ago, she'd been struggling to keep her voice at a low volume so that Trent and Liam didn't hear them arguing. Now, she was biting the inside of her cheek.

"There's no sense in both of us staying here. We can't let the kids get hurt, and you're the one Liam knows and trusts. So, it should be me who stays. Not because I'm trying to coddle you but because they need you more than they need me."

"That's not true." Laurel grabbed Bear's arm and squeezed it harder than she'd intended to. "Trent? You're the closest thing he's got to family now."

At that, Bear looked away from her, out toward the horizon. He breathed out hard and shook his head. When he looked back at her, he said, "Well, hopefully, the plan will work and I'll get off of this thing unscathed. But if it doesn't—Trent will be in good hands."

"There's more to the plan? More than making yourself a decoy target, I mean?" Laurel leaned back against the railing and watched him. As she moved, the structure let out another groan that made her heart jump in her chest.

"Not yet. But I'm not done thinking."

"He's sleeping again." Jim walked over to them and pointed back at Liam. "Poor kid." Pausing, Jim looked from Bear to Laurel. "Heard you lovebirds arguing. What's going on?"

"If you heard, why do you need to ask?" Bear replied snippily.

Laurel ignored his tone and pulled her coat closer as a gust of wind blew across the platform. "Bear thinks I should take the boys and leave. Go fetch help." She looked at Bear sideways and he caught her eye; they both knew it was a bad idea to tell Jim that Bear doubted help would actually arrive in time. He might have helped Laurel back at the river, but knowing what she knew now, she didn't believe that he'd done so entirely unselfishly; looking back, it seemed he'd recognized an opportunity to have three people indebted to him, who he could ask for favors.

Jim shook his shoulders, like a dog trying to release some tension, then nodded. "Okay. Sounds like a plan to me. But if I'm staying, I'll need a gun." He looked over at Trent, who was still watching for Britt.

"No. No way. You're not taking Trent's." Bear took a step back, as if the proximity to Jim was physically uncomfortable for him.

"Laurel's armed." Jim raised his eyebrows, then lowered his voice a little. "Plus, it's not like Trent's the best shot. I doubt he could even put a hole in that giant tree over there."

Laurel flinched as Jim's voice rose in volume. Trent looked over at them as if he'd heard his name, but quickly looked away again.

"Arlo's gun...." Laurel spoke quietly. The words were thick and bitter on her tongue. "He dropped it."

"Ah ah, no way. If they see me going down the stairs, they'll—"

"They won't see you. Right now, it's in shadow. If you strip off that ridiculous orange jacket of yours," Bear was looking Jim up and down as if he really was an idiot for choosing something so brightly colored, "go down there in dark clothes, hat, scarf round your face— they won't see you."

Jim's mouth dropped open a little. "Won't see me? How can you...." He turned to Laurel. "Is he serious?"

Breathing in slowly, Laurel angled herself toward Jim in a way that she hoped implied she was on his side. "We'll cover you," she said, meeting his eyes. "But Bear's right. I don't feel comfortable looking after both boys with only one gun. At least if Trent's armed, we have a spare if I'm out of bullets. And he can create a good amount of noise even if he doesn't hit his targets."

For a long moment, Jim looked as if he was physically having to shove his emotions down from his throat. His Adam's apple bobbed up and down as he swallowed hard. Then he closed his eyes, clenched his teeth, opened them and said, "Fine. Let's do this."

Barely a minute later, Jim had shed his tangerine jacket and was shivering in just his dark brown cargo pants and a navy-blue fleece. He wrapped his navy scarf tightly around his face and pulled his hat down tight over his ears.

"What's going on?" Trent didn't leave his post, but looked over at them.

"We need Arlo's gun," Bear replied matter-of-factly. "Jim's going to get it."

Trent's eyes widened. As Bear stepped over to him, he lowered his voice and leaned toward Bear's good ear. "You're giving him a weapon?"

Bear put a firm hand on Trent's shoulder. "'Fraid we need all the help we can get right now, buddy."

While Bear spoke quietly to Trent, Laurel ducked down behind the railing and watched as Jim began to descend the steps.

Bear was right; it was still in shadow. But it wouldn't be for long.

He was almost there. Laurel cast furtive glances toward the area where Britt disappeared. Were they watching them now, ready to shoot as soon as Jim was visible? The way he was dressed, they could easily mistake him for Arlo or Bear. Jim put his feet on the ground and started to inch toward the gun. Even from here, she could see his hand shaking.

Her breath caught in her chest. Arlo's gun was glinting in the sunlight. If anyone saw him, he'd be an easy target.

Jim squatted and reached for it, his fingers dancing across the barrel as he pulled it closer to him. He tightened his grip, then picked it up. He returned to the bottom of the steps and stopped. He looked behind him, toward the open snowy space that stood between them and Britt's woods.

"He's thinking about running," Bear growled.

"He wouldn't," Laurel said. But even as the words left her mouth, she knew she didn't really believe them.

"He's an idiot if he does. The second he's in the open, they'll see him." Bear's tone suggested that he wouldn't exactly be disappointed if they did.

Finally, Jim turned around, put his foot on the lowest step, and began the climb back up. He'd reached the mid-way point when Jess, who was standing between Bear and Trent, began to growl.

"What is it?" Bear looked at Laurel as if he was missing something that his hearing aid hadn't picked up.

"I have no idea. I can't hear anything."

CRACK!

This time, he did hear it. Below them, Jim cried out. "What was that?"

"Don't panic. It's the weakened strut. She'll hold, just move slowly," Bear called down. When he looked back up, Laurel was staring at him. Pushing her glasses from her nose to her head, she smiled at him. "What does that look mean?" he asked, examining her face.

"It means," she said, "that I have an idea."

As Jim heaved himself back up onto the platform and, shivering, reached for his orange coat, Laurel folded her arms and stood between them. "Okay, listen up—"

27

BEAR

Bear tried not to let himself think about how good Laurel looked when she was in this frame of mind; determined, her brain running at a million miles an hour, ready to tell everyone what to do and not willing to take no for an answer.

"We need to sabotage the platform," Laurel said, barely stopping for breath.

"Sabotage it?"

"The Molotov weakened the strut. We've established that. So it won't take much." She was thinking as she spoke, Bear could see it in her face. She started pacing up and down and pinched the bridge of her nose. She pulled her glasses back down from her head, as if they might help her think. "We have the flare, right?"

"Right." Bear folded his arms and watched her.

"So, if we could fire it at the weakened strut, set it alight, it wouldn't take much before everything came down. Of course, you and Jim would need to be away from the cabin at that point. Somewhere out of sight on the ground so you can fire the flare once Britt and her guys are up here."

"That won't work." Jim was shaking his head.

Laurel raised an eyebrow at him.

"I'm just saying, the flare won't set fire to the strut."

Reluctant to agree with Jim, Bear clenched his jaw and nodded. "Jim's right, just *say* that we found a way to get down from here without being seen, and say that we found a way to entice Britt *up* here."

"Ah ha." Laurel nodded at him.

"It won't catch quick enough with the flare. It might not even catch at all." As she began to frown, he added, "But the fire *is* a good idea. We just need a way to start it. Something to combust with the flare."

Laurel was tapping her foot on the floor. She started to pace, thinking quickly. "The kerosene lamps...." Laurel shook her head. "I don't know. Maybe it's a stupid idea."

"No. It's not stupid." Bear was trying to think it through. He looked up at the sky. It would soon be midday. "Look," he said, inhaling through his nostrils and instantly missing the smell of the air at Thunder Bay, "we have a couple of hours until midday. Let's sit down and eat something. It might clear our heads. Then we'll empty the cupboards and see what we've got to work with." He turned to Jim. "Now you've got a weapon, you can switch places with Trent and take lookout duty."

Before Jim had the chance to object, Bear walked away. "I have some MREs in here," Jim said, reaching gently for his backpack, which was beside Liam.

Laurel started to sift through the packs Jim had been carrying. "Jim has plenty." She glanced over at Liam. "I'm not sure he'll be up to it, though, to be honest."

"How sick is he?" Bear asked quietly as Laurel pulled out some of the MREs and protein bars from Jim's backpack and passed them around along with a bottle of water.

"Pretty sick, but it seems like the treatment he got at Lone Oak did its job." Laurel blinked quickly, the way she did when she was trying not to let her emotions show on her face. "He started coughing a while back, but it seems to have died down. Although I'm not sure how the stress of..." she paused, searching for the right words, "*all this* will affect him."

Next to him, Trent was unusually quiet, and he fingered the package on his meal before setting it aside unopened. In every situation they'd been in so far, he'd remained upbeat, able to think of something snappy to say or to give Bear that cheeky smile of his. But now, he seemed lost in his own thoughts. Bear put an arm around his shoulders and noticed him wiping his eyes with his forearm. "Hey," he said softly, "you don't have to hide your feelings from me, kid."

"I know." Trent sniffed loudly. "Just feel selfish, is all. Liam's the one who just lost his dad. It's just that it's—"

"Reminding you of your folks?" Bear asked, even though he knew the answer.

Trent nodded.

As Bear handed him the bottle of water, he felt his jaw twitch. In all the time they'd spent together, they'd barely spoken about Trent's parents. About his feelings. His grief. How he was coping. He made a note to remedy that as soon as they got off this platform. *If* they got off it.

"What do you have in your pack?" Laurel asked. "Jim brought mainly food. Nothing particularly practical. Not even extra ammo."

Leaving South Minneha felt like so long ago that Bear could hardly remember what he'd brought with him. He brought his pack into the middle of their small circle and turned it upside down so the contents spilled out onto the wooden floor. "First-aid kit, food, knife...." He reached into his pocket and pulled out a magazine. "Plus, three rounds of ammo."

Immediately, Laurel reached for the first-aid kit.

Trent picked up Jess's kibble and gave her a couple of handfuls.

Unzipping the medical kit, Laurel peered inside. "I lost mine when I was stuck in the river."

"You were stuck in a river?" Bear raised an eyebrow at her. She was a good swimmer, so he wasn't sure how that had happened and, if it had, how she'd managed not to freeze to death.

"A dried-up one. Long story." She looked out toward Jim, keeping watch. "That's how we got hooked up with Jim." She continued rifling through the kit, then stopped and looked over to the corner of the room. Arlo's pack was resting against the wall.

Bear was about to tell her he'd check it but she shook her head. "I'll look. You see what's in the cupboards. Check for kerosene in the lamps."

As Laurel gently took items from Arlo's pack and set aside anything useful, Bear headed for the cupboards. Opening each one in turn, he took out the plastic wash bowl, the four old kerosene lamps, a box of latex gloves, some bleach, some liquid soap—at least whoever owned this place was a fan of cleanliness—and a hunting knife. He pocketed the knife. Then in the last cupboard, he hit the jackpot. "Laurel," he waved her over, "I think this just might be our answer."

"Will this work?" Trent picked up a bottle labeled "clear lamp oil" and scrutinized the label.

"Says right there, buddy, *highly flammable*," Bear replied, tapping the bottle.

"So, we coat the strut with this. Fire the flare at it, and…" Trent made a boom sign with his hands.

"That's the idea." Bear nodded. He thought about it for a moment. It was risky. Not foolproof by any means, but not totally hopeless either. "We only have one flare, though."

"That's okay," Laurel said. "You're a good shot." She smiled at him, and he cleared his throat.

"So, we coat the strut, lure Britt up here, then shoot the flare at it once Britt's on board," Trent said, as if he was still struggling to see the plan working.

Laurel picked up one of the kerosene bottles. "If we have enough kerosene left, we can soak the cabin too. Blankets. Anything and everything."

"So that the whole thing goes up?" Trent asked.

"Exactly." Laurel bit her lower lip. "We just have to figure out how we coat the strut in this stuff. Jim might have gotten down there without being seen, but we haven't got the shadows on our side now."

Bear was about to suggest that he go and risk it when Trent let out a *ha* sound and started grinning.

"You have an idea?" Bear asked, raising his eyebrows at the kid.

"You bet." He reached over and grabbed the box of latex cleaning gloves. "A few years ago, me and some kids from my street, we…."

He paused as if he wasn't sure whether he should continue, then shrugged. "We filled a bunch of gloves just like this with red paint. We had this pain-in-the-butt teacher who was just, like, the worst. We found out where he lived and paint-bombed his house." He took a glove from the box and shook it. "If they're full enough, they pop *real* good when you throw 'em."

As Bear gave Trent a disapproving look, Trent dangled the glove in the air.

"It'll work, PB. Trust me."

Bear turned to Laurel. She was looking at him in a way he wasn't sure he'd seen before. "Well, *PB?* Sounds good to me, but what do you think?"

Nodding slowly, Bear said, "Okay. It's good. Not perfect, but good." He clapped Trent's shoulder. "Kerosene bombs it is."

Trent punched the air. "Yes!"

"Doesn't solve the problem of how Jim and I get off this thing, though." He took a bite of the protein bar he'd chosen over the MRE, then started tapping his foot. "We can cause a distraction so that you and the boys can get away down the stairs and into the trees. That's no problem." He felt Trent tense up; it was the first time he'd heard the suggestion that he and Liam leave with Laurel while Bear and Jim stayed behind.

"What kind of distraction?" Laurel asked.

Bear looked up at the sky, then nodded. His mind was starting to slot the pieces together. "When they come to ask for Arlo, at midday, we tell them he wants time to say goodbye to his son, but he'll leave at sunset. That'll put the sun almost directly behind us. Limit their vision."

"Not enough for us to escape unnoticed," Laurel said firmly.

"Right, but as soon as they come for us, which they will, we'll start shooting. Jim and me. We'll switch up positions, make it look like there's more than two of us up here. Attack from this side, so that they're as far away from you as we can get them. Then, once you and the boys are down and in the trees, we'll make it look like we've run out of ammo. They'll take their chance to come up here and finish us off."

Laurel was nodding. Waiting for him to tell her how he intended to get off the platform. To be gone by the time Britt had climbed the steps. "And…?"

"And that's all I've got." Bear pressed his lips together and rubbed the back of his neck. His stomach growled. The protein bar he'd eaten was tiny and hadn't done nearly enough to satiate his hunger, but he didn't think he could stomach much else. "But I'll come up with something." He looked at Trent to reassure him. But Trent simply got up and walked away.

"Time's up!" Britt's voice barely reached Bear's ears. The wind was growing fiercer by the minute, and he had to strain to catch what she was saying. "What's your decision?"

"She's asking what we've decided to do," Trent said, interpreting without needing to be asked.

"It's okay, buddy, I heard her." Bear leaned forward onto the railing. Looking at Britt, imagining the steel in her eyes because he wasn't close enough to see it, he shouted, "We voted. And we're all in agreement. We will give you Arlo Staaf if you give us your word that you'll let the rest of us leave."

Bear didn't have to be close to see the smile that cracked on Britt's face. Pulling off her hat, she waved it in the air. "Well, hallelujah!"

She turned around and yelled something, which Bear assumed was a repeat of his message to her foot soldiers, two men and a woman standing behind her. But who knew how many were in the woods?

When she turned back, she put her hat back on and called, "Now, tell me, was *Arlo* in agreement with this plan? Because I'd really like to hear from the man himself."

Bear glanced at Laurel. Without him needing to ask, she stepped forward. "No. He's not. But we voted."

Britt nodded slowly and tilted her head from side to side. "Harsh." She clapped her hands. "I like it. But I still want to hear it from him."

Laurel turned around and, speaking to no one, said loudly, "She wants to see you. No. She said she wants you to—" Cutting herself off, she turned back to Britt. "He says no. He wants some time with his son. He'll come down voluntarily at sunset if you can give him that."

This was the moment. If Britt said no, which was a distinct possibility because she hadn't exactly proven herself to be the maternal type, Bear had no idea how they would wriggle out of it. It'd be a case of keep shooting and pray for the best.

But after a long pause, Britt finally said, "Fine. Sunset." She offered a jovial salute. "I'll see you then."

Bear and Laurel remained stock still until Britt had disappeared back into the tree line, then left Jim on watch while they returned to the shelter with Trent. Liam hadn't moved from his spot on the sleeping bags. He looked deathly pale, with large bags under his eyes and sunken cheeks, as if everything keeping him whole had been sucked out of him.

Before they spoke to Britt, Laurel had carefully explained what they were planning to do. She'd told him that they needed Britt to think his father was alive for a while longer. He'd barely reacted. "He's in shock," Laurel had said.

After telling Liam, they'd then broken down their plan for Jim. Bear had let Laurel do most of the talking, and had ignored the look on Jim's face when he said he was still working out exactly *how* the two of them would get off the platform before Britt and her gang climbed the stairs to slaughter them.

"Okay, we need to work quickly. There aren't that many hours until sunset." Laurel grabbed the box of gloves and started pulling them out one by one. "Bear, I'll pass them to you, and you fill them as full as you can. Then, Trent, you tie them and put them in the wash bowl *gently* so they don't break. Right?"

Trent nodded. Bear knew he was still sore with him for not telling him that he was planning to stay behind and let Trent go with Laurel and Liam. But he was slowly coming around. "Am I gonna get a turn throwing them?"

"Is he a good shot?" Laurel turned to Bear.

"He's okay." Bear chuckled as Trent gave him a mock outraged glare.

In the corner of the room, Jess gave a small whine. Bear looked up at her. She was wagging her tail, standing beneath the doorframe nearest the bluffs.

"Is she okay?" Laurel asked.

"I think she needs to pee." Bear motioned to the terrace. "Sorry, girl, you'll have to make do with the facilities up here." She tilted her head at him, then made a small *snuff* sound through her nose and trotted off. When she was out of sight, as if he didn't want her to hear what he was saying, Bear lowered his voice and nudged Trent's arm. "Hey, Trent? I have a favor to ask."

Bear handed Trent the first kerosene-filled glove. He tied it tight and gently placed it in the bowl. "Yeah?"

"I'd like you to take Jess." Bear forced himself to swallow the lump in his throat. He could feel Laurel's eyes on him but purposefully didn't look at her. "I want her safe. You think you can carry her in the pack on your front like I did?"

For a moment, Trent simply blinked at him. Then he nodded. "Yeah," he said quietly, "yeah, PB, I can take her." He took the second glove, tied it off and added it to the bowl with the first. "Until you catch up with us. Just until then. Right?"

"Right." Bear patted him firmly on the shoulder. "Right, kid. Until we catch up."

28

BRITT

Britt's scar was itching. It always had in the cold, but out here it was practically burning. She tucked her fingers under her scarf, unzipped her coat a little, and scratched it through the fabric of her fleece. Then she scoffed at herself, zipped the coat back up and held her hands out toward the fire, palms facing the flames.

Overnight, she'd refused to light one. Refused to give away their position. But now that it was obvious they had their prey cornered, she'd stopped caring about the plumes of smoke weaving their way up into the sky.

Karl would probably have told her that was dumb. But Karl was gone. Shot, although she didn't know who by. Possibly Staaf. She'd ask him when she saw him.

Thinking about Arlo, Britt's lips curled into a smile. In just a few short hours, she'd have him.

She'd surprised herself by allowing him the time he'd requested. Time to say goodbye to his kid. She'd never been maternal, but her own parents had died when she was a teenager. Drugs, both of them. So she felt a little sorry for Arlo's kid Liam. Not sorry enough to let his father live, but sorry enough to allow them a goodbye Liam would remember. She'd never had that. Her parents had just been there one day and gone the next.

Looking around at her camp, and the fighters she had left, Britt wrinkled her nose and twitched it from side to side. She'd lost more than half her people, but she still had enough to do the job. Arlo and the others were sealed in a giant wooden box. They had no way out, except the stairs down to the ground, which she had eyes on. She was winning this one. Winning it for Murph. And she knew he'd have been proud.

Beyond the pine trees, the sky seemed to be whitening. She hoped it wasn't going to snow again. She'd had enough of the snow already. Occasionally, wind whipped through the gaps in the trees and made the flames of the campfire flicker. Britt stared at the flames. She still hadn't decided whether she was going to keep to her end of the bargain or not. Part of her wanted to. Murph had always told her how important it was for people to trust your word when you gave it. But then, if it hadn't been for that Army guy, sitting pretty with *his wife*, Murph would have been with her right now, wouldn't he? To tell her himself what to do.

She reached for her pack and took out a candy bar. She'd been saving it and now seemed as good a time as any to tuck in.

She'd just bitten off a chunk and was savoring the feeling of it melting on her tongue when there was a noise in the undergrowth. She sat up and shoved the candy bar back into her pocket.

Panting, wide-eyed, twigs sticking out of his hair like he'd been literally dragged through the bushes, Ryan stumbled as he limped to her and leaned forward onto his knees. He was still mad at her about Bert and about getting shot. But it wasn't her who'd shot either of them.

And Karl probably did Bert a favor, finished him off before he really started suffering.

"How close did you get?"

"Close enough," Ryan said, breathing in heavily. "And you won't believe what happened."

Britt tilted her head.

"The leg we hit with the Molotov… it cracked." Ryan was gesticulating wildly.

"Are they—" Britt stood up, her heart drumming faster in her chest.

"No. They're all still up there. Alive." Ryan took another deep breath. "Except for one."

Britt didn't speak, just raised her eyebrows to indicate he should continue.

"Arlo." Ryan blinked at her. "Arlo's not up there, Britt. I've counted and counted. He's not up there."

For a moment, the words didn't quite sink into her brain. "Then where is he?"

"I don't know, but I know it looked like Karl got one of them before he went down. Maybe Arlo's dead. Or injured. But he's for sure not walking around up there like the rest of them."

"If he's dead or too sick to willingly give himself up…." Britt paused as her brain caught up with her words. "Then they've played us."

Fury began to burn in her throat. "They've played us. Made us think he was sitting there crying with his kid and saying his goodbyes when he could be lying dead in the snow?"

Ryan swallowed hard. Since getting shot, he seemed more afraid of her than usual.

Letting out a howl of anger, Britt tore off her scarf, pulled open her jacket and began to furiously scratch her scar. "What are they planning?" Her eyes grazed Ryan's features.

"I... I don't know," he stuttered. "I just know that no way did Arlo ask for extra time."

"Well, then. We need to come up with a counterattack. Quickly. We'll need to move before sunset if we want to take them out once and for all." Britt turned away from Ryan and clapped her hands loudly. Suze and the guy whose name she always forgot looked up at her. "Okay, you two." She put one hand on her hip and continued to scratch with the other. "Who can climb?"

29

LAUREL

Laurel was looking at the gash on Bear's forehead where he got hit by the broken step. It wasn't a deep cut, but it needed to be cleaned. "You need stitches."

"There's stuff in my kit." Bear gestured to the first-aid kit she'd taken from his pack.

Trent brought it over. "Here." He crouched down next to Laurel. Jim was with Liam. No one was on lookout.

"Someone should be out there." Laurel pointed toward the railing. then opened Bear's medical supplies and fished out the suture kit.

"I can do it." Bear moved to take the kit from her but she sat back on her heels and frowned at him.

"Since when do you have medical training?"

"I learned in the field." He held up his hand and waggled it at her. "Stitched this up a few months back. Did a pretty good job, I thought." He smiled proudly at his scar.

Laurel pressed her lips together and huffed at him. "If you say so."

"I do say so." Bear folded his arms but breathed in sharply when Laurel began her sutures.

Focusing on his forehead, she cleared her throat. "Listen, you still haven't told me how you plan to get out of here once you've fired the flare." She sat back a little and met his eyes. "I can't leave until I know you've got a way out, Bear."

He flinched as she cleaned the wound. "We're going to jump."

"Jump?" Laurel blinked at him and folded her arms. "To the ground? From here? You'll break something."

"No, not to the ground." Bear tipped his head toward the back of the cabin. "Onto the bluffs. The cabin roof extends out far enough that I think if we jump from the edge, we'll make it."

As Laurel's heart began to thud in her chest, she opened her mouth to speak, but Bear stopped her.

"There's a section of cliff that sticks out. I saw it when we moved Arlo's body back there." Laurel winced as he said Arlo's name. "I'm confident we can make it."

"Bear. This idea. It's—"

"It's the best one we've got." He met her eyes. "It'll be okay. I'll be fine."

She breathed in slowly. There was no other option. Trying to sound like she believed it would work, she said, "You'll have a good enough vantage point to fire the flare from up there?"

"Yes."

Laurel bit back the urge to sigh. She was used to these clipped answers. When they were married, answers like this drove her crazy. But she didn't want to fight with him right now, so instead she focused on stitching up his head.

When she'd finished, she sat back and smiled. Gesturing to her own head, she said, "Matching scars. Cute."

Bear smiled back at her. He was about to get up when she put her hand on his arm. "Bear?"

"Mmm?" He met her eyes.

"Before we do this, I need to ask you—"

Bear searched her face. "Ask me?"

"Do you know where Mae is?"

Bear blinked several times, as if he'd misheard the question. "Mae?"

"Do you know where she is?"

"No. Do you?"

"No. I just thought maybe she'd been in touch. She and I haven't been close since…" Laurel trailed off. Although Mae had had disagreements with both her and Bear, she had laid the blame for Bear's decision to run off to the woods solely at Laurel's door. Laurel had never told her the details of what had happened before their separation.

Bear shuffled uncomfortably and coughed. "No. We haven't either."

Laurel sighed a little. "I want to find her." She kept winding. "I *need* to find her."

A hand she recognized—Bear's hand—squeezed hers. He dipped his head until she looked up at him. "When we've dealt with this, we will." He nodded firmly. "I swear we will."

"But we have no idea where she is. Where would we even start?" Laurel finished bandaging him up and rubbed her own thighs to warm them up a bit.

"Last I heard, she was stationed at Fort Sill in Oklahoma. I know she's not there now, but there might be someone who knows where she was moved to. It's worth a shot, and once the weather turns it won't be too bad a journey."

"Fort Sill," Laurel repeated. "See, I didn't even know that."

Bear took her hand and, together, they rose to their feet. Instead of letting go, he took hold of her forearms. "She should know what I did to you. It's not fair that she blames you for what happened to us. It was my fault, not yours."

"I could have done things differently too, Bear. You needed help and I didn't know how… I should have known how…."

Bear was shaking his head at her and had opened his mouth to say something when, from the railing, Trent called over, "You guys, it's snowing."

"Damn snow." Jim waved his hands at the sky and jigged up and down on the balls of his feet.

"The snow's good. It'll cover you when you leave." Bear looked at Trent. "But in case it gets worse, we should hurry up."

Trent nodded. He was holding their wash bowl full of kerosene-filled gloves.

Jim frowned at it as if they were being a little childish, but Bear and Trent ignored him and headed for the top of the steps. Crouching down, Bear positioned himself so he could see the broken strut. "I'll do the first couple. Then you can take a turn."

Trent nodded. He knew it was important they get several good shots. And Bear was more of a sure thing than he was.

Laurel knelt down next to Bear and looked up at Jim. "Keep watch."

He nodded and paced away.

"All right." Bear weighed a glove up and down in his hand. "Here goes...." He pulled his arm back and, aiming for the weak spot in the strut, hurled the glove through the air.

Just as Trent had predicted, when it met with the wood it burst, showering the strut with greasy oil.

"Yes!" Trent high-fived Bear, grinning like they were at a fun fair trying to win a giant soft toy.

Bear took another three shots, then gave Trent a go. He managed two, missed the third, then let Laurel throw the final two.

"She's a good shot," Trent said, eyebrows raised.

"She's not bad," Bear replied, winking at her.

When they'd finished, the brief moment of fun while they threw balloons disappeared and a seriousness settled over them.

"Well, that's the hard part done." Bear wiped his hands on his pants. It wasn't the hard part, and he knew it. But he was clearly desperate to make Trent feel at ease with what was happening.

Reappearing from inside, Jess ran over and licked Bear's face. Ruffling her ears, Bear laughed. "Don't often get me down on your level, huh girl?"

Looking at the two of them made Laurel smile, but then that familiar pang of sadness tugged at her chest.

Why did she feel like she was saying goodbye to him all over again?

"You really think it's going to work?" she asked as she handed him a bottle of water.

Stepping into the shelter, out of the quickening snow, Bear shrugged. "I hope so." He looked over toward the flare, sitting in its case, and chuckled a little. "Guess it depends on how good a shot I am."

"Well, then I guess we'll be fine if the glove balloons are anything to go by." Laurel folded her arms in front of her stomach, partly to stop herself reaching for his hand, partly to keep her own hands warm by tucking them underneath her armpits.

"Liam's awake." Trent's voice nudged her away from Bear's eyes. "He fell asleep again but he's awake and asking what's going on."

Laurel stepped away from the fire. "I'll talk to him."

Over by the backpacks, Liam was sitting with his knees up to his chin. Dark circles had formed beneath his eyes, and he was staring vacantly into the fire.

"Hey, buddy." She sat down next to him, nudging a backpack out of the way so she could put her arm around him. When he didn't lean into her embrace, however, she removed it and simply stayed close. "I'm not going to ask how you're doing."

Liam looked up at her. He didn't smile.

"But I do need to tell you that we have to leave."

"Leave?" His voice was croaky. "Why?"

Laurel tilted her head to the side. "Because we can't stay here, Liam. It's not safe here and when Britt—" She stopped, unsure how to phrase the next part of the sentence.

Liam met her eyes. "When Britt realizes my dad's dead, and that you can't trade him, she'll kill us?"

The expression on Liam's face caused Laurel's gut to lurch up into her throat. All of a sudden, he looked too grown-up. For such a young kid, he'd already been through so much in his life. And now he had to weather this too.

She breathed in slowly and nodded. If he was going to speak to her like a grownup, then she'd try to treat him like one in return. "Yes. She will."

Liam nodded slowly. "How? How do we leave when they're watching us?"

"We have a plan. When it reaches sunset, the light will be in Britt's face, making it harder for them to see. The underside of this structure will be in shadow again. Plus, it's snowing right now. Bear and Jim will create a distraction. You, me, and Trent will escape down the steps and run into the forest."

Sitting up a little straighter, Liam swallowed hard. "Then what'll happen to Bear and Jim?"

"Well," Laurel squeezed his hand, "they're going to climb from the roof to the bluffs. They'll wait until Britt comes up to look for us, then fire the flare gun and set it on fire."

"Set it on fire...." Liam whispered the words. He was looking toward the back of the cabin where Arlo lay under the blanket.

Dipping to meet his eyes, Laurel said, "I know what this means. I know it means leaving your dad behind, and I'm so sorry, Liam. I promise when we get back to South Minneha, we'll have a memorial for him." Again, she squeezed his hand. "I promise."

But this time, Liam simply pulled his knees closer and turned his head away from her. "Let me know when we're going."

Finally the sun began to dip below the horizon. Beyond the forest, Laurel could picture the buildings of South Minneha. The skyline she'd seen so many times from her mother's room at the hospital or from the top floor of the parking lot. The skyline she'd grown to love when she'd moved here.

"It's time." Bear and Jim were standing by the railing, weapons ready. Bear had the flare in his pocket.

With Trent and Liam on either side of her, Laurel had strapped Jess to her chest and was carrying Arlo's pack. They'd kept his things in it and added some of Jim's so that they had enough to keep them going until they reached South Minneha. Bear and Jim had lightened their own packs, but had enough equipment and supplies to keep them alive on the bluffs until Laurel returned, If that was what needed to happen.

Quickly, as if they were each trying not to become too emotional, Trent and Bear embraced one another. As they hugged, Bear patted Trent on the back and Trent returned the gesture.

Laurel smiled softly at them. Sometimes, they were like father and son. Sometimes, like military buddies. It was nice to see Bear forming relationships again. Perhaps because Trent didn't know him *before*, it was easier.

When Bear let Trent go, he turned to Laurel but didn't put his arms around her. "I'll see you soon, Rivera," he said, locking his steely eyes onto hers.

"Soon, Peterson." Laurel nodded at him in return.

Standing beside Bear, Jim interrupted with an exaggerated shrug of the shoulders. "Well, seeing as no one wants to hug me goodbye, I guess this is it?" He glanced toward the trees where they knew Britt and her people were hiding. "Everyone take your positions?"

Laurel nodded in agreement, put her arms around the boys, and herded them toward the steps. They'd just reached the top and were crouched out of sight, ready to descend, when Bear raised his hand.

"I see someone," he hissed.

Making the boys stay low, Laurel peered around the side of the railings. Sure enough, there was Britt. Lifting her arms in the air, she approached the cabin steps. A man and a woman were walking alongside her.

Bear remained upright, gun in his hand but hidden behind the railing. Jim looked at him, then copied his stance.

"A little birdy told me you've been telling porkies…" With the snow still swirling, Britt's voice barely reached them on the wind. Laurel looked at Bear and could tell he hadn't heard what she said. To her surprise, Jim seemed to have noticed too and leaned in to repeat Britt's words.

"A bird told *me* that Arlo Staaf isn't up there with you. Not a sign of him. So we think our friend Arlo is either very badly injured or already dead!" Britt was grinning. Laurel cast a glance at Liam. Trent had put his arm around the younger boy, but Liam looked as if he was somewhere else. Trying not to see or hear anything that was happening around him.

"In which case…" Britt continued. "I think we need to come to a new arrangement."

As Jim repeated Britt's message, Bear twitched his fingers at Laurel. He didn't turn his head, didn't look at her, just motioned for her to be ready.

Any minute now, it would be time.

Ducking back behind the railing, she nodded at the boys. "On my cue. Me first. Then Liam. Then Trent. Okay?"

Trent nodded back. Liam closed his eyes.

Then it started. Before Britt could say anything else, Bear fired a shot. Jim followed suit.

Immediately, Britt yelled, "Take them down!" and bullets began to tear through the snow, hitting the struts, the railings, the walls.

"Now. Go." Laurel crouched down as she descended the stairs. Her gun was in her belt, where she could reach it if she needed to. But with Jess on her front and Arlo's pack on her back, she was struggling to move quickly, especially with her ankle.

Purposefully not looking at what was happening, trusting that Bear had her back, she kept moving.

Finally, they were at the bottom of the steps. Laurel landed with a soft thud in the snow. She helped Liam down, then Trent. Then they ran.

Bear had been right about the shadows. There was no one here. Pausing behind a tree, she checked. It was clear. Over on the other side of the platform, Bear and Jim were keeping to their side of the plan. Britt and her two soldiers were returning fire, getting closer and closer, but they hadn't seen Laurel and the boys.

Running for the tree line, they paused. "You okay?" she asked, looking from one to the other. "Both of you?"

Trent nodded but said, "Liam's tired."

"I know." Laurel rubbed Liam's back. "I know you are, buddy. But we're on the home stretch now. Come on."

Leaving the sound of gunfire behind them, Laurel led the boys into the forest.

30

BEAR

"You have the rope, right?" Jim yelled as he fired another shot, moving toward the side of the platform and aiming at Britt's feet.

"I have the rope." Bear took aim at a nearby tree. Britt was hiding behind it and he hadn't been able to get a clear shot. Changing position, he looked over toward the trees on the other side of the lake. He hadn't seen Laurel reach the ground, but he had to believe she'd done it. "They must be in the trees now. Nearly time to move."

Jim nodded.

"Give them a few minutes to get away, then stop shooting. I'll stop after you. Then we retreat to the back. Up onto the roof and over to the bluffs. Got it?" Bear looked at him as if he couldn't be sure Jim had understood what was supposed to happen.

"Yeah," Jim said. "I got it." He fired at the woman who'd ducked out from behind a large rock, but missed. "Then we fire the flare, set this thing on fire, tie our rope to a tree and abseil to safety."

"Right." Bear nodded. "Exactly." He looked down. He only counted three down there. Were there more hiding somewhere or was this it? Three fully armed, with more ammo than sense, was still too many. "Okay, stop." He gestured for Jim to stop shooting.

Jim looked at his gun, flexed his finger on the trigger, then grimaced. "I'm out." He shoved the gun into his back pocket.

Taking his place. Bear took a few shots and stopped. "I've only got two bullets left. I thought we'd last longer." Bear looked down. The snow had slowed and he could see Britt waving her arm, signaling for the others to peel off and head for the stairs. "Well, I guess this is what we wanted. Here she comes."

Turning around, they hurried back inside. The place smelled of kerosene. They'd laced the floors and walls with it. Bear just hoped Britt didn't realize when she got up here.

"Okay. This is it."

At the rear of the tower, Bear hopped onto the railing, then heaved himself up onto the roof. Jim copied him. Although his upper body strength was a little lacking, he made up for it with his legs.

"Here we go." Bear dipped low, so that no one on the ground saw them, and started to head for the bluffs. From here, they'd be able to jump, grab hold of the protruding section of cliff, and clamber up to the top. No problem.

They were almost there when a shot sounded out. Close. Closer than he'd expected. Bear stopped, dropped to his stomach, and looked up.

Another shot.

His hearing aid began to whistle. He pressed his finger to it but the whistling got worse. He couldn't tell where the shots were coming from. Where were they coming from? "Jim? Where are they?" Bear rolled onto his side, searching for Jim.

Next to him, Jim too was on his stomach. But when he looked up, the expression on his face told Bear that he was not okay.

"I think they're on the bluffs." Jim was pressing his palm to his stomach. Blood was blooming beneath it, soaking his orange jacket.

Bear clenched his jaw. Then he looked up. Above them, one of Britt's soldiers was clinging precariously onto the side of the bluffs. Moving toward them, he'd stopped shooting and was clinging to the rocks. Any minute now, he'd be close enough to jump onto the roof.

"How did he get up there?" Bear jumped to his feet. The guy on the bluffs reached for his gun. Bear reached into his pocket and took out the hunting knife he'd found in the cabin. He weighed it in his hand. The guy was struggling to keep his grip and aim at the same time. Bear raised the knife, aimed, and hurled it through the air. It struck the guy's upper arm. He cried out, grabbed for it, lost his grip and plummeted to the ground.

Reaching down, Bear grabbed the straps of Jim's backpack and started to drag him across the roof.

"Leave me." Jim looked up at Bear and shook his head. "You can't get me up there. Leave me."

Bear crouched down, letting go of Jim's pack. "I should have seen it coming. I didn't think they'd get up there. No way I thought they'd get up there."

Jim shuffled sideways and pulled his backpack from his shoulders, wincing, moving slowly. He leaned onto it and looked down at his bloodied jacket. "Probably what I deserve," he said. "I left you for dead. You and the boy. Now it's your turn."

Bear looked at Jim for a moment, then gritted his teeth. "No way you're getting out of it that easy." Bear ducked down and, before Jim could protest, hauled him up onto his shoulder. "*I don't leave soldiers in the field.*"

When they reached the edge of the roof, Jim started to groan. "Bear. Put me down, man. Put me down. I can't."

Bear stopped and lowered him to the roof. The snow was slowing. Good for helping the whole structure go up. Not good for hiding their climb from the roof to the bluffs. Although now they were here, Bear had no idea how he was going to get both him and Jim over there. Without his pack, he might stand more of a chance, but even then, he'd seen how slippery the limestone was.

He'd been telling the truth when he said he'd never leave a soldier in the field. But did he value Jim's life above his own? If they both fell to their deaths, who would that help?

As if he'd been reading Bear's mind, with a raspy breath, Jim shuddered and said, "You've got to go, Bear. Even if you could get me up there and down to the ground, get me to the doc… it'd be no good." He breathed in a long shaky breath. Bear crouched next to him. Shouts from down below told him Britt was coming up the stairs to the platform.

"Besides…" Jim had been holding his stomach, but now his hand dropped to his side. "I'm ready."

"What do you mean, ready?"

Jim closed his eyes tightly as pain surged through his body. "I had a family once, too. I'm ready to see them again."

Jim tapped his coat.

Taking the cue, Bear unzipped it and reached for the inside pocket. He pulled out a crumpled photograph of a woman and a child. A girl, about the same age as Liam. He pressed it into Jim's hand.

"My daughter..." Jim swallowed hard, then coughed. "Guess my wife didn't...." He paused to cough again. When he took his hand away, there was blood at the corner of his mouth. "Didn't think there was anything left to live for."

Bear lowered his head. "I'm sorry."

From below, Britt's voice carried up to them although Bear couldn't hear what she was saying.

"They're close." Jim motioned to Bear's gun. Bear looked at it, then handed it over. "I'll hold them off as long as I can."

"You've only got two—"

"I know." Jim wheezed and groaned as he tried to sit up.

Bear hesitated for a moment, then nodded. "I hope you see your family again."

"Oh, I will." Jim smiled, a genuinely happy smile. "I will."

By the time Bear got to the edge of the roof, Britt's cries were closer. He stood looking at the limestone. There was a craggy section just above head height that should give him the leverage to get up. If he could maintain a good grip.

Without looking back at Jim, and without letting himself think about it too much, Bear fixed Laurel's face in his mind and leaped. His fingers scratched the limestone, grappled to get a hold. His feet were pressed up against it, toes bent, trying to find purchase.

His leg slipped, but he steadied himself. With a strength he wasn't sure he even had anymore, he climbed. It was just a few feet to the top but it felt like a thousand.

He was hauling himself over the rim when a gunshot fired. Then another. Then a third. A bullet whizzed past him, hitting the limestone. Jim yelled.

At the top, Bear turned, flattened himself onto his stomach and looked over. Jim was lying still. Britt was alone. She'd been hit. She was limping. Jim got her. He got her.

Bear looked sideways. He couldn't see the weakened strut. On his belly, he crawled until it came into view. Then he took out the flare gun and without even blinking fired it.

An arc of bright light shot through the air. Bear had a good aim. A great aim. The flare hit the strut. A few seconds later, the flames started small, but quickly spread thanks to the kerosene. Bear looked back at the roof. Britt was still trying to reach the edge. She wavered but kept going, dragging her injured leg with her.

Jim wasn't moving. She walked right past him and stopped at the edge of the roof. She spotted Bear and called up to him, but he couldn't hear her. She lifted her gun and fired. She was a poor shot, hitting a spot on the bluffs several feet below him. She went to shoot again, then cried out and tossed her gun down. Looked like she was out of bullets too.

Turning away from him, she ran back to the place where she'd climbed up, then stopped.

Flames had migrated from the strut to the steps and were now snaking up toward the platform. Laurel had laid a slick kerosene trail all the way inside. The fire followed it. The structure was creaking.

Britt looked back at Bear as if she had no idea which direction to go.

Down below, a woman Bear recognized was on the platform. She was yelling up to Britt. She turned and ran, but the steps were on fire. There was nowhere for her to go. She stopped at the railing, looked like she was contemplating jumping over, then clambered up and hauled herself onto the roof.

Running toward Britt, she waved her arms in the air.

Britt gestured for her gun, took it and turned back to Bear. Stalking forward, she fired another shot, then another, then another. All of them missed.

When she ran out of bullets for a second time, Britt screamed and tossed that gun down too. The woman tugged her arm, but Britt pulled free and headed for the edge. The woman hesitated, then turned and clambered back down, taking her chances closer to the ground.

The entire cabin and platform were creaking now. The weakened strut was ready to go. Britt was staring up at the cliff. She looked like she was getting ready to jump. Bear readied himself to run; he could make it down the other side before she reached him. But before Britt could move, there was an almighty crack, the cabin shifted, then the roof crumpled beneath her.

One second, Britt was there. Then she was gone. And so was Jim.

31

LAUREL

Deeper in the forest, the canopy blocked most of the light from outside, leaving Laurel, Liam, and Trent moving slowly through the trees. At first Liam refused help, moving like a zombie; trudging, one foot after the other, behind Laurel. But when he tripped and stumbled, he finally let Trent put his arm around him. As Laurel moved to support Liam's other side, Trent shook his head at her. "You should keep watch." He nodded at her gun. "I got him."

With Jess on his front and Liam at his side, Trent was clearly using all his strength to keep walking, but he didn't show it. He was stoic, like Bear. Laurel wondered if he'd always been that way or if Bear had instilled it in him during their time together.

"Hey, Trent?" Laurel asked, adjusting her pack and peering into the shadows up ahead. "Can I ask you something?"

Trent nodded. "Sure."

"Why'd you call Bear 'PB'? What's it stand for? Peanut butter? Because I distinctly recall him *hating* peanut butter."

Laughing a little, Trent helped Liam over some tangled tree roots. "First off, he hates peanut butter? I did *not* know that. Second, PB—Papa Bear?"

"Ohhh," Laurel chuckled.

"Which, I guess, makes you Mama Bear." Trent smiled at her.

Laurel straightened her shoulders and took her glasses off, shoving them into her pocket. With her hat, it was hard to balance them on top of her head. "I'm not sure about that."

"You think you'll get back together?" Trent tilted his head.

"Are you always this direct?" Laurel had slowed down and widened her eyes at him.

"PB would say so, yeah," he replied, a flicker of sadness crossing his face.

Laurel stopped and put her hand on his arm. "He'll be okay. Once we're at the edge of the woods, we'll stop and set up camp for the night. We'll wait for him. I've made sure to leave a trail for him to follow."

"I thought he told us to keep walking? Back to the hospital?" Liam's voice was small and a little hoarse.

"He did." Laurel nodded. "But if everything goes to plan, he should make it here before nightfall. If it doesn't, well, then we'll leave." In truth, she was still contemplating leaving Trent and Liam with the campfire, once they got set up, and going back to make sure Bear didn't need her help. But as she looked at the boys, she knew she couldn't leave them.

Nodding at her, Liam started to cough. It had been a while since he'd shown signs of his breathing problems, but stress could exacerbate all kinds of illnesses. Laurel just prayed that the trauma of losing his father wouldn't undo all the progress Liam made at Lone Oak.

"How about we stop and rest for a moment?" She looked behind them. They were far enough away that they could no longer hear gunshots. But that might be because they'd reached the part of Bear's plan where guns weren't required.

Liam nodded, stepping away from Trent and sliding down the trunk of a nearby tree to sit on the ground. Shuddering, he wrapped his arms around himself. Laurel passed him a bottle of water.

On Trent's front, Jess was starting to wriggle. "I don't want to put her down in case she runs off after Bear." Trent stroked her head and bent to whisper to her. "It's okay, girl. Your pop will be along soon. I promise."

Swallowing down the emotion that always surged to the surface when she thought of Jess and Bear being separated, Laurel lifted her pack from her shoulders and pulled out a pair of Arlo's sweatpants, turning her back so Liam didn't see. Holding up a finger to indicate to Trent "one minute," she pulled the tie string from the pants, then pulled out the one from the bottom of her coat too. After tying them together, she waved them at Trent. "Use these as a leash." She handed them to him.

Trent tied the cord loosely around Jess's neck, just tight enough so he could stop her from running off, then unclipped the makeshift carrier and let her jump to the ground.

Instantly she peed on the pine-needle covered ground nearby, then started frantically sniffing, as if she might be able to figure out where Bear was.

Laurel crouched down next to Liam and put her arm around him. He coughed again, his breath making small white clouds in the cold air. Rubbing his shoulder, she said, "We better not rest here for long. We need to get to the edge of the woods so we can start a fire. Get you warmed up."

"It'll be a squeeze in the tent." Trent looked at the small popup tent strapped to Laurel's backpack.

Before she could answer, a voice she didn't recognize floated toward them. "Oh, I wouldn't worry about that. No one's going to be sleeping tonight."

Laurel jumped to her feet and stared into the undergrowth. In the shadows, a silhouette moved. Trent was watching it too but before he could reach for his gun, the silhouette jumped from the shadows and grabbed hold of him.

It was a man. A young man, perhaps mid-twenties, no older. He had a bloodied bandage wrapped around his leg and limped as he struggled to keep hold of Trent. With one arm around Trent's torso, pinning his arms to his chest, the man pulled out a gun and pointed it at Trent's face. Jess started to bark. Trent dropped her leash and she scampered backward to stand beside Laurel. The man stared at her, wide-eyed, as if he didn't know who to point his gun at—Jess or Trent.

"Make her shut up," he shouted.

"She's scared." Laurel raised her hands slowly, palms out. On the ground next to her, Liam had tucked his knees up under his chin and was rocking a little, back and forth.

Laurel tried to step forward but Jess was still barking and the man holding Trent waved his gun in the air. "Back off, and shut that dog up, or I'll shoot him. I swear!"

"Okay, okay," she said slowly, "you're calling the shots. I'm going to crouch down and get hold of her leash, okay?" Laurel asked, maintaining eye contact.

The man nodded.

Bending down, Laurel patted her leg. "Jess, here girl. It's okay."

Jess looked at her, then trotted over. She was trembling. Taking hold of her leash, Laurel backed up slowly. "I'm going to give her to Liam. He'll keep her quiet. Is that all right?"

The man bit his lower lip and said, "Do it."

Without turning her back to him, Laurel did as she'd said she would. To Liam, she said, "Sweetheart, will you look after Jess?" As he nodded at her, she lowered her voice and whispered. "It's going to be okay, just stay calm and still."

"All right."

She stood up. Her gun was in her waistband, hidden by her coat. But going for it was far too risky while Trent had a gun to his head. "So, you're in charge here. Tell me what you want me to do."

"Damn right, I am. Move away from your stuff." The man gestured to Laurel's backpack. She stepped forward but he shook his head. "Not this way. That way." He indicated for her to move sideways. Good, away from Liam.

The way he was handling his gun told her he was *not* an experienced fighter. Plus, he looked terrified. If she played this right, she might just be able to get them all out of it unharmed.

"You're with Britt? Right?" she asked gently. "What's your name?"

"Ryan," he said defiantly. "Remember that. 'Cos that's the name of the guy who's going to kill you. *Ryan.*"

Pinned to Ryan's chest, Trent's eyes widened. Laurel caught his gaze and gave him the smallest shake of her head, hoping he knew she was telling him to stay calm. That everything would be okay.

"Kill us? Is that what Britt asked you to do?"

"No." Ryan tilted his chin up as if he was trying to look more confident. "She doesn't know I'm here. But I saw you sneaking into the woods, and if I go back and tell her I got two of Rambo's men *plus* Arlo Staaf's kid, well, she might just finally realize I'm good for something."

Ah, so that was it. He was trying to prove himself to Britt.

"Ryan, you seem like a good kid."

"Don't patronize me!"

"I'm not." Laurel remained calm, even though she could see Trent beginning to sweat with fear. His fingers twitched at his side, but his own gun was too far out of reach. "You really do seem like a good kid. I was a medic in Iraq. I've seen young soldiers, younger than you. A lot of them have a look in their eyes, like their soul has already been damaged. But you?" She examined his face. "You're not there yet. There's still hope for you."

Frowning at her as if he couldn't quite believe what he was hearing, Ryan opened his mouth and closed it again.

"Trent's only… how old are you, Trent?" she asked, widening her eyes to indicate he should answer.

"Fourteen," he said croakily.

"And Liam is seven. Is that right, Liam?"

Liam nodded.

"Now, I'm sure you could shoot me if you wanted to. In fact, I don't doubt it. But do you really want to kill a couple of kids?" She looked over at Liam, then back at Ryan.

His eyes flickered to the boy sitting on the ground. "His dad. Was I right? Is he dead?"

Liam let out a small whimper.

"Yes," Laurel said solemnly. "Arlo is dead."

Ryan sucked in a deep breath.

"I have a proposition for you." Laurel still had her hands raised.

Ryan blinked at her.

"I'll give myself up. I'll even let you shoot me. But you have to let the boys go."

Scoffing, Ryan rolled his eyes. "Yeah. Right. You've tried bargaining before and you *lied*. Remember? You told us you'd give us Staaf. And the whole time, he was dead."

"Not the whole time." Laurel pressed her lips together. "One of your men killed him."

Ryan inhaled through his nostrils. He shuffled, his leg clearly hurting. "What's in it for me?"

"You show Britt you're capable of making calculated, clever decisions."

He frowned.

"This way, I hand over my weapon. You let them go. They run off into the woods. Then you can shoot me or take me prisoner. Whatever you decide. Any other way we play this, well, it'll get messy."

Ryan was blinking quickly, as if his thoughts were racing. "You hand over your weapon. I let them go. Then you come with me?"

Laurel nodded.

After a long pause, in which no one moved, Ryan finally said, "All right. But you take the leash off the dog, and after you throw me your weapon, you tie your hands together. Right? I don't want you thinking you can disarm me."

"Clever." Laurel made an *I'm impressed* face. "So, if I tie up my hands, we have a deal?"

Ryan chewed his lip. "Yeah. Okay. We have a deal."

"In that case, I'm going to reach very slowly into the back of my pants and I'm going to take out my gun. I'll lower it to the ground and kick it over to you. All right?"

Ryan pulled Trent farther in front of him. "Do it." But when the gun was on the ground, as she was about to kick it, Ryan said, "Not to me. Over there. Into the bushes."

"All right." Laurel did as he'd said.

"Now, you, Liam. Untie the dog, then get over here and tie up her hands."

Liam looked wide-eyed from Laurel to Ryan and back again.

"It's okay, honey." She held out her wrists. "Go ahead."

Shaking, Liam unlooped the leash from Jess's neck. Instantly, she started to bark again. Binding Laurel's hands together, Liam's fingers could barely tie the knots.

"Tight," Ryan yelled. "Tighter than that."

"It's okay," Laurel whispered. "It's going to be okay."

When he was done, Liam sat back down and pulled Jess into his lap. Her bark quieted to a deep, throaty growl.

"Now it's your turn." Laurel looked at Trent. "I trusted you to keep your side of the deal, Ryan. It's time to let the boys go."

Ryan looked at Trent. He was stock still. "When I let you go, you run straight for the bushes and you don't look back. Right?"

Trent nodded. "Right. I promise. Straight for the bushes."

"You too, kid." Ryan pointed at Liam. "Get up. Get ready to run."

Slowly, Liam rose to his feet, lifting Jess in his arms. She was still growling, looking from Trent to Ryan as if she couldn't understand why no one was doing anything to get Trent out of harm's way.

Laurel met Trent's eyes. Very purposefully, she moved her gaze from his face to his side, where she knew his gun was tucked into his belt. In return, he offered her the smallest nod.

"Go!" Ryan released his grip on Trent and shoved him forward. Trent made a show of stumbling a little but as he righted himself, Laurel saw his hand go for his belt. Swiftly, he pulled out his weapon and raised it.

"What the—?" Ryan yelled and pointed the gun back at Trent. Then he fired. He missed, the bullet ricocheting off a nearby tree.

Liam cried out. Jess had leaped from his arms and, in a flurry of fur and barking, charged at Ryan.

Ryan fired again, this time, pointing at Jess. A high-pitched yelp bounced off the trees.

"Jess!" Trent lifted his gun and, with fury in his eyes, pointed it at Ryan.

"Put the gun down or I'll shoot!" Ryan's gun wavered as he tried to hold it steady.

"You shot her!" Trent was almost growling.

"Trent, give me the gun." Laurel was at Trent's elbow and started tugging at the leash with her teeth. If Trent shot another person, he'd never be the same again. She'd seen it before, too many times. With her hands finally free, she put her fingers on Trent's arm. "Trent, give me the gun now."

On the ground, Jess whimpered. Finally, Trent looked at Laurel and pressed the gun into her hands.

"Get out of here. Now."

In front of her, Ryan was shaking. He was moving from pointing his gun at her, to Trent, to Liam. But he seemed unable to fire it.

"Take Liam, I'll bring Jess. Go!" Laurel gave Trent a shove.

He took one last look at Jess and bolted, taking Liam with him.

Silence settled. Jess wasn't making any noise at all now. "All right, Ryan. Now it's just you and me. We're both armed, but I'm a quicker shot than you so I'm giving you a chance to—"

Before she could finish her sentence, Ryan's trigger finger twitched.

But Laurel's was faster.

He wavered for a moment, then fell to the ground.

32

BEAR

For a long time, Bear was unable to move. As the cabin turned into a tinderbox, and flames licked the sky, it became impossible to tell ash from snow. After the cabin caved in on itself, the strut was the next to go. The entire structure tipped sideways, crashed into the bluffs, then crumbled so it was nothing more than a heap of burning wood. A giant bonfire, lighting up the darkening sky.

He knew he should move before darkness set in. If he was fast, he might even be able to catch up with Laurel; having Liam in tow, and with her still-sore ankle, she would be moving at half his pace.

But by the time he tore himself away from the edge of the cliff, the sun had dipped below the horizon, and it was far too dark to attempt the climb down.

Pulling his sleeping bag free of his pack, he huddled beneath the shelter of the trees. It was still snowing, but not hard. Not enough to make the next day's journey more treacherous, but enough to make his night cold and uncomfortable.

With the cabin still smoldering down below, it felt strange to light a fire, but he needed hot food, a hot drink, and something to keep him warm as the temperature plummeted.

Slowly, he gathered kindling and stones, shredded some bark to make a tinder nest, then took out the almost empty bottle of kerosene from his pack; he'd deliberately left enough in the bottom of it to make absolutely sure he'd be able to create and keep a fire going if he ended up stuck on the bluffs waiting for help.

It wasn't long before the fire took, so he crawled into his sleeping bag and sat, sheltered by the trees, watching his small kettle of hot water boil. Even with nothing to add to it, drinking something warm was soothing. He wrapped his hands around the mug and, as he waited for his beans and rice to cook, he thought of Thunder Bay.

He'd camped out by the lake like this many times. Just his sleeping bag, a campfire, and Jess for company. It was the reason he'd left home; because he'd wanted a simpler life. A life where he could be alone and where nothing was expected of him except the daily tasks required to survive.

How ironic that now all of those things had been thrust on him, he could think of nothing better than being surrounded by his family again.

As the word *family* danced through his mind, he saw not only Mae, and Laurel, and Jess, but Trent too. And suddenly, he could picture it; all of them, back in Thunder Bay. Forging a new life together.

Bear wrapped his arms around himself and looked up at the small slice of sky that was visible through the branches. When he told Laurel they'd find Mae, he truly hadn't expected to live long enough to make that happen. Now, though, a fire was stirring in his belly. A fire he hadn't felt since he first decided to leave Ontario and find Laurel.

He'd promised her they'd look for Mae, so that was what they were going to do.

After finishing his supper and making sure the fire was stoked, he drifted into a half-sleep. Just under the surface of consciousness, he dreamed he could still hear the crackling of the burning cabin. But by the time he woke the next day, it was nothing but a pile of smoking charcoal. Gone. Taking Britt, Jim, and Arlo with it.

As the sun rose in the sky, Bear packed his things and headed for the lake side of the bluffs. Looking down, he found he was higher up than he'd anticipated. The cabin side must have been lower. From here, the height made him a little dizzy.

Heights had never been his strong suit. The few helicopter jumps he'd done in his time with the Army had been a true test of his mental strength. Now, looking down and trying to plot the best route, nausea gripped his stomach.

He contemplated going back to where he'd climbed up from the cabin, but he didn't fancy trying to land amid the still smoldering ruins.

Turning to the tree line behind him, he took a deep breath.

"Let's hope your knot-tying skills are as good as you think they are," he muttered as he took the rope from his pack. Looking at it, he was pretty sure it wouldn't reach all the way to the ground. But he'd identified a section of rock that looked easy enough to climb down. All he needed to do was get to it.

Looping the rope around a sturdy medium-sized tree trunk, he tied a bowline knot to secure the rope, then wrapped it around his waist and tied a figure eight knot. Walking backward, pack on his back, he stepped to the edge of the cliff and breathed out. Hard.

Testing the rope, his stomach lurched as it pulled tight. It would hold, but that meant it was time to go over.

Without looking down, concentrating solely on where his feet were going, Bear leaned back and began to walk himself down the bluffs.

He was about halfway when he began to gain some speed. But before he could get much farther, the rope jarred. His foot slipped and he crashed forward, slamming his knee into a protruding piece of limestone.

Cursing at the cliff, he struggled and ended up swaying on the end of the rope, back and forth. He'd reached the end of it. It wouldn't go any farther.

Hesitantly, a knot of hot nausea lodged in his stomach, he looked down. He was dangling about fifty feet from the ground. If he fell, he'd be toast.

Looking back up, he leaned his weight into the rope and swung close enough to grab the section his knee bashed into. His fingers struggled to grab hold but when they finally did, he stopped moving.

Checking either side of him, then below, it seemed like there was no better or easier place to descend. So, without allowing himself to stop and think about it, like jumping out of a helicopter, he pressed his feet into the limestone, gripped as hard as he could with his left hand and swiftly freed himself from the rope with his right.

In the split second between the rope falling and his right hand joining his left, his stomach dropped out from under him and a cold sweat covered his brow.

He was panting, hanging on, unable to move.

For several minutes, he stayed like that, trying to calm his breathing. *Okay, PB, time to roll.*

He took one more breath, then continued his climb down.

Moving slowly, checking each foothold and handhold before he changed position, he scaled the remainder of the bluffs. Ignoring the pain that shot from his knee down to his ankle, and the seasick sensation that took hold whenever he focused on the ground below, he kept moving.

Six feet from the ground, he was tempted to jump, but his knee stopped him; he couldn't afford to damage it further or he'd never catch up with Laurel.

Four feet from the ground, he finally let go and dropped.

Aware that if he gave himself a moment to catch his breath, the pain in his knee would take hold, Bear headed straight for the forest. Beneath the canopy, it was dark and quiet. Moving toward the area he imagined Laurel would have entered, he scoured the ground for tracks.

Finally, he found some. It felt strange to be traveling alone, without Jess or Trent to talk to, but he pressed forward. He'd been traveling a little over an hour when he came to a small clearing. He stopped and was bracing his hands on his thighs, breathing through the pain in his rapidly swelling knee, when he saw something in front of him.

A foot.

He looked up. There on the ground was a body. A young man, blood pooled beneath him, soaking into the forest floor. Eyes open, staring unblinking at the leaves above him.

Bear crouched down, wincing as pain shot from his knee to his foot. He felt for a pulse, even though he knew there wouldn't be one. The boy was one of Britt's men. Bear recognized him from the frozen lake. Ryan, she'd called him.

Unfortunately for Ryan, he'd taken a bullet to the stomach.

Standing back up, Bear scanned the area. A few feet in front of Ryan was another bloodstain, smaller. But it didn't lead anywhere. Whoever this stain was from had been carried from the clearing.

His throat constricting as he thought of the boys, of Laurel trying to carry them, or the two of them trying to carry her, Bear searched the undergrowth until he re-found the trail. Before following it, he snapped a branch off a nearby tree. Using it as a cane, he plowed on.

He was almost at the edge of the woods when he smelled smoke. Campfire smoke.

Up ahead, orange flickered through the trees. Bear slowed his pace and approached as slowly as he could. Each step made him wince and lean harder on his makeshift cane.

Straining his ears, he thought he could make out voices, but couldn't hear well enough to catch what they were saying. Finally, he was close enough to see. Pressing against a tree, he peered around it and his heart leaped into his throat.

"Laurel!" He called her name before he could stop himself, and stepped into view as she stood up and whirled round, holding her weapon in front of her.

It took only seconds for her to lower it, a smile breaking out on her face. "Bear...." She whispered his name, so he couldn't hear it, but he knew its shape on her lips. Running over, she wrapped her arms around him and squeezed. Close to his ear, she said, "I knew you'd make it. I knew you would."

For a long moment, he held her, breathing in the faint smell of her hair mixed with smoke and pine trees. When he stepped back, still leaning on his cane with one hand, he left the other on her waist. "You're okay?" he asked, meeting her gaze. "You're all okay? I saw a kid back there, one of Britt's guys. There was blood…."

Interrupting, rushing over to thump Bear on the shoulder, Trent widened his eyes and said, "The dude had a gun to my head but Laurel was *awesome*. She tricked him. Took him out. She saved us."

Bear raised his eyebrows and took in Laurel's *it was nothing* expression. "That doesn't surprise me at all," he said.

Over by the campfire, Liam was sitting cross-legged, a pile of blankets in his lap. He looked up at Bear and rested his palms on the blankets.

"You okay, kid?" Bear asked. "You managed the journey okay?"

Liam nodded but looked at Laurel.

Something crossed between them and it made Bear's heart thud a little faster in his ribcage. Looking around, he frowned. "Where's Jess? She off chasing rabbits? You probably should have kept her on a leash. She didn't go looking for me, did she?"

No one answered.

Bear looked from Laurel to Trent. While Trent averted his eyes, Laurel breathed in deeply. "Bear…."

He inhaled sharply, his gut twisting violently. The blood on the ground. If Ryan had a gun to Trent's head, he could only imagine what Jess would have done. "Where is she, Laurel?"

Suddenly, Laurel's eyes softened and she shook her head. Putting her hand firmly on his arm, she said, "Oh, no, no. She's okay. She's fine. She has a war wound, though."

Bear turned as Liam stood up. He held his pile of blankets out to Bear, and it was in that moment he saw a white flash of fur. Taking it from Liam, Bear pulled back the blanket. Jess looked up at him and let out a small but happy whimper.

"You silly, silly dog. What have you done?" Bear sank to the ground, not even caring that his knee felt like it was going to crumple beneath him. "Silly girl." He lowered his head to Jess's, then saw the wound on her front leg.

Crouching down next to him, Laurel said, "I cleaned the wound and stitched it. The bullet hit her at a shallow angle, so it's not too bad. She'll be okay."

"Why isn't she moving?"

"I gave her some pain meds and a little valerian. Liam foraged some a while back." Laurel looked at Liam and smiled approvingly. "So she's a little spaced out, is all."

"Valerian?"

"It's totally fine for dogs. The pain meds are meant for humans, but a small amount to get her through the next few days won't hurt." Catching Bear's eyes, Laurel added firmly, "She'll be *okay*, Papa Bear."

At the use of his nickname, a smile twitched on Bear's lips. Holding out his arms, he beckoned Trent and Laurel in for a hug. When Liam didn't join them, Bear waved at him and said, "You too, kid. Looks like your Boy Scout skills really came in handy for Jess here."

Tucking into the bundle, Bear saw Liam smile a little. He breathed out slowly. They were together and they were safe. Laurel and the boys, and Jess. Just like he'd promised.

When he sat back, returning Jess to Liam so he could take her over to the fire, Bear rubbed his knee and stretched his leg out in front of him.

Patting his leg, Laurel raised her eyebrows at him. "Now it's my turn to ask questions."

"Questions?"

"What happened to your leg? What happened to Jim? And is Britt...." She trailed off, pressing her lips together.

Still rubbing his knee, Bear's jaw twitched. "Britt and the cabin are gone. The plan worked. The flare hit it and the kerosene lit the place on fire. My knee smashed into the bluffs when I abseiled down this morning."

"And Jim?" Trent was next to Laurel. He seemed more curious than concerned about their former robber's fate.

Bear shook his head. "He didn't make it."

Trent shrugged. "No great loss there."

"No," he replied. "But to give him his due, he came through at the end. He stayed and tried to fight off Britt. I owe him that, at least. I could have tried to carry him, but there was no way I'd have gotten off the roof with him on my back."

As Trent lowered his gaze, Laurel took Bear's hand in hers and squeezed. "You came back to us. That's all that matters." After a pause, she took her fingers back and said, "Right. Now, let me look at this knee."

33
DEB

ONE WEEK LATER

It was almost sunset. Deb's breath billowed in thick clouds into the early evening air. Pulling her coat closer, she rubbed her hands together. She was wearing gloves, but her fingertips were still freezing cold.

Picking up the gun that lay in her lap, she flexed her index finger on the trigger. Her finger was so numb she could barely feel it.

She'd been out here too long. She knew that. Any minute now, Henry would come looking for her. Or Hannah. Or Bulldog. Even Chris Jenkins had taken to keeping a watchful eye on her.

It was as if everyone knew—even without her telling them—that something had changed. That her body was growing weaker.

She tried her best to hide it. She still played cards, helped in the kitchen, helped the nurses. But when no one was looking—or at least when she thought no one was looking—it was like a balloon inside her deflated and she could barely pull herself up out of her chair.

Tightening the blanket that she'd laid across her thighs, she narrowed her eyes at the woods. Despite the snow, she knew the deer had been venturing out, attempting to find blades of grass to nibble. And she was determined to shoot one.

For whatever reason, that morning she'd woken with a feeling deep in the pit of her stomach that *this* was what everyone needed today. Real food. Something to take their mind off the fact that the hospital was cold and bleak without Laurel, and that Peter was getting sicker and had no meds to help him.

Something to bring back the jolly atmosphere of those first few nights in the new joint dorm that Bear had helped to create.

She'd hunted many times over the years, with Laurel's father and by herself. And since Bear left, she'd taken to visiting the place where he taught Trent how to shoot so she could hone her skills once more.

It was something to distract her from the monotony of waiting for Laurel. Thinking about Bear. Wondering if Trent ever caught up with him.

How she *wished* she'd stopped him from leaving. How she wished she'd seen in his eyes what he was planning to do and locked him in one of the offices to prevent him walking out the door.

Chewing her lower lip, wishing she had a nicer shade of lipstick than the harsh red she was wearing, which did nothing to compliment her ever-paler complexion, she once again scanned the tree line.

Half watching the trees, half listening for the sound of feet in the snow behind her, she tried to push Henry from her mind. She'd been thinking of him a lot lately. Probably too much.

He was such a kind man, possibly the best man she'd ever known. But she didn't want him to have to go through what was coming next. Because even if Laurel did return, Deb knew in the pit of her stomach that it would not be to save her. It would be to say goodbye to her.

She blinked hard and wiped a tear from her eye. Then something moved. She froze. Waited. Waited some more. Then as the large white-tailed deer stepped out of the trees, she fired.

It fell instantly.

Deb's heart was pounding in her rib cage. She could hear it, thud, thud, thud in her ears.

"Nice shot." Henry's voice made her jump almost clean out of her seat. Spinning around, she slapped him gently on the arm.

"Don't sneak up on a woman holding a gun, Henry. I could have done you some real damage."

Henry looked down at her and smiled. Then he gestured for her to move over and sat down beside her. "How long have you been out here?" He put an arm around her shoulders and rubbed the top of her arm. "You're a block of ice."

"A block of ice who just caught us some dinner." Deb raised her eyebrows at him. She wanted to cough. The itch was building in her throat. Her chest was tightening, but she swallowed it down and shakily stood up. "Will you help me get it back up to the hospital?"

Henry stood up too and folded his arms in front of his chest. "You think the two of us can haul more than a hundred pounds of deer all the way up the lawn?" He turned and looked back toward the rear of the hospital. In summer, this was a large, green, beautifully manicured lawn, strewn with staff and patients. Now, it was simply an expanse of snow that took forever to wade through.

"I tell you what. Come back inside with me. Get warmed up, and I'll ask Bulldog to come help me with the deer."

Deb inhaled slowly, still fighting the cough. She had straightened her shoulders and was tipping up her chin rather defiantly. A few years ago, she'd have strode down there and helped him herself.

"All right." She softened a little when Henry smiled at her. Slipping her arm through his, she nodded. "All right. I suppose it is rather chilly out here."

It took them longer than usual to get back across the lawn. Henry had noticed. He must have noticed that she was slowing down. But he didn't say anything, simply kept pace with her and steadied her with his arm.

When they were finally inside, he put his hand on the small of her back and guided her down the hallway. Before they reached the canteen—which was still serving as the hospital's living quarters—Janet appeared up ahead and Henry waved to her.

"Janet, would you mind getting Deb a hot drink? She's just caught us our supper."

Janet raised her eyebrows and grinned. "Have you now?"

Deb smiled back, a little thinly; Janet had a habit of speaking to Deb as if she was ancient and hard of hearing. She meant well, but she was still irritating.

"Well, then. A hot drink's definitely in order. What did you catch? A rabbit?"

"A deer." Deb pulled off her gloves, shoved them into her pocket, and untucked her arm from Henry's. Turning to him, she said, "I'll tell Mrs. Johnson to expect it."

Henry nodded, and in a gesture that was becoming ever more natural between the two of them, he squeezed her hand. "Will do."

As Henry headed for the foyer to find Bulldog, Deb set off in the direction of the canteen. Janet stepped into line with her. But before they reached the doors at the end of the hallway, Deb found she could hold back her cough no longer. At first, she cleared her throat. It helped a little, but then the tightness in her chest threatened to overwhelm her. She coughed a little. Then again. Then before she knew it, she was bent double and could hardly catch her breath.

"Deb. Deb?" Janet put her hands on Deb's shoulders. She was moving her. Where was she moving her to? "Sit down." She ushered her into a chair.

Deb waved her hands. "I'm fine." It was a wheelchair. She didn't need a wheelchair.

"You're not fine. You've been out in the cold too long." Janet crouched down and inhaled slowly through her nose, gesturing for Deb to copy her.

For a few moments, they stayed like that, breathing in and out, in and out. Finally, her breathing returned to something close to normal.

"Deb...." Janet put her hands on Deb's knees and looked up at her. "You're not a well lady. You need to look after yourself."

Deb fought the urge to scoff, in case it set off another coughing fit. Had she always been this indignant? Or had that happened since Laurel left?

"Laurel wants you in one piece when she gets back. She'll kill me if I let anything happen to you." Janet smiled and patted Deb's knee.

Looking at Janet's face, Deb softened a little. Gently, she tapped her fingers on the back of Janet's hand. "Point taken. I'll be more careful in future."

Janet nodded. "And if there's anything you need to tell me… anything about your health…."

"There's nothing." Deb looked away because her eyes were becoming moist. "But I'll tell you this… I really do need that hot drink now, I think."

Smiling thinly, Janet gave a small sigh but stood up. For a moment, Deb thought about insisting she could walk back to the canteen. But when Janet started pushing the chair, she found she didn't have the energy to protest.

An hour later, after watching Henry and Bulldog wheel her deer into the canteen on a gurney, and hearing the entire room erupt with whoops and cheers, Deb quietly removed herself and headed for the stairs.

At the bottom, she looked up and grimaced. She shouldn't do this now. She knew she shouldn't. Not after the coughing. But it had become a ritual, and it was one she wasn't willing to give up on.

She'd made it just a few steps when she began to cough again.

This time, it wasn't Janet who steadied her. It was Henry. Catching hold of her elbow, he tilted his head and smiled at her. "Come on, Duchess. Don't keep trying to hide from me."

Deb steadied herself on the banister. "Oh, Henry." She lowered her eyes. "I'm so sorry…."

Tucking his finger under her chin, Henry gently raised her face up to his. "You have nothing to be sorry for," he said, stroking a strand of hair from her cheek. Hair that used to be dyed dark but was now displaying shiny silver roots that she was desperate to cover up. "But please don't try to do this on your own."

"It's only stairs. I've done it a million times."

"I'm not talking about the stairs." Henry caught her gaze and refused to let go until she nodded.

"Oh." She smiled. "All right. I promise."

"Good." He looked toward the top of the steps. "In that case, shall we?"

"It might take me a while."

"I don't have anywhere to be."

When they reached the top, after stopping more than once for Deb to catch her breath, Henry once again held out his arm and, together, they walked toward Deb's old room. The one with the view of the front lawn and the parking lot.

Settling into her chair by the window, she allowed Henry to wrap a blanket around her shoulders. Nudging her gently, he said, "Don't tell Bella but…" and he held up a box of matches. Shaking them, he gestured to the trash can in the corner of the room. "Shall I?"

Deb smiled. Her muscles relaxed and she eased back into her chair. "Yes. You should."

By the time the fire was lit and crackling, the sun was dipping down beyond the parking lot. It would soon be dark. The end of another day. Another day without Laurel.

Deb reached for Henry's hand. He wrapped his fingers around hers and she was about to suggest they stay a while, enjoy the warmth and the solitude, when he squeezed. Tight. "Deb."

"Henry, I don't really feel like talking." She almost laughed. Since when had *she* been the one telling Henry to be quiet?

"Deb," he repeated. He was starting to stand up.

Deb followed his gaze. Rising from her chair, she braced herself on the window ledge. "It can't be...."

There in the distance, five silhouettes had appeared on the path. A man, a woman, two boys and a very small dog.

34

LAUREL

By the time they made it to the lawn in front of the hospital, a crowd had gathered in the foyer. The doors were open, Laurel's mom at the front, Henry by her side.

Laurel desperately wanted to run, to hurtle forward and wrap her arms around her mother's small frame. Everything in her body was telling her to, but Liam was struggling to keep up with their already-slow pace and Bear's knee had only just healed enough for him to ditch his cane. So, she kept walking — slow but steady.

Finally, someone broke through the crowd. Laurel instantly recognized Peter as he ran through the snow, with no coat or hat, toward his friend.

When he reached Liam, he stopped as if he wasn't sure whether to hug him or not. Chris wasn't far behind, striding up next to Peter and saying, "Liam, buddy, we missed you."

As Peter slung his arm around Liam's waist and helped him the rest of the way, Chris looked at Laurel and mouthed, "Arlo?"

Laurel shook her head. Hanging back a little, she said, "He didn't make it, but we have meds for both boys." She patted Arlo's pack. At least they kept those safe.

Rubbing his stubbled chin, Chris sighed. "Is Liam doing okay?"

"He could use a friend." Laurel put her hand lightly on Chris's arm and smiled. As he smiled back, she caught a glimpse of his sweater, beneath his coat. Sticking out from the top of it was her necklace. He was still wearing it.

Catching her looking, as they made their way forward, he hurried to unfasten it.

"It's okay," she said. "You can return it to me later. We have a lot to catch up on."

Nodding, Chris turned to Bear, shook his hand briefly, said, "Good to have you back," then jogged off to follow Peter and Liam inside.

When they reached the door, as others filtered forward to greet Bear, slapping his shoulder, beaming at him, Laurel's mom opened her arms and ushered her in for a hug.

Feeling her entire body relax, as if all the fear and worry she'd been holding onto had suddenly been given permission to evaporate, Laurel folded herself into her mom's embrace and wrapped her arms around her. She felt smaller, thinner, but she looked good.

Grinning at her, Laurel's mom cupped her face in her hands and smoothed her hair. "I knew you'd make it." She looked over at Bear. "I knew Bjorn would find you."

Laurel chuckled. Her mom was pretty much the only person in the world who insisted on calling Bear by his real name.

"Come inside." Henry stepped forward and motioned for Laurel to give him her pack.

Next to her, Bulldog was hugging Trent.

Slipping the pack from her shoulders, Laurel sighed as the weight she'd carried for seven full days was finally taken away from her.

"Come." Her mom squeezed her hand. "Come in. You're just in time for supper."

As they were ushered into the foyer, Laurel exchanged a look with Bear. He was next to a tall, dark-haired woman who was talking to him as if she had weeks' worth of information to fill him in on. He nodded at Laurel, the corner of his mouth twitching into a smile, and she knew what it meant; *we did it. We made it back.*

In the foyer, Laurel stopped and looked around. It was empty. No beds, no chairs, no nurses' station.

"Where is everyone?" She stopped and looked around, a sense of panic settling in her chest. Was this it? This small group? This was all the people they had left?

"A lot left," the dark-haired woman answered. "After Murph, some decided they'd take their chances on their own. The rest are in the dorm."

"The dorm?"

Putting his hand on her elbow, Bear nodded. "We converted the canteen into a dorm room and a rec room before I left. This space was too big to heat."

Laurel took in the size of the foyer. She hadn't thought about it before, but Bear was right; with the high ceilings it would have been almost impossible to keep warm through the winter months. "Good idea," she said. "What are you using for heat?"

A little way ahead, Trent—who'd been taking a turn with Jess strapped to his chest—turned and called over his shoulder, "Bear built us a fireplace. It's awesome. Wait till you see it."

Meeting Bear's eyes, Laurel raised her eyebrows. "You didn't tell me you'd been quite so busy in your short time here."

Bear shrugged. "I filled you in on the most interesting parts."

"The siege and the poisonous gas," she replied. "But you forgot to mention you'd single-handedly renovated the place."

"I don't know about that." Bear slung his arm around her shoulders. It was a gesture that made Laurel pause. For a whole week they'd been on the road together, and while they'd spent plenty of time talking about what they'd been through since the EMP hit, they hadn't been physically affectionate with one another.

She caught her mother watching them and ducked free, taking her mom's arm in hers instead.

Behind them, Henry was helping Bulldog pull the doors closed and securing them with an array of heavy cabinets which had clearly been transported from elsewhere in the hospital.

As they were sealed shut, and the draft from outside disappeared, Laurel tugged off her hat. For the first time in weeks, she'd soon be truly warm.

"You can have a hot shower if you want, my dear." Her mom squeezed her arm close to her body. "Bear built a second fireplace in a smaller room, in case we needed to separate any patients or give them their own space. We've been using it to heat water, and Henry and Bulldog figured out a shower system. Every day, they bring snow in, melt it, then—"

"I'm not sure Laurel wants to hear all the details right now, Deb," Henry said softly.

Laurel watched as her mother blushed a little, laughed, then nodded. "Of course, I'm sorry, I'm showing you off, aren't I?"

As Henry tilted his head, Laurel smiled. She was glad her mom had someone to take care of her all this time. Henry had clearly done a good job.

"Here we are." Bear stopped and gestured to the canteen doors. Then, looking at Bella, he added, "Can't wait to see what you've done with the place."

Inside, a wave of warmth greeted them and Laurel didn't know where to look first.

The room had been divided into two halves, one containing beds, the other with a large table (the canteen tables pushed together) and what looked like the contents of various staff rooms: two large couches, a rug, a coffee table, a bookcase.

On the couch, Peter and Chris were helping Liam tug his boots off. A woman Laurel recognized, but couldn't name, came bustling over with a large cup of water and handed it to Liam.

The smell of cooked meat drifted through from the serving hatch.

Suddenly, it was all a little too overwhelming and Laurel realized she was exhausted. As if she could tell that her daughter was about to fall down if she didn't sit, her mother guided her to the couch and sat her down next to Liam.

The woman with the water handed Laurel a glass too.

Bear and Trent joined them, and the four of them sat and watched as everyone buzzed around them. Peter had already taken Jess over to the fire and settled her on a pillow. Bear laughed and muttered, "She'll milk her injury for weeks. You'll see."

From somewhere, Janet appeared.

"Good to have you back, Dr. Rivera," she smiled. "But where are my sneakers?"

Laurel looked at her feet and laughed. "I'm sorry. They weren't quite up to the snow. I owe you a new pair."

Shaking her head, Janet laughed and helped Laurel tug off her boots. "I'll let it slide," she said, "if you let me look at these poor feet."

Wincing, Laurel let Janet peel off her socks and start tending to her many blisters. She'd become numb to them after a few days, but now realized they were sorely in need of being cleaned and covered with Band-Aids.

In a chair opposite, Hannah was doing the same for Bear. "Any other injuries we should know about?" Hannah asked.

"Bear hurt his knee, but it's healing." Laurel winced as Janet pressed an alcohol swab to an open blister on her toe.

"Looks like you both hurt your heads," Hannah said, pointing from Bear's forehead to Laurel's.

"That was a while back. We're okay."

"And Jess?"

"Bullet wound to the leg, but she's good too." Laurel sighed a little and sank back into the couch cushion. "We're all okay." Her eyelids felt heavy. She yawned and put her hand over her mouth. Janet was still tending to her feet. The room was warm, and the food smelled so good.

Her stomach rumbled.

But it wasn't enough to stop her from falling asleep.

When she woke, the others were gathered around the table. Bear was at the head with Bella on one side and Trent on the other. Laurel looked down at her feet. They were in thick socks now, but she could feel the Band-Aids Janet had applied.

She sat up slowly.

Liam wasn't at the table.

She scanned the room and found him over by the fire. Someone had pulled a bed close to it and he was eating sitting up, with Jess at the foot of the bed and Peter on a chair next to him. Peter was showing him a comic book. Liam laughed, and Laurel's heart relaxed. He lost his dad, but he didn't lose everything.

Slowly, she stood up and walked over to the table. There was a spare seat next to her mom. By the time she reached it, Bear had spotted her. "Just in time," he said, gesturing to the spread laid out in the middle of the table.

Plates had been filled and half emptied, but there was plenty left.

"Sit down, my dear." Her mom gestured to the chair, then pushed herself up from the table, took Laurel's empty plate, and began to fill it with food. A dark meat, which looked like it had been slow-roasted. Rice. Canned tomatoes.

"Is that fresh bread?" Laurel's stomach lurched into a growl.

Her mother smiled and handed her a chunk. Laurel held it to her nose and breathed in the smell, not caring whether she looked ridiculous. "Oh, my word. How did you…?" She looked around the table until her eyes landed on the woman who was clearly the chef.

"I'll teach you one day, my dear," she said. "It's not hard, if you know what's what."

Next to her, Laurel's mom hissed, "That's Mrs. Johnson. She won't teach you. Can't stand the idea of anyone else being in the kitchen."

Opposite Laurel's mom, Henry nodded and chuckled, "You're so right."

"Well, tuck in." Her mom squeezed Laurel's leg under the table.

Laurel studied her mother's face. She was pale, but she was wearing her customary red lipstick. She looked good. Her eyes were bright. She wasn't wheezing and didn't seem to be having trouble standing. After slowly chewing and swallowing a mouthful of the most heavenly bread she'd ever tasted, Laurel said quietly, "How are you, Mom? Are you doing okay?"

Laughing quickly, her mom moved a forkful of tomatoes around her plate. "I'm fine, dear. Just fine. Right as rain." But she didn't look up. Didn't meet Laurel's eyes.

And when Laurel looked at Henry, she saw something cross his face. Worry. Sadness. Something she couldn't place but which gave her a gnawing, uncomfortable feeling in the pit of her stomach.

She opened her mouth to prod further, then stopped herself.

There was plenty of time for that. Tonight, all that mattered was that they were back. They'd made it. Plans for what happened next could wait.

35

BEAR

Being back at South Minneha was an overwhelmingly surreal experience. One minute they were on the road, trudging through snow and feeling like their journey would never end. The next, they were eating a hot, home-cooked meal at a large table. Surrounded by smiling faces. Band-Aids on their feet and beer in their cups.

"Where did you find this?" he'd asked Bella as she produced it from a large backpack.

In response, she'd simply shrugged and said, "I know a guy who knows a guy."

By the time they'd finished eating, consuming every scrap of food so there were absolutely no leftovers, Bear's stomach was achingly full and Trent looked a little queasy.

"You didn't drink any beer, did you?" Bear asked.

Trent shook his head. "No, I swear. I just don't think my stomach's used to such good food."

Looking down the table, Bear noticed Mrs. Johnson grinning at the compliment. *Good work, kid. Keep the cook on our side.*

Even Jess had been spoiled rotten with a small helping of deer and some kibble that Bulldog had scavenged a few weeks ago in anticipation of her return.

"Looks like everyone's really pleased to have us back," Trent said later as they settled into their cots by the fire.

"Looks like it." Bear watched as Trent's face dropped a little.

Clearing his throat, Trent turned on his side and said, "How long till we, ah, leave? To find Mae?"

Bear's eyes widened.

"I heard you and Laurel talking about it."

"You sure you want to come with us?" Bear asked, leaning up on his elbow.

At that, Trent made a *pfft* sound and rolled his eyes. "You really need to ask that? After everything?"

Bear allowed a smile to curl his lips. "I guess not, kid. I guess not." Breathing in sharply, he rubbed his beard. "We'll wait till the spring thaw," he said. "So, don't worry. We have a while to get comfortable."

The next morning, Bear woke before the rest of the room, scooped Jess up and took her outside for a bathroom break. Heaving the cabinets free from the door single-handedly wasn't easy, but he managed, watched as Jess relieved her bladder, then hurried back inside and sealed the place back up.

He was on the way back to the dorm when he remembered what Deb had said about the hot shower.

Just down the hall from the dorm and rec room was the old staffroom where he'd built the second fireplace. With Jess under his arm, he pushed the door open. A curtain from the ER had been placed like a shower screen in front of the fireplace. Sticking out above it, he could see a wooden structure with a bucket and a rope.

He stepped around the curtain, wondering how they got the hot water into the bucket, but was met by a loud scream.

"Bear! What are you doing?"

Bear blinked rapidly and spun back around. "I didn't see anything!" he said, covering his eyes even though he was now facing the other way.

In a still high-pitched voice, Laurel replied, "You could have knocked! Or said something?"

"I didn't know anyone was in here." He folded his arms in front of his torso, tapping his foot on the floor.

"You didn't hear me?" She stepped in front of him, hands on her hips, now wrapped in a towel.

A little sarcastically, Bear tapped his hearing aid.

Laurel blinked. Her features were sharp, annoyed, her forehead creased into a frown. But as she looked at him, she started to laugh. "Oh well," she said, squeezing water from her long dark hair, "I suppose it's nothing you haven't seen before."

Awkwardly, aware there was no right thing to say in this situation, Bear cleared his throat and looked past her at the shower.

She'd been standing in a large plastic tub. Next to the fire was another tub made of metal.

"So, how does this work?" he asked, deliberately not looking at her damp shoulders.

"They fill this one with snow, let it melt and heat up. You lower the bucket, ladle the warm water into it, then lift it back up. There are holes in the bottom. Small ones." She laughed and shrugged. "Not the *best* shower I've ever had, but it's warm, and I finally feel clean."

"I'm sure we could do something with this. Get a proper system rigged up somehow." Bear scratched his chin, then realized Laurel was staring at him.

"You did good work here," she said. "Thank you."

"I knew you'd want everyone taken care of," Bear said. "Didn't want to get into trouble for leaving them all to fend for themselves while I came looking for you."

Gesturing for Bear to step back on the other side of the curtain while she took her pile of fresh clothes from by the fire, Laurel said, "Well, I appreciate it." After a pause, she added, "My mom looks good, don't you think? You said she seemed a little weaker when you were here before, but she looks good to me. Maybe Janet and Hannah changed her meds. Found some new ones. I'll catch up with them this morning because—" She pushed the curtain aside, now wearing a striped navy-blue sweater and jeans. She frowned at him. "What? You're looking at me weirdly."

"Nothing. You just...." Bear brushed his fingers through his hair and shrugged. "You look nice. Haven't seen you without a layer of dirt and a huge, padded coat since I found you."

Laurel twitched her nose from side to side but ignored the compliment. "So, my mom. You think she's doing okay?"

Breathing in slowly, Bear looped through various different responses before settling on, "Let's talk with Hannah and Janet later. They'll be able to fill you in."

Laurel nodded. "She says she's good."

"Yeah, but you know what patients are like—never quite tell the whole truth. You've said that yourself."

He watched as she pressed her lips together and sighed. "Mmm."

"I think we should also talk about Mae later." Bear was lingering next to the shower curtain, eager to have his turn under the warm water but also to make the most of their first moment of true alone time since reuniting.

"Mae? Yes. We should." Laurel put her hands into her jeans pockets. "We said we'd wait until the spring thaw, but we still need a plan."

"I've been thinking about that, actually…." Bear looked over at Jess, who was sniffing the bowl of warm water next to the fire. Turning back to Laurel, he said, "You know what? We can talk about it later. Maybe dinner? Tonight?"

Laurel pushed her glasses up her nose and smiled at him. "Sure. Dinner. But first, I need to check on my patients. Catch up on how everyone's doing, get Liam settled in, give Peter his new meds."

Nodding slowly, Bear watched Laurel walk away, still muttering to herself. She was back where she belonged. He just hoped she'd have the strength to leave again when the time came.

Because their family would not be complete until Mae was back in the fold.

Laurel, Mae, Trent, and Jess. They were his people.

Stepping under the bucket of warm water and letting it drizzle down onto his skin, Bear repeated their names in his head. Laurel, Mae, Trent, and Jess.

One more person to find, then back to Thunder Bay.

Just one more person.

36

MAE

Before they even made it back to the fence, it started to rain. Not gentle rain. Hard, unrelenting rain that battered Mae's dark blue jacket and left a ringing in her ears.

She broke into a run, striding through puddles and letting the water splash up to her knees. She'd be freezing later, but right now all she felt was the pulse of adrenaline in the pit of her stomach.

Next to her, Neve was breathing heavily. She caught him looking over his shoulder. "They're still with us!" he yelled.

Mae simply nodded and kept running.

After weeks holed up in this godforsaken town, she knew it like the back of her hand. The locals couldn't outsmart her. Not anymore. "This way!" She tore down an alleyway between two large buildings. Neve grabbed her arm.

"Are you sure? Where does it—"

"Trust me." Mae pulled herself free and kept running. At the end, a tall wire fence loomed in front of them. Without even stopping, Mae bounded onto a nearby dumpster, propelled herself at the fence, grabbed the top of it and vaulted over, scrambling halfway down, then throwing herself to the ground.

She landed crouched, knees bent, palms on the slick concrete. When she looked up, Neve was struggling. He was shorter than her, having trouble heaving his leg over. When he did, for a too-long moment, he simply hung there—as if he was hoping the fire department would arrive with a trampoline for him to fall onto.

"Move it, Neve. Let's go!" Mae straightened herself up and looked past him. There they were. The group of locals who now called themselves the Freemen.

Jacob was at the front, practically salivating as he locked eyes with Mae. He was tall and skinny with tattooed arms and pierced nostrils. He made her skin crawl.

The rest of them were different, mostly ordinary townsfolk who'd got caught up in the idea that Jacob and his cronies could protect them. From what, Mae hadn't yet figured out.

Right from the beginning, when the Militia had tried to take charge, tried to *help* the people of the town, there had been problems. Mae had always known that the locals hated the base being taken over — ever since it was turned into a high-tech training facility, the conspiracy theorists had been having a field day—but she had genuinely thought they would welcome the military taking control.

Surely, the one thing everyone wanted when the power went out was to be assured that law and order still existed? Still counted for something. That people weren't going to be allowed to start doing whatever they wanted whenever they wanted.

But when Mae's captain had stumbled upon looters, and a local teenager had been killed, Jacob had seized his chance. He'd tasted blood, and like a vampire, sucked the town dry of compassion. He had painted the soldiers as the bad guys, and himself as the town's savior.

And they had been fighting him ever since.

More than once, Mae had asked Neil why they didn't just pack up and leave. "Because we can't abandon the folks of this town, Mae. That's why," he'd said, again and again.

Finally, Neve let go of the fence and tumbled to the ground. He landed on his side with a thud, cried out, and rolled over. Looking at him, Mae wasn't sure how he ever passed basic training.

"This way." She barely gave him a moment to catch his breath before tearing off down the alley.

Behind her, Jacob let out a loud whistle. She heard feet hitting wire as he and his men began their ascent. If she was wrong, if she'd miscalculated their position, then this could be it. She and Neve could finish the day as Jacob's captives. And she knew what he did to captives who were soldiers.

Halfway down the alley, this time approaching a true dead end—a large brick wall—Mae spotted what she'd been looking for. A beaten-up black door.

Spinning on her heels, she turned and charged toward it. It clattered back on its hinges and she pulled Neve inside with her.

"A bar?" Neve looked around. The room they'd entered was dimly lit, just the smallest amount of light filtering in from the street. Rain pounded the windows. "It stinks." Neve wrinkled his nose but Mae ignored him.

Striding into the middle of the room, she grabbed a long wooden table and began to drag it toward the door. "Help me," she grunted.

Neve stepped up and took hold of the opposite end. Together, they hauled the table to the door and positioned it in front, then lifted a second on top and stacked some chairs in front.

"That'll hold them off for a few minutes." Mae glanced up at the windows. They were high, unreachable, and too small for a person to get through. The only way for Jacob to get in would be to use brute force, or to go back the way he'd come and use the front entrance.

And by that time, she and Neve would be long gone.

They were at the end of the bar, heading through an archway that led to another room and the door onto the street, when they heard gunshots.

Mae counted. One. Two. Three.

Neve turned and shouldered his weapon.

"Ignore it, keep going. They're just making noise. They can't get through." Mae quickened her pace. When they reached the front door, she stopped, pulled it open just a few inches and looked out. Then a bit farther. Then farther still. There was no sign of movement in the street.

Long-abandoned, it was now nothing more than two long lines of empty stores. Most had been looted, windows broken, cleared of anything useful. She'd made a midnight trip to the pharmacy last week, to see if there was anything left that they could use to boost their own medical supplies. But the only thing she found was a box of gel icepacks that had to be kept in the freezer in order to work.

Briefly, as often happened, an image of her previous life flashed through her mind. Her parents, standing in their kitchen in Texas. Beads of sweat on her father's forehead. Her mother's cheeks flushed. The freezer open and dripping onto the floor.

"Of all the days for it to die," her mom had laughed, tucking a strand of dark brown hair behind her ear and wrinkling her nose, "it had to be the hottest day of the darn year."

"I don't care," Mae had said. She'd been sitting on the countertop, swinging her legs, staring at the glorious stack of ice cream cartons they'd have to work their way through to save throwing them away.

"I'm with Mae," her dad had said, tweaking Mae's chin with his index finger. "I've always wondered what it would be like to have ice cream for breakfast, lunch, *and* dinner."

Mae blinked hard and forced the image from her mind.

These were the hardest to bear. The memories from when she was younger. Six. Eight. Ten. From when they were stupidly happy. An in-sync little unit, the three amigos. She wondered whether it was strange that remembering happy times was harder than remembering the sad ones.

She'd asked Neil about it once, but as usual, talking about anything close to feelings or their personal lives had made him twitchy. It was an unwritten rule between them; don't tell me about your life and I won't tell you about mine.

As they jogged across the street, Neve looked back over his shoulder. He was always doing that; using his senses all wrong. Relying on his eyes when his ears could do the job. If her dad's injury had taught her anything, it was that—as soldiers—they should use every tool at their disposal and use it in the right way. In the rain, they'd hear the splash of footsteps if someone was following them.

She was about to tell him to concentrate on where they were going when the crack of a gun made her jump. She stopped, whirled around, ready to return fire but completely unable to see where the shot had come from.

The sky was thick and gray, the rain blurring her sight. She looked at the broken storefronts of nearby buildings, then up at their roofs. Nothing.

"Let's go!" she yelled. But as soon as they moved, another shot rang out. And this time, Neve fell to the ground.

Mae wavered on the spot. The bullet had hit his neck. There was blood. Too much of it. She'd seen wounds like that before, but she'd never seen one bleed into the rain and pool in the street that way.

"Neve...."

He blinked at her. He was holding his neck. "Don't leave me."

Mae screwed her eyes shut. Another shot. But the sound was distorted. She had no idea where it was coming from. When she opened them, she shook her head.

Another shot.

"I'm sorry, Neve."

Another.

"I have to go."

Another.

"I'm sorry."

Before he could reply, she turned and ran.

By the time she reached the fence that surrounded the base, she was shaking. Whether it was from the cold that was seeping through her clothes and into her skin or the image of Neve's face as he pleaded with her to stay, she had no idea.

Approaching the checkpoint, she shouted, "Sergeant Mae Peterson." She searched her brain for today's password. "Delta Gamma Upsilon." She winced at the irony: *don't give up.*

Helen was on duty. She gestured for the others to pull back the barrier and escorted Mae through it.

"Jacob was following me. I think I lost him. Don't know if he'd have the guts to come this far." Mae stopped when she reached the shelter of the overhang, leaned forward onto her thighs and took three deep, heavy breaths. Behind her, the barracks was in darkness.

"What happened?" Helen put her hand on Mae's shoulder, looking from Mae to the barrier and back again. "I thought Neve was with you?"

"He was." Mae was still panting. She stood up, reached for her hair—tied back into a braid that almost reached down to her waist—and twisted it until water dribbled out. "They got him."

"Who?"

"I didn't see. We were on Main Street. Shots were fired. I think it was a lone shooter, but in the rain, I couldn't say for sure." She steadied herself, then stepped back to lean against the wall. Suddenly, the strength had gone from her legs and she wasn't sure how long she could remain standing. She pressed two fingers to her neck. "Here." She tapped it. "There was nothing I could do."

Helen pursed her lips and looked down at her feet. "Dammit." She shook her head. "Thankfully, we're moving out."

"Moving out?" Mae's eyes locked on Helen's as the slightly older woman tilted her head to one side.

"First light. Cornell says—"

"Cornell? What about Ne—" Mae stopped herself. Bit her lower lip. "What about Captain Mackenzie?"

For a moment, Helen simply frowned. Then her features softened. She put her hand on Mae's arm. "Mae... Mackenzie left. This morning."

Mae blinked. "Left?"

"He said..." Helen cleared her throat. "He said he needed to go find his wife."

A rushing sound filled Mae's ears. Like she was going through a tunnel on a fast-moving train. Neil had gone to find his wife. Of course he had. And the way Helen was looking at her told her that she knew precisely why Mae was upset about it. Her cheeks began to flush. She stood up and brushed down her sopping-wet clothes.

"Thank you for telling me." She stood up straight, feet together, shoulders pushed back, chin up. "I should inform Captain Cornell about Neve."

Helen offered Mae a sympathetic smile.

Mae didn't let herself look at it for long. "Stay on guard," she said as she walked away. "If I know Jacob, he's not going to let us go without a fight."

She was barely inside the side entrance near the training square when she came face-to-face with Captain Cornell. Previously Neil's right-hand man, he was now in charge. And the look on his face told her he was relishing every moment of it. "Ah. Sergeant Peterson. I was wondering when you'd return." He looked behind Mae. "Sergeant Jenkins not with you?"

"I'm afraid not, Captain. Neve... Sergeant Jenkins was wounded in the field. Shot by one of the Freemen. He didn't make it, sir." She swallowed hard, praying to whatever god might exist that Neve was already gone, not still lying there.

"Ah." Cornell's jaw twitched. "Well, then it's a good thing we're moving out. Sounds like the *Freemen* are determined to run this town into the ground."

"Captain." Mae nodded.

The way Cornell was looking at her made her think he was waiting for her to ask about Neil. She wasn't going to give him the satisfaction.

"We leave at first light." He stepped to one side, ready to end their conversation. "Go to the mess hall and you'll be assigned duties for the coming hours. We need to move fast. Come morning, there should be no sign we were ever here."

Mae resisted the urge to point out that the giant Army barracks and signage was a bit of a giveaway. Instead, she said, "Captain, if you don't mind me asking, where are we moving out to?"

Looking her up and down, Cornell narrowed his eyes. "Actually, Sergeant, I do mind." Then he walked away.

In the mess hall, Mae was surrounded by movement. Soldiers clearing up, packing, preparing to leave as the Captain had said, at first light.

"Peterson?" A sergeant holding a clipboard looked her up and down. "You're to report to Bay Six and help load ammunition into the wagon. When that's secure, you may pack your own things. I'm sure you're aware, we leave at sunrise."

"We have wagons now?" Mae couldn't help her clipped tone. If they'd procured wagons and horses, leaving had been on the agenda for a while. Yet this was the first she was hearing about it.

The sergeant folded her arms and gave Mae a withering stare. "Any more questions, Sergeant?"

"No." Mae's jaw twitched. "No more questions."

In Bay Six, she reported to another sergeant with another clipboard, then set about carrying weapons and ammo from the store. Four horse-drawn wagons were lined up beside the building. Each was surrounded by armed guards.

Mae looked up at the sky. Cataloging and moving their supplies would take all night. At this rate, she doubted there would be time for her to pack her own things as well as finish the job here.

It was nearing sunrise when they loaded the final box of ammo.

"Permission to return to the dorm and pack, sir?" She stood, straight as a board, in front of the sergeant in charge.

He didn't speak, but nodded curtly at her.

As soon as she was out of sight, Mae broke into a run. In the mess hall, she slowed to a quick march, then once through the door ran toward the dorm.

Hers was the only bed that hadn't been stripped. The others were all bare and the locker doors beside them were hanging open, completely empty.

Mae grabbed her sleeping bag and rolled it tightly, then secured it with its thick black strap. Pulling her pack from beneath her bed, she opened her locker and began pulling things out. Spare clothes, boots, socks, a book. She stopped as she picked up the final object. A phone. Her cell phone, which hadn't worked in months. She turned it over in her hand. She looked at the open pack on the bed and contemplated throwing it in; it barely weighed anything. What would be the harm?

Her hand was hovering over the backpack when she changed her mind, tossed it back into the locker, and closed the door.

Checking the pockets for her other supplies—water, protein bars, first-aid kit—her fingers brushed the small inside zipper. The tiny, concealed pouch inside the back pocket. She sat down on the bed and slid the zipper across. Her fingers instantly found what she was looking for, a small, crumpled photograph. She smoothed it out in her lap. It was a photo of her, her parents, and their dog Jessamine. Back home in Texas, sitting on the porch. Her gran took the picture. It was her mom's birthday. There was a cake on the table.

On the back of the picture, her father had scribbled the date it was taken and the message: *Come and visit me in Thunder Bay any time you like. I love you, Mae Flower. XXX*

He'd sent it to her when he'd first arrived there, but she'd never responded. In fact, she remembered it irking her that he'd sent a family photograph when he'd made the decision to excommunicate himself from the family and move to the middle of nowhere.

Now, all she felt looking at it was a tug of nostalgia.

"Thunder Bay," she whispered. "Are you still there, Dad?"

She brushed her thumb across her parents' faces, then looked at her pack. She was alone. There was no one here. She could take her things, sneak out, and head for Ontario right now. Join him and Jessamine. Maybe even find Mom.

But even as the thought entered her mind, she pushed it away. Leaving wasn't an option. She'd made a promise to serve, and that was what she was going to do. She was fighting for a greater cause, one she would not—could not—abandon, no matter what the cost.

END OF DANGEROUS WORLD
EMP AFTERMATH BOOK THREE

Broken World, July 13, 2022

Chaotic World, August 10, 2022

Dangerous World, September 14, 2022

Divided World, May 10, 2023

PS: Do you enjoy prepper fiction? Then keep reading for exclusive extracts from **Divided World, No Rescue,** and **Crumbling World.**

THANK YOU

Thank you for purchasing 'Dangerous World'
(EMP Aftermath Book Three)

Get prepared and sign-up to Grace's mailing list to be notified of the next release at www.GraceHamiltonBooks.com.

Loved this book? Share it with a friend, www.GraceHamiltonBooks.com/books

ABOUT GRACE HAMILTON

Grace Hamilton is the prepper pen-name for a bad-ass, survivalist momma-bear of four kids, and wife to a wonderful husband. After being stuck in a mountain cabin for six days following a flash flood, she decided she never wanted to feel so powerless or have to send her kids to bed hungry again. Now she lives the prepper lifestyle and knows that if SHTF or TEOTWAWKI happens, she'll be ready to help protect and provide for her family.

Combine this survivalist mentality with a vivid imagination (as well as a slightly unhealthy day dreaming habit) and you get a prepper fiction author. Grace spends her days thinking about the worst possible survival situations that a person could be thrown into, then throwing her characters into these nightmares while trying to figure out "What SHOULD you do in this situation?"

You will find Grace on:

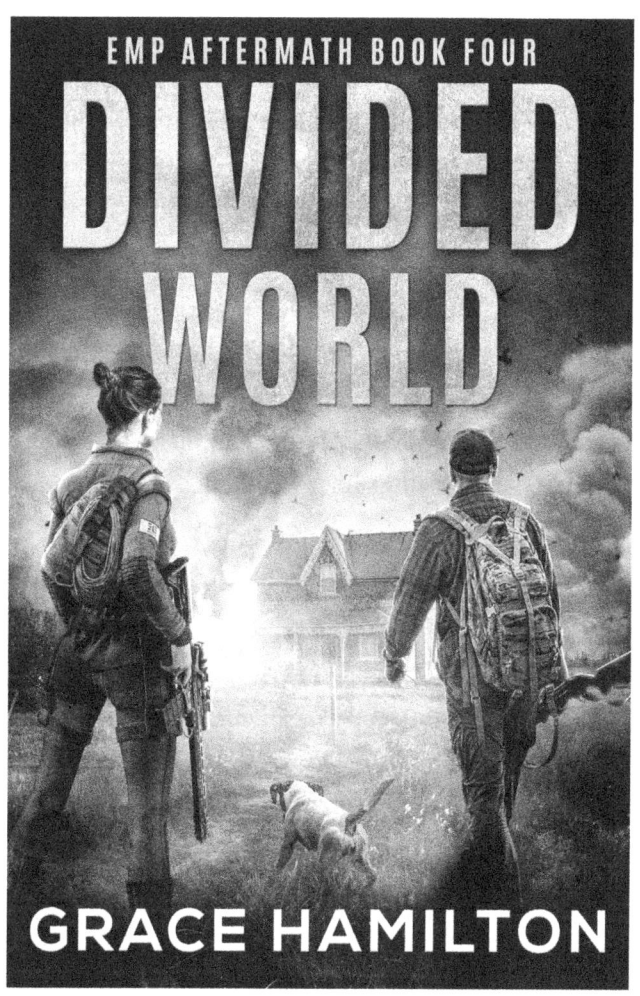

BLURB

They went looking for their daughter. They found a civil war…

Laurel and her husband Bear are finally reunited. But South Minneha Hospital is no longer the haven it once was. Together, they take on a new quest: leaving the hospital behind, and setting off to find their daughter, Mae.

Accompanied by Trent and Jess, Laurel and Bear leave the safety of Minneha and begin their search, knowing only that Sergeant Mae Petersen was serving in the US Army when the EMP hit. The Internet is just a memory, and phones are now quaint relics. Finding out where one soldier was stationed—and where she might be now—will take a miracle.

Laurel is up for the challenge, but the world changed while she was fighting to save South Minneha. Roving bands of gunmen have given way to organized paramilitary groups. The land she and her companions must cross is contested by two factions, the Militia and the Freemen. Tensions are rising, lines are being drawn, and one fact is painfully clear…

If Laurel and Bear are to reunite their family, they're going to have to fight.

Get your copy of *Divided World*
Available May 10, 2023
(Available for pre-order now)
www.GraceHamiltonBooks.com

EXCERPT

Chapter One

Laurel

"All set?" Laurel crouched down and tucked the blanket a little closer around her mom's legs.

"Stop fussing, darling." Her mom smiled and tweaked her index finger beneath Laurel's chin. She was wearing her customary bright red lipstick and a splash of mascara, but her complexion was paler than normal.

"It won't hurt to wait until it's a little warmer out." Laurel glanced at the large glass windows that enclosed the hospital foyer. Still only March, while it was sunny outside, it was also bitterly cold. Especially when the wind blew.

For a long moment, Laurel's mother looked at her. Her eyes softened, as if she was feeling sorry about something. But then she said, "Nonsense, come on. I need some air. I've been stuck inside for weeks."

Standing up, Laurel moved to the back of her mom's wheelchair and flexed her fingers on the handles. Since her return to South Minneha, no one had ventured outside unless it was for hunting, scavenging, or one of their weekly trips to look for townsfolk who might need medical help; it had been too cold for leisurely walks. But the last snow fell more than a week ago now, and the ground was starting to thaw. So, Laurel had promised her mother a short outing. Looking at her mom's diminutive frame, however, she was beginning to wonder whether it was a good idea.

That morning, once the sun was up, and the snow a little softer, Bear and Henry had cleared something of a path around the building using Henry's special salt mixture and two large shovels. Laurel intended to start at the front, exiting from the foyer, and loop around until they were back where they'd started. She had packed a thermos of coffee and some cookies for them to enjoy when they reached the bench that looked out at the forest. *If* her mom was doing okay.

Over the past few weeks, she'd been quieter than normal. When she caught Laurel watching her, she made an effort to smile and pretend to be upbeat. But Laurel knew she was hiding the true extent of her discomfort. As Bear pulled open the doors for them, she made a mental note to discuss her mother's meds with Hannah later. The new combination they'd started her on was never going to have the same effect as the trial meds had, but Laurel would have expected to see at least *some* improvement.

"See you soon." Laurel allowed her hand to graze Bear's as she walked past him. He smiled at her and nodded. Once he was out of earshot, Laurel's mom reached up and patted Laurel's hand. "Things seem to be going well between the two of you?"

Pulling her scarf tighter around her neck, Laurel laughed. "Well, that took all of thirty seconds."

"What did?" Her mom folded her arms around her middle.

"Asking about me and Bear. We've been out of the building less than a minute."

"Well," her mom chuckled, "I don't get any other chance to ask you. Lately, it seems that wherever you are, he's only a few steps behind you." She looked over her shoulder and gave Laurel a knowing glance. "So…?"

"So, nothing." Laurel pushed the chair over a difficult patch of ground and winced at the twinge in her ankle. Although the injury had healed, she was still experiencing discomfort and it was starting to irritate her. She was *not* used to being unable to shake something when she wanted to. Several times, Bear had offered to give her some PT but she'd refused, telling him it would sort itself out soon. Now, however, she was beginning to wonder whether she should give in and allow him to help.

"Not nothing." Her mom's tone had become sharper, the way it was when she was about to tell Laurel off about something. "Laurel, the world crumbled around our ears. Bear came all the way here from Thunder Bay to find you. You were the first thing he thought of. *You.* That has to mean something."

Laurel pressed her lips together and pushed her glasses up the bridge of her nose; the cold was making them slip. "Maybe, but do we need to figure it out right now?"

She expected her mom to answer right away, but instead there was a long pause. She watched her mother's shoulders gently rise and fall as she took several deep breaths. "I'd like you to figure it out before—"

"Coffee," Laurel interrupted. She knew what her mother was about to say and, not for the first time, stopped her from saying it. She couldn't hear talk like that. Not now. Not ever. Not after such a long, hard journey to get back here. "I brought coffee and cookies. We're nearly at the bench. Do you feel up to stopping for a snack break?"

After a short, sharp sigh, her mom replied, "When have I ever turned down cookies?" then laced her gloved fingers together in her lap and remained quiet while they made their way around the side of the hospital building toward the picturesque lawn and forest out back.

"I have to say," Laurel spoke up — feeling the need to fill the silence with words — "You know I'm not Robert Sullivan's biggest fan, but it was a good idea to keep this area open. Part of the hospital grounds. It's good for the soul to be close to nature."

"Is that a scientific opinion?" her mom asked, slightly sharp.

"Yes, actually." They were almost at the bench. Bear and Henry had cleared a path directly to it. On the brow of the dip that led down toward the trees, it gave a perfect view of the forest and the sky beyond. "There was a study. I remember reading about it—"

Mid-sentence, Laurel stopped.

"Did you hear that?" She stepped sideways, so she was standing next to her mom, and strained her ears. "I swear I heard something." She looked down at her mother. She too was listening intently but shook her head.

"No, dear. I can't hear anything."

"I'm sure…" Laurel peered down the slope at the trees. The spaces between them were dark and uninviting. She'd ventured in there a couple of times with Bear and Trent on their hunting expeditions, but on the whole, had left food gathering to them; they were better at it and Trent seemed to revel in the alone time with Bear. He hadn't said anything, he was too sweet a kid for that, but Laurel could tell he was finding it hard to adjust to sharing Bear's attention with someone else.

She was shaking her head, about to take out the coffee, when something moved in the periphery of her vision. She stepped forward, watching the tree line.

"Is someone there?" Her mother asked, following Laurel's gaze.

"I'm not sure." She turned and flicked the brakes on her mom's chair. "Mom, can you wait here a moment?"

"I can't exactly make a run for it," her mother quipped.

Striding away from the path Bear cleared for her, Laurel inched through the thinning snow until she was a few feet away from the bench. There. Something was definitely moving.

Reaching for her gun with one hand, she waved the other and called, "Hello? If there's somebody there, I'm a doctor. This is a hospital. Do you need help?"

For a moment, nothing moved. A cold breeze whipped across Laurel's face. Then a voice carried forward on the wind. "Help! Help! My sister-in-law. She needs help!"

As Laurel took another step forward, a figure emerged from the trees. A woman. Waving frantically, she called again, "My sister-in-law needs help. Please!"

"Mom," Laurel turned to her mother. "I'll be right back. Wait there."

Then she charged down the slope in the direction of the trees.

By the time Laurel reached her, the woman was no longer alone. She'd been joined by another, who was clutching her stomach and seemed barely able to stand. When she looked up and moved her arm, Laurel realized why.

"You're pregnant…" Laurel rushed forward and took the woman's other arm. In answer, she simply groaned and clutched her stomach harder.

"Her name's Tory. She's thirty-six weeks. I'm Kate. She's my brother's wife." The woman who'd shouted at Laurel from the trees adjusted her friend's weight on her shoulder and winced.

"Okay, Kate. We're not far from the hospital. Let's get Tory inside. Is your brother—" Laurel glanced back at the trees, but Kate replied with a solemn shake of the head. Laurel nodded in understanding, then motioned for them to start moving. Slowly, they began to help Tory up the slope.

"Tory, I'm a doctor, can you tell me what happened? When did you start experiencing pain?"

Tory breathed in hard, gritted her teeth, then replied, "This morning. It just started this morning."

"Are you having contractions?"

"I don't know." Tory gripped Laurel's arm a little harder. "How do I know?"

"Does the pain come in waves? Or is it constant?"

"Constant. All the time. No waves." Tory winced and wobbled, but Kate steadied her. Then, stopping, she looked up at Laurel. "This is a hospital, so you can help me? Right?" Her voice wavered and moisture sprung to her eyes. "I can't lose my baby."

"We can help you, Tory." Laurel nodded firmly. "We just need to get you inside."

As they drew closer to the bench, and Laurel's mom realized what was happening, Laurel saw her push herself gingerly out of her chair and shuffle to the bench itself. "Mom," she called, "sit back in your chair!"

But when they reached her, her mother simply said, "This young woman needs it more than I do. Take her inside and send someone back for me. I'll be fine for a few minutes."

Laurel bit her lower lip. Her mom had already been outside for almost half an hour. But there was no way Tory would make it to the foyer without the chair.

"All right," she said, lowering Tory into the wheelchair. "But I'll send someone right away." She grabbed the blanket and wrapped it firmly around her mom's shoulders. "Just hang tight, okay?"

Her mother's answer was drowned out by another pained cry from Tory. "It hurts," she moaned. "Please. Help me. It hurts."

"Help her!" Kate grabbed Laurel's elbow.

"Okay, Tory. Here we go." Laurel looked briefly at her mom. "I'll send Henry right back." Then she nodded, and began pushing.

**Get your copy of *Divided World*
Available May 10, 2023
(Available for pre-order now)
www.GraceHamiltonBooks.com**

No Rescue

BLURB

A rising storm. A sudden catastrophe. No hope of rescue…

A storm looms on the horizon as Ruth Garber and her granddaughter Stella travel by helicopter to an offshore drilling rig. Ruth, a world-class geologist, is there to consult on a software upgrade. Stella, a geology student, just wants to prove herself to her legendary grandmother. They don't know their trip will become a grim struggle to survive…

When the helicopter goes down after dropping them off, they realize they're in trouble. The platform loses power. Cell phones don't work. Everything electronic is dead. Stranded with a skeleton crew on a steel platform miles from shore, battered by massive waves, the deadly truth of their predicament slowly sinks in.

Meanwhile, John and his son Curtis are in a fishing boat, suddenly adrift when the engine fails. The waves are getting higher, and the storm has them on a collision course with the rig.

As the castaways on the rig struggle to survive, they discover the back-up generator has been deliberately damaged. When people begin to disappear, they come to a grim realization.

Someone in their tiny group is a saboteur.

**Get your copy of *No Rescue*
Available December 14, 2022
www.GraceHamiltonBooks.com**

BLURB

Family comes first—and he'll do whatever it takes to protect his from the looming storm.

Even before becoming a husband and father, safety had been Shane McDonald's priority for most of his forty-five years. As a nuclear engineer, it's his responsibility to keep the Sequoyah Nuclear Plant functioning at optimum levels to avoid what protesters fear most—a meltdown.

But when a coronal mass ejection from the sun wipes out power across the globe, stopping a nuclear chain reaction is no longer his primary concern.

Now Shane must trek across hundreds of miles to ensure the safety of his loved ones in a world rapidly disintegrating into lawlessness. Yet with few functioning automobiles and a blind teenage daughter to protect, it'll require careful planning to reach his prepper mother-in-law's and reunite with his family.

His wife has her hands full as well. When her brother's chemo drip suddenly stops working and her son gets stuck in the hospital elevator, all Jodi McDonald wants is the security of her husband's steady presence. But with a weakened brother and inexperienced son to look after, Jodi must remain strong amid the chaos and help guide them to her mother's.

However, even the best laid plans go awry as the miles stretch out between them. Supply thefts run rampant. Those who have necessities prey on those who don't. Minds broken by hardship kill on sight.

But the fatal mistake comes when thugs threaten the McDonald's little girl.

Shane must find the strength to do the unthinkable—or watch his family suffer the consequences.

Grab your copy of *Crumbling World* (Surviving the End Book One) from www.GraceHamiltonBooks.com

EXCERPT

Chapter One

Violet must have sensed the furious crowd gathered in front of the gate. In the rearview mirror, Shane saw her sit up straighter and cock her head to one side. Ruby, her black lab guide dog, responded to the sudden change in her body language and looked at her with concern. Roughly two dozen people had gathered in a grassy area alongside the entry road to the Sequoyah Nuclear Plant, some of them carrying neatly stenciled signs as they marched back and forth. On the other side of the road two police officers stood watching in front of their patrol car.

"Dad, what's going on?" Violet said. "I can hear a crowd of people. It sounds like they're chanting."

He hadn't intended to tell her about the protestors. He had been hoping to avoid having to explain to his daughter why people were protesting his place of work on Take Your Child to Work Day. She was fourteen, but she was also somewhat naïve. Shane had perhaps sheltered her too much as a child, waiting to protect her from danger, from bullies, from so many possible problems, particularly because of her disability. This had only recently become difficult, as she began to push back, growing into a questioning teen who would no longer accept easy answers.

"Just some people," he said. "Don't worry."

As the car drew up alongside the protestors, the words of their chant became clear.

"Shut it down! Shut it down! Shut it down!"

Ruby had been sprawled across the back seat, but she rose now and placed her head on Violet's lap. Some would have mistaken this for a gesture of affection. Shane recognized it as a protective move.

"Why are they saying that?" Violet asked, pushing her sunglasses up the bridge of her nose. "Is something wrong? They sound angry."

Trying to ignore the hateful stares of the protestors, Shane slowed as he approached the guard station next to the front gate. He fumbled in his shirt pocket for his work ID, trying to think of the best way to explain the situation to his daughter. Violet tended to think the best of people, and he didn't want her to lose that optimism.

"They're just exercising their first amendment rights," he said. "Freedom of speech is a beautiful thing, even if the things being said are questionable."

"So they're protesting the power plant?" she asked.

"Well...yes," he replied, hoping she would leave it at that.

"That happens a lot here, huh?" she said. "A lot of people protest?"

"No, only occasionally. Generally, when we make the news for some reason or another."

"Why are they so mad this time? Did your company do something wrong?"

"They're upset because of the talk about adding a third reactor to the plant. Our service area is growing, and we could use another reactor, but as soon as it hit the news, people in the community started complaining. I imagine they organized some kind of protest gathering on social media, and here they are. It's fine. People are entitled to voice their concerns." He flashed his ID to the guard, who gave him an anxious smile and waved him through the open gate. The parking lot beyond was emptier than usual. At two minutes to four in the afternoon, they were smack-dab in the middle of a shift change. Had the protestors planned it that way, hoping to catch the bulk of the second shift workers as they pulled into the gate? It seemed likely. "If you ask me, they're being rather alarmist. People like this, I don't think they get it."

"They don't get what, Dad?" Violet asked.

He carefully considered his words before answering. Would his daughter think less of him if she understood the controversial nature of his chosen industry? "Well, Violet, sweetheart, nuclear energy is the cleanest and safest form of energy in the world—hands down, no question—but the word *nuclear* makes some people nervous. They assume radiation is seeping into the environment and creating three-eyed fish in the river."

Violet laughed at that. "Is it?"

"No, of course not. The radiation is fully contained."

Ahead, the vast gray cooling towers rose on either side of a domed containment building, billowing steam into a crisp late-April sky. Shane could see the curve of the Tennessee River where it slipped behind the plant in a broad arc. It was a sight that never failed to impress him, even after these many years, and he wished his daughter could enjoy it. As he pulled into the closest row of parking spaces, he considered ways he might convey the majesty of this place to her.

"Dad," she said, "we talked about nuclear power in our science class at school. Our teacher said nuclear power plants are dangerous because if they overheat, they can go into a meltdown. She said meltdowns have happened before, and they hurt a lot of people, even poisoned whole cities. Is that true? Could it happen here?"

"It's true. But did your teacher mention that more people die in coal mines *every year* than have ever died from nuclear meltdowns?" Shane said.

Violet persisted. "But a meltdown could happen here?"

Shane grunted unhappily. "That would require a very severe accident."

"But they've happened before," Violet said. "At Chernobyl in the Ukraine, and somewhere in Japan. One even happened in America, she said, at a place called Three Mile Island."

"Don't worry," he said. "Something like that is not going to happen here. The Chernobyl accident was mostly caused by the poor design of RBMK nuclear power reactors. We don't have that problem here. And Fukushima in Japan was caused by a tsunami, which probably isn't going to happen in the mountains of Tennessee. We're safe."

"But how do you know for sure?" Violet asked.

"Because I'm a nuclear engineer," he replied. "It's my job to know. It's my job to keep everyone safe, and I will. I will keep us safe."

"Promise?" Violet said.

"Promise."

The hallways were emptier than usual because of the shift change, but they met Landon just outside the control room. He was coming from the direction of the break room, his sleek black wheelchair making its gentle *whirring* sound. It had wheels with fat spokes that were slanted inward, a heavily padded seat and backrest, and a sturdy frame. As Landon had explained in the past, it was technically an athletic wheelchair, but he'd gained an affinity for them during his years of playing wheelchair basketball. He was broad-shouldered and strong, a former athlete with a well-built upper body. His legs had atrophied from spina bifida, but this had rarely been an issue on the job.

"Hey there, buddy," Landon said, when he spotted Shane rounding the corner. "I don't usually beat you to the office. What's the holdup?"

"I brought a guest with me this morning," Shane said, "so watch your salty language today."

"What are you talking about?" Landon replied. "I haven't even said my first four letter word of the day."

Shane shuffled slowly down the hall, holding his daughter's hand and guiding her. She came somewhat reluctantly, her other hand sliding along the wall. Passing through security had made her nervous—the great hum and hiss of the metal detector, x-ray machine, and radiation monitor—and she kept fiddling with the small radiation monitoring device hanging around her neck. Like the workers, she had been given an orange hardhat, and it was slightly too big for her head, pushing against the rims of her sunglasses.

To make matters far worse, security had insisted she leave Ruby behind. They'd made a place for her beloved black lab in the security office, but Violet had balked at the idea. It was Shane's fault. He'd pulled strings to get approval for Violet to come to work with him—no easy feat—but he'd forgotten to get clearance for Ruby.

That'll put a damper on the day, he thought.

Fortunately, Violet knew Landon well—he was practically family—so when she heard his voice, she relaxed a bit.

"Hey there, Vivi," Landon said. Only Landon could get away with calling her Vivi. "Where's your furry sidekick? I've never seen the two of you apart." He was particularly fond of the dog.

"They wouldn't let me bring her into the building," Violet said. "Even though she's a trained guide dog, they said it's not safe to bring an animal—any animal—into the plant, so she's sitting back there by herself."

"Not by herself," Shane said gently. "The security team will take good care of her, and we can check on her from time to time. We'll bring her something to eat during my lunch break."

"I don't know what they're afraid of," Violet said. "She never bites, and she doesn't get into anything. She doesn't even bark unless I'm in trouble. If we brought her inside, she would sit quietly and mind her own business all day long, except for pee breaks."

"It's just company protocol," Shane said. "Sorry, I should have tried to clear it first. I didn't realize it would be a problem."

"Don't you worry about it, Violet," Landon said. "I won't let this injustice stand. I'll file a formal complaint. It's not nice separating a kid from her loyal sidekick. If we have to take this all the way to the board of directors, so be it. Policy must be rewritten."

Shane shook his head at Landon. "It's fine. It's only for a few hours. Ruby will be okay. We'll check on her at lunchtime, get her something to eat, take her potty, and everything will be okay."

"She doesn't know that," Violet said. "She doesn't know we're coming back at lunchtime." Finally, Violet shrugged and rolled her head back on her shoulders. When she did, the orange hardhat almost fell off, and she had to grab it. "Oh well, nothing we can do about it, I guess. I'll give her an extra treat after we get home tonight."

"There you go," Shane said. "Great idea."

"I don't know why you wanted to come here anyway, kid," Landon said. "Should've gone to work with your mom at the CDC. You know your dad's job is incredibly boring, right?"

"Dad says his job is to keep everyone safe," Violet said.

"He's not wrong." Landon turned and wheeled toward the control room door, beckoning for them to follow. "But you'd be surprised how boring it is keeping everyone safe."

"Now, now," Shane said, laying a hand lightly on his daughter's shoulder. "Don't undersell the experience, Landon. She's been looking forward to this."

"All I'm saying is you should have gone with your mom," Landon said. "She works with diseases. She's battling deadly viruses on the daily, keeping world-devouring pandemics at bay with nothing but grit and determination."

"That's not exactly true," Shane said. "She does have a lot of grit and determination, though, I'll give you that."

"Centers for Disease Control. That's her place of employment, right? Disease *control*, man. They're protecting us from mutating Ebola and bio-engineered smallpox. Those are the real dangers right there, not some silly old nuclear power plant. Nothing exciting happens here."

"Dad said yes first," Violet said.

"I did," Shane said. "Plus, your mom is technically a statistician for the CDC. She's not battling bio-engineered smallpox, but they do work to prevent diseases. He's right about that."

"It's fine," Violet said. "Except for poor Ruby, I don't mind coming here. I can visit Mom's place next time."

The curve of a long green console took up most of the center of the control room, its surface covered in a complex array of gauges, screens, buttons, and knobs. A low hum filled the room. Violet reacted upon entering the room, perking up and turning her head first one way and then the other.

"The air is different in here," she said. "Feels kind of weird. Sort of electric, if that makes sense."

"Lots and lots of warm electronics," Landon said, wheeling himself up to the console and leaning in close to one of the monitors. "That's what you feel. It kind of smells plasticky, doesn't it?"

"Yeah," Violet replied.

Landon's elbow crutches were leaning against the end of the console. He kept them close, but he preferred using the wheelchair. When Shane took a seat, they started to slide so he caught them and set them on the floor. As Landon began cycling through system menus, Shane called his daughter over, took her right hand, and laid it on the console beside his keyboard.

"You feel that?" he asked. "That's my computer. I spend a whole lot of time at this computer."

"I can almost see it," she said. "The screen is bright right now, isn't it?"

"That's right. The starting screen is a light blue color."

Though Violet was visually impaired, Shane knew she could perceive light. She described bright lights as vague, distant blobs. She could also tell when she was in a completely dark room. Beyond that, she was incapable of perceiving shapes or colors.

"We monitor every system in the station from this room." Shane turned to Landon. "In fact, we can pretty much determine everything that's happening from right here, and we can call other departments if we need to talk to them."

"On rare occasions, we even leave the room," Landon said.

"That's true," Shane said. "In fact, I was thinking about giving her a tour of the facility when the rest of the staff get here. She could meet some of the department heads and hear what they do. What do you think?"

"Sorry, pal," Landon replied. "After the software upgrade, we've got to run through the rest of those scenarios this morning. The tour will have to wait until after lunch."

"Oh, man, I thought we finished those yesterday."

"Not even close," Landon said. "They're being especially comprehensive this time."

Shane guided his daughter's hand to the next seat, and she sat down.

"Sorry, sweetheart, I'll take you on a tour a little later," Shane said. "Just hang out here for a bit while we get some work done. Do you need a drink or anything? I could run to the break room and get you something."

"I'm fine, Dad," Violet replied, feeling the edge of the console and resting her forearms against a spot that was clear of buttons, gauges, or knobs. "Don't worry about me. Just do your work. I don't want to be a bother."

"You're never a bother," he said.

"Brace yourself, Vivi," Landon said. "Running through end-of-the-world scenarios while pretending they can never happen gets dull after a few hours."

Shane almost shushed his friend, but it was too late. The words were out. Violet pushed her sunglasses up the bridge of her nose and frowned.

"End of the world?" she said. "What do you mean by that?"

"Just scenarios," Shane said. "Not real life. We're testing a recent software upgrade by seeing how it responds to theoretical situations."

"What kind of situations?" Violet asked.

But at that moment, a harsh squawk came out of one of the tiny speakers beside Shane's computer console as a window popped up on his screen. A red message flashed brightly: CORONAL MASS EJECTION EVENT IMMINENT TWO MINUTES. It flashed a few times before he registered what he was reading.

"Coronal mass ejection," he said. "Landon, did you start the simulation already?"

Landon leaned back in his chair to get a look at Shane's screen. "I haven't done anything," he said. "I haven't pressed a single button yet." A two-way radio sat near the edge of the console, and he grabbed it. "Let me see if I can find out what's going on. Maybe they're running some kind of remote drill. Is that possible? I mean, it can't be real."

"If it was real they would have given us a lot more than two minutes warning," Shane said, feeling a flutter of anxiety despite his words. "It has to be some kind of test."

"Okay, let me see if I can get hold of someone," Landon said. "If it's an unplanned simulation from on high, I'm going to pitch a fit. We have enough scenarios to run through without the higher-ups messing around. Sometimes, they're too clever for their own good."

"Dad?"

Violet managed one plaintive word before the power went out. Every light and screen went dark, and Shane heard cooling fans winding down.

"Well, that's not good," Landon said. "We just lost everything."

Shane had been trained to handle this kind of scenario—he knew the steps—but having his daughter present changed everything. He could hear her panicked breathing, the squeak of her chair as she fidgeted. It was distracting. He wanted to comfort her, but he also knew they had to act fast.

"Dad, what's happening? What's a coronal…whatever?"

"Coronal mass ejection," Landon said. "A massive burst of plasma from the sun. Causes an electromagnetic pulse which can knock out the power grid, fry electronics, and do all sorts of bad, bad stuff. I'm going to take a wild guess here and say it's not a simulation."

The control room was quiet, too quiet, but Shane heard shouting in the hallway—panic throughout the building just as the second shift was arriving. Terrible timing.

"Backup power's not coming on," he said. "Could the CME have taken out the generators?"

"Doubt it," Landon said in the darkness. He sounded breathless. "If it's a CME, the backup generators might be fine. They're just old-fashioned diesel engines. No electronics in them to be fried. We'll have to start them manually though."

Shane was still half-convinced it was a test, but he didn't like the nervous edge in Landon's voice. The man was usually so calm and collected.

"I'll take care of it," Shane said. He started to rise from his chair, but Violet's hand clamped down on his arm.

"No, Dad. Don't leave. I'm scared."

"It's okay, honey. I just need—"

He heard the whir of Landon's wheelchair. "I've got it. You two stay here. I know the way, and I can move faster than either of you. We need to act quickly."

"No, I'll come with you," Shane said. "It might require two of us to get the generators working. Violet, you can come, too. I won't leave you here by yourself."

"Are we in trouble?" she said. "What happens if you don't get them working?"

"If the main power is knocked out, the control rods drop into the core, and the reactor is flooded with water to drive the temperature down," Shane said. "That can't happen until we get the backup generators on, but we will. It'll just take a minute."

"You're talking about a meltdown," Violet said, her voice quavering, her hand squeezing his arm tighter. "That's it, isn't it?"

"No, no, we have…plenty of time to get things under control." He had to force the words out. *But it's a test, right? It has to be? If it's a real CME, they would have warned us a lot sooner.*

Shane heard the hiss of the control room door as Landon heaved it open and wheeled into the hallway. Shane rose and grabbed Violet's hand. Then he followed after Landon.

He wanted to believe they had plenty of time. He almost did believe it, but he'd never heard Landon sound so scared.

Grab your copy of *Crumbling World* (Surviving the End Book One) from www.GraceHamiltonBooks.com

Made in the USA
Las Vegas, NV
31 October 2023